D1011236

POTBOILERS

By the same author

The Method as Means

Theatre at Work (ed.)

The Encore Reader (ed.)

The Tragical History of Doctor Faustus

Confessions of a Counterfeit Critic

Open Space Plays: An Othello *and* Palach
(In collaboration with Alan Burns)

The Act of Being

Artaud at Rodez

The Marowitz Shakespeare:
Hamlet, A Macbeth,
The Shrew, Measure for Measure
and The Merchant of Venice

Sex Wars: Free Adaptations of Ibsen and Strindberg
Hedda, Enemy of the People
and The Father

Prospero's Staff

POTBOILERS

Sherlock's Last Case
Ah, Sweet Mystery of Life!
Clever Dick

Three black comedies by

Charles Marowitz

Marion Boyars · New York · London

Published in the United States and Great Britain
in 1986 by Marion Boyars Publishers
262 West 22nd Street, New York, NY 10011 and
24 Lacy Road, London SW15 1NL

Distributed in the United States by
Kampmann & Co., New York

Distributed in Australia by Wild and Woolley

Printed in the United States of America

Contents

Introduction

When I was Artistic Director of London's Open Space Theater, it some-times befell that a play, duly announced and verbally contracted, was gazumped by a larger, better-heeled theater. This was the case several years back when we were about to begin rehearsals for the première of a new British work which we had every reason to believe was ours for the staging. In the event, we found ourselves with a blank slot and about three weeks to fill it or suffer the displeasure of our subscribers and, more to the point, sustain some hefty financial losses at the box office. To avoid such a fate, I was exhorted by my partner to 'pull something out of the bag'. "Can't you write something," she hectored, "you've got two weeks!" The unimpeachable logic of her remark penetrated the softer regions of my skull. No matter that most playwrights worked two, three or four years on their magnum opus, confronted with a hiatus of fourteen days, there was no good reason in the world why an industrious chap couldn't come up with a play.

As it happened, I'd had this idea for a play for some seven or eight years before but, like most writers, found good reason to postpone its creation. Now, however, confronted with the yawning void of our 'blank slot,' I was impelled to see if the bugger could indeed be written. God knows, it had been gestating long enough! To make a long, tedious story into a short tedious one, I wrote the first version of *Sherlock's Last Case* in the appointed fourteen days. It was a long one-acter running about ninety minutes and it finished where the first act of the present version now ends. It was a very different play—inexorably black and culminating in the Grand Guignol murders of both Mrs. Hudson and Liza Moriarty—each of whom was discovered hanging upside down in a closet.

Being both the Artistic Director of the theater as well as the director of this hastily assembled work, I felt it was pushing nepotism to insuf-ferable limits also to be announced as the author, and so concocted an imaginary playwright called Matthew Lang. Mr. Lang, I told the com-pany and anyone else in earshot, was an old GI buddy of mine who was essentially a painter. He lived at some *poste restante* address near Marrakesh and was constantly on the move although, whenever the need arose, I could (miraculously) get him on the long distance telephone.

We began rehearsals; I trying conscientiously to fulfil the author's demands as I understood them. On several occasions when disputes arose and I insisted that I knew precisely what the author meant in a particular phrase or speech, the actors asked how I could be so certain. I could only reply that we had been very close buddies in the army and I felt I had the measure of Matthew's mind instinctively. As these disputes began to arise with some regularity—I continually insisting I knew exactly what the author intended—a cloud of suspicion settled over the rehearsals and more and more questions were asked about our absent playwright. I parried all thrusts with an aplomb developed over the years of outwitting troublesome actors and the play finally got on. I garnered some very upbeat notices and one or two critics prophesied that, no doubt, we would be hearing more from Matthew Lang.

Then a development ocurred that I had not foreseen. Alexander H. Cohen, the Broadway impresario, became interested in the script and began negotiations for the New York rights. I, as Lang's appointed representative conducted these negotiations as tactfully as possible. "Do you mean he's not going to be here for revisions and rewrites—even if the play's going to be done on Broadway?!" asked an incredulous Cohen. Yes, I'm afraid that's the case, I had to reply fixedly, stone-faced. Lang is a peculiar chap who has very little interest in theatrical matters, I explained, and considers himself primarily a painter. Nothing can dissuade him from his art-researches in (I believe by this time it was) the Negev, however I am empowered to act on his behalf in any matter that may arise.

These strained and somewhat incongruous discussions continued for something like fourteen months—with regular requests for Lang to make an appearance and Lang tenaciously refusing to do so. You see, by this time, Lang had acquired a genuine persona and I was stuck with the eccentricities of his wilful nature. In any case, after protracted letters and telephone calls with Cohen and The Open Space Theater, the impresario's patience snapped and negotiations were discontinued. Although disappointed, I was also a little relieved as the double life, as any full-time schizophrenic will tell you, is a very taxing business.

Skimming the pages of The Dramatists Guild Quarterly, I came across a blurb from the producer George W. George of Saga Productions saying that he was interested in 'thrillers' that had a strong core of 'character' about them. Believing my long one-acter to be just such a work, I sent the manuscript to him. To my astonishment, he not only replied but said he was intrigued with the play and would the author be prepared to expand it into a proper, full-length work with the inclusion of a new second act. As I had no desire to exhume the defunct Matthew Lang, I replied Yes, *I* the author, would be happy to do so.

At the same time as George offered to option a revised and expanded version of the play for Broadway, Alexander Cohen resurfaced and offered an Off-Broadway production of the ninety-minute version. Feeling that the hastily written first version left much to be desired and tempted by the challenge of restructuring a play I had previously closed down for good and all, I opted to go with Saga's offer, wrote Cohen accordingly and began meetings with George W. George on the expansion of the work.

Here, I must digress slightly to say that over the years, I have had dealings with a wide variety of commercial producers both in America and England and found them to be uniformly imbecilic. Their language consisted of theatrical clichés and they were forever going on about 'beefing up the second act,' 'cutting the flab' or injecting more 'thrust' or 'pizazz'—but when asked to explain their recommendations in detail, they took refuge in woolly-minded generalizations or pure fudge. Their exhortations to the writer were really a kind of pep-talk intended to convey the inspiration of the Muse without providing the nuts and bolts of an editorial intelligence. Happily, George was very unlike the producers I'd known before. He thought in specific images and made sweeping, sometimes sound—sometimes untenable—suggestions as to which direction the new play might take. Reading my rewrites, he was lucid in his judgments, frequently confirming my own niggling suspicions that a scene was diversionary rubbish and should be abandoned. With his help, the play dropped several of its original scenes and turned into something much more practical and stageworthy.

Through my association with the Los Angeles Actors' Theater—and particularly due to the enthusiasm of its Consulting Director, Alan Mandell, the play was accepted for production in the summer of 1984 as the official offering of the Olympic Arts Festival. Despite a rocky start during which we replaced the lead three times and lost the original director in the second week causing me to step in, it finally got on and received a sympathetic press response and a somewhat rhapsodic public reception.

As I expected would happen, several spectators and other pernickety types with knowing looks confronted me with the charge that they knew this play very well from England (where, incidentally, it had been performed in several repertory theaters such as Liverpool, Pitlochry, Peterborough, etc.) and that its true author was one Matthew Lang and what did I think I was trying to pull anyway? Where possible, I explained the convoluted origins of the piece; where not, I simply said that Yes, there once had been a writer named Matthew Lang associated with the original work but that I had murdered him in order to take the credit for the piece myself. This usually silenced my more vituperative critics but, I fear, did very little good to my reputation.

Having been a director much longer than I have been a playwright, I must resist the tendency to tell others how this play should be staged. Of course, every company develops its own Rosetta Stone in translating the hieroglyphics of a play into acting-terms, but for what it's worth, I would enjoin my colleagues to bear in mind what, for me, are three cardinal points.

The language of *Sherlock's Last Case* is bogus 19th century English and intended to be spoken at a rapid pace. Indeed, I do not believe the play's verbal ideas can be properly conveyed unless it rattles along at a good clip. Secondly, there is a parodic element in the work without which much of the humor must fall by the wayside. What is being parodied is not only the mythos of the Holmes-Watson relationship, but the melodramatic conventions of the late 19th century and an understanding of that is integral to its style. And lastly, despite the appearance of traditional thriller-elements—plot twists, suspense, unexpected revelations—I see the play as a moral combat between arrogance and subjugation and feel it is closest to my intent when it dramatizes the paradox of a familiar public relationship with a very different private face. If this play is approached merely as a thriller, it delivers only half of its cargo. If it can be seen as an exploration of ego and envy, it stands a much greater chance of unloading all of its goods.

Most of *Ah, Sweet Mystery of Life!* was written in the Canary Islands where I went with an understanding Norwegian girlfriend to try to recover from a shambolic marriage which, after some two and a half years, had turned me into something of a zombie. That quintessential and unquenchable instinct which, previously, had enabled me to recover from a variety of lesser emotional calamities assured me the only way to survive this one was to fasten onto its absurdity. Writing a comedy about my abysmally depressive state seemed an utterly logical course of action. Given the size of the trauma, it had to be something of a 'black' comedy and, given my Old Testament desire to exact retribution, there had to be an element of revenge in it. But that part of me that still retained objectivity, warned that if one went too far in making the play a reprisal for a rough ride, its therapeutic value would nullify any merit it might have as a play. Consequently, let me say at once to all those readers who voyeuristically scan the piece for cryptic autobiography, the circumstances of the play are entirely fabricated, although the feelings generated by the put-upon hubby and his emasculating spouse are traceable to emotions knocking around inside of me at the time of writing.

My feeling about the play, which received its première at the Pioneer Square Theater in Seattle, is that production must soften the prejudice with which I imbued the character of Lueen. Whoever plays this role must be cast for attractive and sympathetic personality traits which do not telegraph or overstate the bitchiness which eventually engulfs her. By the same token, the more one can demonstrate that Matt is actually responsible for his own decimation, the more the moral balance of the play is maintained.

To an extent, and in a way that should be palpable to an audience, the play, apart from its marital preoccupations, is also about opposing definitions of 'romance', a term which in my experience can be applied to candlelit dinners beside casement windows filtering moonlight as they can to brokerage transactions. These ideas are basic to the characters and largely determine the way they behave with one another.

For those who complain *Sweet Mystery* is in fact two plays, one light, the other dark, I would say in its defense, the nature of black comedy is to change complexion when one least expects it. A schizoid play is as capable of providing diversion as a schizoid personality and, recalling Emerson's stricture about inconsistency being the hobgoblin of little minds, readers should resist that overweening impulse which insists a play must be one thing or the other.

And finally, not to infer a seriousness of purpose which the material may not justify, but simply to make others privy to the gestation process behind it, let me say that during the period the play was being hatched, I was directing a production of *The Father* at the Trondheim Theater in Norway. As much by design as by osmosis, Strindberg's obsessive, sexist and paranoid ideas filtered their way into the piece. The

Captain, in Strindberg's play, is also done in by a conniving and blood-sucking wife, and I have always believed that behind*The Father*'s taut and classical contours lies the possibility of an outlandish farce which, had Strindberg possessed a comic bent, could have stood head and shoulders above the dark tragedy he *did* write.

Just as *Sherlock's Last Case* is not a thriller, neither is *Clever Dick* a whodunnit, and just as I confess to no great partiality for the work of A. Conan Doyle, I must admit I have never seen a play of Agatha Christie's all the way through to the end. Why then, you will ask, move out conspicuously in the direction of a genre that is of no particular interest? The answer is that within the rigid conventions of the thriller and the whodunnit lie immense possibilities for extrapolations of content not usually associated with those forms.

Clever Dick is clearly (perhaps too clearly) about class where whodunnits of the Agatha Christie variety are only obliquely about class. It is the tangential quality of that subject in a framework which appears to be about other things which makes it stand out so sharply.

In England, the working class has always believed that the most despicable thing about the upper middle class is that it derives more pleasure out of sex than they do; that while they are laboring in the factories or in the pits, the 'toffs' are swapping sexual partners, flagellating one another, dressing up in erotic lingerie and having a whale of a decadent time. Regular scandals like those of Christine Keeler and the Profumo Case feed this fantasy and two hundred years of romantic fiction has embedded it in the popular imagination, which is what makes it a perfect subject for farce comedy. To the extent that a play can be said to have an object, the 'object' of *Clever Dick* is to explore these class myths within a context which purports to be about murder, criminal investigation and Hitchcockian and Christie-an notions of mystery and suspense.

Finally, a definition of 'potboiler' without which I could never rest easy with this egregiously titled collection. A potboiler is a crafted work of art which clearly has in view the appetites and predilections of the audience for which it has been fashioned. The degree to which it satisfies the predictable appetites of that audience confirms its status as a potboiler. The length of time it continues to do so eases it out of that invidious category and into the realm of art. Shakespeare wrote a lot of potboilers that have become classics. I, in the latter part of the 20th century, have written only potboilers. Should they still be around to please the taste of audiences two and three hundred years from now, this collection may well have to be retitled.

C.M.

Characters

DR WATSON
SHERLOCK HOLMES
MRS. HUDSON
LIZA
INSPECTOR LESTRADE
SHERLOCK LOOK-ALIKE

TIME—September 1897
PLACE—Victorian England

Sherlock's Last Case was first presented at the Los Angeles Actors'
Theater in association with George W. George on June 29, 1984. It was
directed by the author; the production was designed by Timian Alsaker:
the lighting and special effects were created by Russell Pyle and the
sound was designed by Jon Gottlieb. The cast was as follows:

DR. WATSON	Dakin Matthews
SHERLOCK HOLMES	David Fox-Brenton
MRS. HUDSON	Toni Lamond
LIZA	Judith Hansen
INSPECTOR LESTRADE	Peter Bromilow
SHERLOCK LOOK-ALIKE	Edgar Llandudno
DAMION	Leif Farraday

The play was presented in New York by Alfie Productions, The Ken-
nedy Center/ANTA, Ray Larsen and The Landmark Entertainment
Group at the Nederlander Theatre on August 20, 1987. It was directed
by A. J. Antoon with scenery by David Jenkins, costumes by Robert
Morgan and lighting by Pat Collins. The cast was as follows:

SHERLOCK HOLMES	Frank Langella
DOCTOR WATSON	Donal Donnelly
MRS. HUDSON	Jennie Ventriss
LIZA	Melinda Mullins
INSPECTOR LESTRADE	Pat McNamara
AN IMPOSTER	Morris Yablonsky
DAMION	Daniel M. Sillmun

Sherlock's Last Case

Act 1

Scene 1

HOLMES' Baker Street Flat, Victorian. DR. WATSON and SHER-LOCK HOLMES.

WATSON: I can see why the topaz earring led you to Madame Neander, and I can even see why the chipped tooth ruled out Graves as a suspect, but how in heaven's name did you deduce that Guy Heatherington and Madame Neander were one and the same person?

HOLMES: Almost transparent, my dear Watson.

WATSON: Well, I confess I can't see it.

HOLMES: Pass the tea like a good fellow, will you? Do you remember when the maid asked Madame Neander for a light . . . just before the guests arrived?

WATSON: I vaguely remember something about . . .

HOLMES: If you hadn't been preoccupied with Lady Carlton's decolleté at just that moment . . .

WATSON: Confound it, Holmes, she was brushing the hem of her dress and her cleavage practically spilled onto the carpet.

HOLMES: Be that as it may; had your eyes been with Madame Neander, you would have noticed an involuntary movement of her right hand as it half-darted to her breast pocket.

WATSON: But Madame Neander had no breast pocket.

HOLMES: Precisely, Watson. A breast pocket is not a normal accoutre-
ment on women's clothing, although it is fairly standard on a man's.

WATSON: I must say, Holmes, that was a piece of luck.

HOLMES: Luck had nothing to do with it, my dear Watson. Two sugars
old chap.

(WATSON *spoons them in.*)

Earlier the same evening, as the guests assembled in the great hall
. . . you remember how the women all arrived in a great bunch . . .
well, did you notice anything odd as they were standing before the
looking-glass in that great hall?

WATSON: Only that they were preening themselves like jackdaws, as
they always do.

HOLMES: All but one.

WATSON: *(Suddenly realizing)* Madame Neander!

HOLMES: What woman who truly was a woman, would miss a chance
of admiring herself in the glass. That, I fear, was Heatherington's
fatal giveaway. No milk, Watson.

(WATSON *stops just before adding milk.*)

WATSON: Well, I must say, he led us a merry dance. It looked for a
while as if we were all goners. Still, I suppose it's always darkest
before the dawn.

HOLMES: Not strictly true, Watson.

WATSON: Eh?

HOLMES: I mean not meteorologically speaking. The hours between 3
a.m. and 4:15 are usually the hours of densest darkness as the sun is
furthest both from sunset and sunrise. Just a twist of lemon.

(WATSON *twists it into* HOLMES' *cup.*)

WATSON: Dash it Holmes, I wasn't talking about meteorological whatsi-callit, but about our hopeless situation. Before Lestrade strode in with fifteen of his burliest constables and turned off the gas jets, I thought we were all for it.

HOLMES: Precisely what Heatherington would have liked you to think, but being as poor a scientist as he is a female impersonator, he never realized when you have a roomful of plants photosynthesizing carbohydrates, the effect of carbon monoxide is considerably diluted.

WATSON: Do you mean we wouldn't have snuffed it?

HOLMES: Not a chance, my dear Watson.

WATSON: Well I certainly didn't know that.

HOLMES: Nor did he, and since his aim was our collective asphyxiation, I didn't think it prudent to volunteer the information. *(Looking towards teacup.)* Have you stirred it?

(WATSON *automatically stirs tea.*)

WATSON: Holmes, you astonish me.

HOLMES: Nonsense, my dear Watson. Any schoolboy using elementary intelligence and an applied grammar-school education could have arrived at exactly the same conclusion. *(Beat)* Assuming he was supremely gifted, of course.

(The mechanism of the cuckoo-clock suddenly activates itself. HOLMES *removes his watch from his vest pocket and holds it up as if to confirm the hour. The cuckoo springs out—but suddenly it stops in its tracks and stands there motionless without uttering a sound.* HOLMES, *surprised, looks towards the clock as does* WATSON. *After three or four seconds of static silence, the bird very, very slowly withdraws until it is out of sight. This is followed by a slow, even funereal, closing of the cuckoo-clock's doors.)*

HOLMES: *(Looking at* WATSON) The only other time that clock refused to cuckoo was the fateful day I set off for the Reichenbach Falls for my last encounter with Professor Moriarty.

WATSON: *(Confused)* But what . . . could it possibly . . . ?

HOLMES: An omen Watson—that something untoward is about to happen.

(There is an electric pause—suddenly broken by MRS. HUDSON*'s noisy entrance. She is clearly in a state.)*

MRS. HUDSON: I'm so sorry, Mr. Holmes. I hate to bother you—*(Controlling herself)* It's this letter, Mr. Holmes, that Dr. Watson brought in. It's from my cousin in Dundee. It seems my grandfather is in a terrible condition and will probably not last out the week.

WATSON: I'm terribly sorry to hear that, Mrs. Hudson. You were very close were you?

MRS. HUDSON: No, not what you would call close.

WATSON: He was a distant relative, then?

MRS. HUDSON: Not what you'd call 'distant'.

WATSON: He was neither distant nor close.

MRS. HUDSON: To tell you the truth, I never even knew he was still alive.

HOLMES: *(Sternly)* In that case, my dear woman, why indulge in this charade of melancholy?

WATSON: Come, come Holmes—the woman is upset, can't you see?

MRS. HUDSON: I'm very attached to all my relations because there's so few of 'em. The idea of any one of them passin' away is just terrible, terrible.

HOLMES: What you mean is you're a sentimental old sop and haven't a clue as to who you're wailing about.

MRS. HUDSON: That's not true, Mr. Holmes. I remember my grandfather very well. My mother talked of him often. He was a caretaker by profession; took great pride in tending the flowers in the local cemetery. It's very confusin' to have to suddenly mourn someone you never even knew was alive. It's hard enough keeping track of the dead ones.

WATSON: I can quite see that, Mrs. Hudson; quite.

HOLMES: Do stop sobbing, Mrs. Hudson.

MRS. HUDSON: I can't help it. My whole family's always been very emotional. They cry at weddings, anniversaries, baptisms, communions. *(Fondly)* They could never contain themselves.

HOLMES: Incontinence, Mrs. Hudson, is nothing to boast about.

WATSON: Holmes, you're being deucedly callous to an employee and a good friend. Can't you see the poor woman is in a state?

HOLMES: Is there something specific we can do for you, Mrs. Hudson?

MRS. HUDSON: I must go to him.

HOLMES: Ah, I see.

MRS. HUDSON: He's askin' for me. It says so in the letter.

HOLMES: Even though he never knew you.

MRS. HUDSON I'm his only other livin' relation.

HOLMES: I see. And how long do you imagine the pilgrimage will take?

MRS. HUDSON: I don't know. It only says he's near the end. I don't know when he's actually going to pass over.

HOLMES: Given the tendency of the Scots not to part with anything already in their possession, he may linger on for a decade or two. That would leave this flat in a rather disconsolate condition.

WATSON: Holmes, how can you think of your own comfort when Mrs. Hudson is so bereaved?

HOLMES: She isn't bereaved yet, Watson.

MRS. HUDSON: But I must see the poor man if he's askin' for me.

WATSON: Of course you must. You go along, Mrs. Hudson. There's a train later this afternoon. We'll be able to cope quite well till you come back. Won't we, Holmes?

HOLMES: If you really feel you must, Mrs. Hudson . . .

MRS. HUDSON: Oh thank you, Mr. Holmes. I knew you would understand.

HOLMES: Naturally, we will stop your wages until your return.

WATSON: Holmes, really! I think you can do better than that.

HOLMES: Since you are leaving on a Wednesday, strictly speaking, I'm entitled to hold back this week's wages as well.

WATSON: Don't you fret, Mrs. Hudson. Holmes likes his little joke. You go right along. You can take my hansom. It's standing just outside. If you need any assistance while you're in Dundee, wire me immediately.

MRS. HUDSON: Oh, you're a saint, Dr. Watson you truly are.

HOLMES: Do try to be philosophic, Mrs. Hudson. If your grandfather *is* going to die, your bedisde lamentations will only provide irrelevant musical accompaniment. Whereas here on Baker Street, you are tending the living who have a very real need of you.

MRS. HUDSON: I worry about you, Mr. Holmes. Especially since you've started smoking all that—you know what.

HOLMES: I beg your pardon.

MRS. HUDSON: *(Under her breath)* Smells like flamin' pig manure.

HOLMES: *(Piqued)* Your impertinence, Mrs. Hudson, is almost as odious as your sentimentality. Take your week's wages and go tend the dying. God knows if it doesn't prepare them for heaven, it will give them a very tart foretaste of hell.

WATSON: Don't you mind him Mrs. Hudson. We know how crotchety he gets after a bad case. And remember, if you need anything, just telegraph.

MRS. HUDSON: God bless you, Dr. Watson.

(Sulky look to HOLMES *and muttering as she leaves.)*

Smells just like cat-poo. Stinks to high heaven. Wicked, wicked.

WATSON: Holmes, you behaved abominably to that old woman. You should be thoroughly ashamed.

HOLMES: I never heard such a cock-and-bull story in my life.

WATSON: You don't believe her?

HOLMES: I do not speak of proof, Watson, but as we all know, the twin obsessions of the working class have always been absenteeism and tardiness.

WATSON: If you're an emotional kind of person, it's quite understandable to wish to visit an ailing relative.

HOLMES: It's more likely if you fancy a vacation with pay.

WATSON: Well, she's hardly got that, has she?

HOLMES: Mrs. Hudson, my dear Watson, has always known on which side her scone is buttered. They're a beastly lot, these Scots—thought by some to be the Lost Tribe of Israel and there's good reason to believe it. They're as mean as buggery—as tight as six toes in a sock. Scotsmen have been known to return from the dead to claim the pennies on their eyelids.

WATSON: Holmes, I don't know what's been getting into you, but some of your views, of late, are almost barmy.

HOLMES: If all the timber in the North American continent were laid end to end, it would never even begin to bridge the gap between my insights, Watson, and your perceptions.

WATSON: Holmes, if I didn't know you better, I'd take offence at every tenth word you uttered.

HOLMES: Which would make me fiercely scrutinize why the nine were having no effect.

(The bell rings.)

Drat! the first bitter fruit of Mrs. Hudson's untimely departure. Now I must answer the front door myself.

WATSON: Don't fret, Holmes. You're getting to be like an old woman. I'll get the door.

(HOLMES *alone, takes out tobacco and stuffs some in his pipe. Peers around cryptically, fishes out a small leather bag from a coal scuttle, takes out a pinch of its contents and shoves it into the bowl of his pipe. Begins to puff languidly, a serene expression on his face.)*

(WATSON *re-enters holding a letter. He sniffs, discerns the peculiar smoke aroma and frowns reprovingly.)*

HOLMES: What is it, Watson?

WATSON: A hand-delivered letter.

HOLMES: *(Taking it)* Too early for bills and too late for birthday greetings. I wonder what . . . *(Reading it, puffing)* Hello.

WATSON: What is it?

HOLMES: What indeed.

WATSON: Well, what's it say?

HOLMES: It's from a Moriarty.

WATSON: *(Aghast)* Moriarty, but he's dead. How could it . . .

HOLMES: Not *the* Moriarty, *a* Moriarty—a Mr. Simeon Moriarty; son, as it appears, of the deceased professor.

WATSON: I never knew that Moriarty had a son.

HOLMES: Villain that he was, I suppose he was still capable of biological reproduction.

WATSON: Read it out, for goodness sake, Holmes. I'm dying of curiosity.

HOLMES: "Mr. S. Holmes" is the salutation. Blunt and to the point. "Having recently returned from foreign parts, I have only just been advised of your role in my father's untimely death which, to put a finer point to it, one could call 'murder'. You should understand that the Moriarty Clan was fired in the crucible of family pride and the inevitable corollary of that pride is the appetite for revenge; a revenge which is implacable and which neither God nor Man nor Sherlock Holmes can possibly gainsay. Be advised, therefore, that appropriate measures will be taken to redress these heinous wrongs and due punishment meted out to their contemptible instigator. Your obedient servant, Simeon Moriarty." Copies to The London Times and Scotland Yard.

(HOLMES *and* WATSON *regard each other for a moment.)*

WATSON: It's just a hoax. Wouldn't give it a second thought.

HOLMES: Hello, what's this? An enclosure. Hmm.

(Opens paper.)

"If you would know the hornet's sting
Seek the insect in his nest.
But do not dare to cut his wing
Or never shall your heart know rest."

(Looks at WATSON.*)*

WATSON: Balderdash. Hornet's sting . . . cut his wing . . . Rubbish!

HOLMES: It won't stand comparison with Tennyson, I grant you, but then the intention is quite different.

WATSON: What intention?

HOLMES: "If you would know the hornet's sting
Seek the insect in his nest . . ."

WATSON: Poppycock. Some crank, I shouldn't wonder . . .

HOLMES: "But do not dare to cut his wing
Or never shall your heart know rest."

WATSON: Doggerel. Pennyfarthing rhymes!

HOLMES: And yet the intent is crystal clear.

WATSON: What *do* you mean? I can't make head or tail of it.

HOLMES: It means, my dear Watson, that within a very short period of time, only days perhaps, there is every likelihood that I shall be murdered.

(Turns firmly to WATSON *who gapes and pops his eyes and involuntarily spits his tea into the cup.*

Music sting and blackout.)

Scene 2

Lights up.

Same as previous scene except that teacups and saucers are piled on the desk and elsewhere conveying a somewhat dishevelled impression. In the background, a solo violin (obviously played by HOLMES) is performing Boccherini's Minuet.

A PALE YOUNG GIRL stands Center Stage, bag in hand. After a moment, she stifles a cough in her gloved hand. The violin music cuts out and, as HOLMES enters, the GIRL draws herself together.

HOLMES: *(Placing violin case in cabinet)* So sorry to have kept you. I find I can't go a day without Boccherini's Minuet. One of my many addictions. *(Turns and sees the GIRL for the first time)*

You wished to see me?

LIZA: Mr. Sherlock Holmes?

HOLMES: At your service, Miss . . . ?

LIZA: Moriarty—Liza Moriarty.

HOLMES: *(after a beat)* Do take a seat.

LIZA: I see my name has had some effect on you.

HOLMES: Did you expect it should not?

LIZA: Indeed, I would have been quite astonished had it not.

HOLMES: *(Cordial)* Would you like some tea and scones?

LIZA: That would be very nice. It has been a rather long dusty journey.

HOLMES: *(Irate)* Damn! My blasted housekeeper is away. *(Cordial)* I'm afraid I shall have to withdraw that impetuous offer of hospitality.

LIZA: No matter. I had half a glass of barley water before boarding the train.

HOLMES: Very prudent of you. Now then . . .

LIZA: Mr. Holmes, I know you have received a letter from Simeon.

HOLMES: Simeon?

LIZA: My brother.

HOLMES: I see, you are . . .

LIZA: I am Professor Moriarty's daughter.

HOLMES: Quite a prodigious progeny for a confirmed bachelor. I'm sorry. I've touched a nerve.

LIZA: Mr. Holmes, I cannot begin to defend my father. I, and the whole world beside, know what he was, and what evil he wrought. But, when all is said and done, he *was* my father, and I still experience the odd twinge of filial respect.

HOLMES: And so you should, my dear. "The good that men do lives after them. The evil is oft interr'd with their bones."

LIZA: *(Beat)* I believe you have that the wrong-way-round, Mr. Holmes.

HOLMES: I know. I find Shakespeare so much more amusing that way.

(LIZA *stifles a cough*)

  (Cordial) Would you like a little sherry?

LIZA: That would be refreshing.

HOLMES: *(Irate)* Blast! The sherry's all gone! That confounded old
. . . *(Cordial)* I do apologize.

LIZA: Not at all. Sherry is a trifle reckless so early in the day.

HOLMES: You were saying . . .

LIZA: Allow me to explain. I have only recently come to know my
brother for, being much given to self-abuse, he spent his formative
years living in America. I have only renewed my acquaintance with
him at a belated memorial service for my father.

HOLMES: At . . .

LIZA: The Memorial Hall in Bermondsey.

HOLMES: Quite, I remember receiving the invitation, but unfortunately
I was in Marrakesh at the time.

LIZA: I was quite relieved. A parental tie, Mr. Holmes, is like a hoop of
steel, and no matter how Christian one tries to be, I doubt I'd have
been able to suppress a natural animosity towards the murderer of
my father.

HOLMES: You do know the circumstances of our final encounter?

LIZA: Perfectly, and there is no need for explanation. The reason my
father never mentioned Simeon or myself is surely self-evident. He
felt if you, or members of the police, were made aware of our existence, our lives would become a torture, and every pressure imagin-
able would be put upon us in order to ferret him out.

HOLMES: Your mother . . .

LIZA: I was coming to that.

HOLMES: I don't mean to pry . . .

LIZA: If anyone is entitled to these facts, Mr. Holmes, you certainly
are. Do you remember the case of The Vinegar-Stained Hatband?

HOLMES: Quite clearly.

LIZA: Then you will recall that after a variety of unfortunate circumstances, you stalked my father to an old mill near Haddlesby, Dorset, where you, temporarily, lost the scent.

HOLMES: Yes, I remember it vividly. The search was called off for five days and then Moriarty was sighted at Christchurch Abbey disguised as a choirboy. He was uncovered by the deacon during a routine examination of the children's genitals and fled immediately.

LIZA: What you never knew was that during those five days when he appeared to have vanished off the face of the earth, he was being hidden by my mother, a coloratura soprano who used that old mill as a practice studio.

HOLMES: Your mother—Moriarty. But where in heaven's . . .

LIZA: There was a trap door that led to an old cellar and in that dark dungeon my mother, who, due to the turbulence of her musical talent, was prevented from practising anywhere else in Dorset, used to run scales, from dawn to dusk. It was only after balancing on a precarious rafter for twenty-four hours that my father realized he was not alone in that old mill. He heard sounds of the diatonic scale emanating shakily from somewhere behind the mill, traced the sound to a trap door and eventually found my mother. At first she was frightened out of her wits. He made a clean breast of everything, told her he was being hounded by the police and threw himself on her mercy. She immediately responded to his entreaties, being softhearted and Episcopalian.

Nothing more would have come of this encounter had it not soon transpired that my father possessed a plangent baritone voice and knew, by heart, most of the selections my mother had been practising. Keeping to a tremulous sotto voce, so as not to give away their whereabouts, the two began to perform a series of duets from Mendelssohn to Spohr. The softness of their tone, made necessary by the precariousness of my father's situation, gradually engendered an intimacy for, as you may know, Mr. Holmes, it is not possible to sing duets from Mendelssohn to Spohr in hushed tones without some kind of bond springing up. Before long my father realized he had met the woman of his heart. During a rather impassioned allegro vivace from 'La Forza del Destino' my father, who virtually dissolved before the sway of Verdi, succumbed to my mother's E above high C, and intimacies followed hard upon.

HOLMES: But surely Moriarty didn't just leave after that?

LIZA: He had no intimation that his musical duet was to bear fruit. For, despite his cunning and his guile, he knew virtually nothing about biology. It was only months afterward that my mother had the courage to inform my father of the birth of twins.

HOLMES: How did she manage to track him down again?

LIZA: Before he left her at the old mill, he devised an ingenious scheme for communication by way of the personal columns of the public prints. He instructed my mother to advertise the passing of imaginary clergymen from remote parts of the British Isles, using a code known only to him and her. And in this way, one fateful Sunday, he read the words: "In eternal and loving memory of Vicar Aspinall Pratt late of Aberystwyth—now resident in Paradise." He knew at once that he had become the father of twins.

HOLMES: And your mother . . .

LIZA: My life, no less than my father's, has been pockmarked with tragedies, Mr. Holmes. As a result of assistance from a mysterious benefactor, who was undoubtedly my father, my mother soon achieved the concert stage. She gave a premiere recital at the Wigmore Hall on the 24th of November, 1889.

HOLMES: 24th of November, 1889 . . . but wasn't that the day . . .

LIZA: You remember it. I thought you might—though not half so well as I.

HOLMES: It was a macabre incident. There was a short notice of it in The Times, if I remember rightly.

LIZA: During the last encore, as a result of a tremendous ovation in a rather unstable hall, the castors of the concert-grand came loose from their moorings and, as the pianist hit the first chords of Spohr's "Blumen in Meinem Herz" which, as you probably know, is a wild cascade of B-Flats, the instrument came hurtling down upon the unsuspecting soloist, pinned her against the side of the stage, and lodged itself in her diaphragm. The hammers of the upper octaves were wedged lethally into her abdomen, and although a series of delicate operations managed to remove everything from E flat to F above high C, the damage was irreversible.

HOLMES: A grim and fascinating account, madam, but I fail to see what all this . . .

LIZA: Has to do with you? I was just coming to that.

HOLMES: Pray do.

(LIZA *coughs.*)

HOLMES *(continued)* Can I offer you an apple or some grapes perhaps?

LIZA: That would be . . .

HOLMES: *(Reaching for them)* Blast that jade! Even the fruit bowl is drained dry. *(Cordial)* I'm not usually so bereft, but my odious housekeeper . . .

LIZA: Think nothing of it. Fruit is somewhat binding before dinner. That letter, Mr. Holmes . . .

HOLMES: Letter?

LIZA: I know all about it. Simeon told me he was sending it, just as he described the gory details of the ruin he intends to wreak upon you. You must leave London at once.

HOLMES: My dear young woman, I am touched by your regard for my welfare but as you surely must know, a day without a threat against my life is like "un jour sans soleil."

LIZA: But so long as you remain here, he will continue to make attempts on your life.

HOLMES: And if I leave, why would he not pursue me, as indeed, I pursued his notorious father?

LIZA: Once he has had time to assimilate the shock of our father's death, he will forego his desperate plans.

HOLMES: My dear, if he is a true Moriarty, and your story leaves little doubt on that score, he will pursue his fiendish aims to their pre-ordained conclusions.

LIZA: But I wish to make an end of this hideous enmity. My father is dead. My mother is dead. My brother is all I have left, and I know if he continues on this course, he will certainly come to ruin.

HOLMES: I do understand your dilemma, my dear Miss Moriarty, but you do see, don't you, that I have no alternative but to defend my life if it is threatened.

LIZA: There is one.

HOLMES: And that is . . .

LIZA: If I can find him—if I can lead you to him, would you promise to reason with him? The actual confrontation with Sherlock Holmes would be enough to disperse his wild fancies.

HOLMES: And what if I cannot dissuade him? What if the sight of me so incenses him, he strikes immediately and eventually hangs for it? Then you will have the blood of two men on your hands.

LIZA: If he cannot be dissuaded from his course, then I myself shall arrange for his detention, for I would rather have him under lock and key than standing trial for attempted murder.

HOLMES: My dear Miss Moriarty, there is another aspect to this problem which you do not seem to have considered. I am Sherlock Holmes. That is a name and reputation well known throughout these

British Isles and, I daresay, beyond them. You are asking me to go to a young hothead and dissuade him from a vengeful course of action, the inference being to the uninformed that I fear his designs.

LIZA: But you know that isn't true.

HOLMES: I know it, and you know it, but the press invariably scrutinize the hole rather than the doughnut.

LIZA: But if you can restrain Simeon, I will tell the world the true circumstances and when I have done that, your behavior, rather than smacking of cowardice, will be wreathed in magnanimity. Here is a boy whom you could have crushed—as you did his father. Instead you have given him a stern reprimand and an opportunity to mend his ways.

HOLMES: *(Savoring it)* Put that way, I must say it has a certain ring to it.

LIZA: Will you do it?

(HOLMES *puffs and thinks.* LIZA *waits tensely.*)

LIZA *(Continued)* I have always heard that one of the things that made Sherlock Holmes the Great Sherlock Holmes was that he managed to temper justice with charity.

(HOLMES, *struck by the thought, has a moment of silent self-idealization, then false humility.*)

HOLMES: Miss Moriarty, you are as eloquent as you are charming. You have a bargain. Find the hothead, and I shall endeavor to cool his brow with the cold compress of reason.

LIZA: Oh thank you; thank you. *(Impetuously kissing him)* I'm sorry. I lost my head.

HOLMES: Recover it immediately, Miss Moriarty. Emotional effusions of that sort are the dry-rot that weakens the timbers of masculine resolve.

LIZA: I'm very sorry. It will never happen again.

HOLMES: On the other hand, don't make long range plans you may have to amend.

LIZA: Of course.

HOLMES: But be advised, Miss Moriarty, that if after two weeks you have not located him, it were better that you retired from the scene and let destiny take its inexorable course.

LIZA: Your terms are completely fair, Mr. Holmes. If I cannot bring him to you in two weeks' time, I shall steel myself for the consequences of his actions, and your own.

HOLMES: Good.

LIZA: Oh, one last point. If Simeon learned of my coming here, he would be furious—so when I next have news of him, rather than risk a return visit, I will send it by carrier pigeon.

HOLMES: And how, pray, will you manage that?

LIZA: During a brief family reunion in Capistrano, my father taught me to train birds expressly for that purpose. He believed written messages sent by normal means were certain to be tampered with. It was one of my father's many fanciful ideas.

HOLMES: On the contrary, I suspect the theory is sound and may well account for the longeurs of our atrocious postal service.

(LIZA *smiles at* HOLMES' *gallantry in acceding the point.* HOLMES *receives the smile and smiles back.*)

It strikes me, Miss Moriarty, there is one refreshment I *can* offer. *(Suddenly producing it)* A bottle of Chateauneuf-de-Pape 1794 which I keep for very special occasions, of which this is certainly one. *(Pouring the drink. Close to* LISA*)* Would you be rash enough to indulge with me?

(LISA *after a pause, slowly nods 'yes' and is given a glass.* HOLMES *slowly pours the drink looking directly into her eyes.*)

You have the brightest, most intense and exciting eyes I have ever seen in a woman.

LIZA: *(Close)* Everyone says I get them from my father.

(HOLMES *slowly pulls back as the lights fade.*)

Blackout

Scene 3

Lights up.

The Baker Street flat is even more untidy than before, strewn with teacups, piles of clothes that need washing, papers, etc.

HOLMES: *(Entering)* Lestrade, you're making a bloody nuisance of yourself.

LESTRADE: *(On his heels)* That is as may be, Holmes, but the fact remains this letter constitutes a threat on your life and I'm obliged to take it seriously.

HOLMES: *You* may take it as seriously as you wish.

LESTRADE: 'N so should you, Holmes. This is no ordinary crank, y'know. This is the son of the most notorious scoundrel that ever prowled the streets of London. If he's even half the man his father was, he's a threat to every decent person for miles around. In any case, we've taken some subtle precautions.

HOLMES: If you're referring to those beefy bobbies you've posted outside my front door, I can tell you right now, Lestrade, they will have to go. All those brass buttons and brogans are lowering the tone of the entire neighborhood.

LESTRADE: I could always put them into plain clothes.

HOLMES: If *your* plain clothes are anything to go by, it'd be a veritable slum.

LESTRADE: You may think all of this is a big joke, but Dr. Watson and I feel that . . .

HOLMES: Ah ha, so you've consulted with Dr. Watson . . .

LESTRADE: When I received a copy of that letter, I felt it my duty to discuss the problem with all the people directly concerned.

HOLMES: Excluding myself who is, of course, the most directly concerned.

LESTRADE: Dr. Watson and I—and all of Scotland Yard—have your best interests at heart, Mr. Holmes.

HOLMES: Bollocks.

LESTRADE: Still Dr. Watson and I thought it would be a good idea. *(Checks watch)* I wonder what's become of him. We arranged to meet here at 2:30. It's not like him to be late.

HOLMES: To meet here?

LESTRADE: To try to persuade you to take some protective measures in this matter, Holmes.

HOLMES: I must say, Lestrade, your cloying sense of paternalism is really becoming quite obnoxious. I've never before required the aid *(Sounds of thumping in the closet)* of Scotland Yard in my personal or professional dealings and I would rather . . .

LESTRADE: *(Jumping back, with pistol)* Stand back, Mr. Holmes.

(More thumps from closet.)

There's someone in that closet.

HOLMES: Astonishing deduction, Lestrade.

LESTRADE: Stand back, he may be armed.

HOLMES: Highly unlikely—or he wouldn't be thumping the door with his elbows.

LESTRADE: Eh?

(HOLMES *approaches closet and opens it.* WATSON, *entirely trussed up and gagged with a letter pinned to his lapel, stumbles out and into* HOLMES' *arms.* HOLMES *helps him onto bench.*)

Good Gawd, Dr. Watson! What are you doin' in there? How'd you get into that closet? What in heaven's name has happened to you?

HOLMES: I believe the answer to all of those questions might be facilitated if you removed the gag, Lestrade.

LESTRADE: What? Oh. *(Begins to remove gag and untie him)* Dr. Watson, are you all right?

WATSON: Ugh . . . ugh . . . drink . . . drink!

LESTRADE: *(Pouring brandy)* Good Gawd, man, you look terrible. How long've you been in there? You gave me a start I can tell you. *(Gulps down the brandy he has poured out for* WATSON*)* Gave me quite a turn, it did.

(HOLMES *takes brandy.*)

HOLMES: Are you all right, Watson?

WATSON: Barely.

HOLMES: Have a swig. Ropes, Lestrade.

WATSON: *(Drinking)* Thanks, Holmes.

LESTRADE: What's happened for Gawd's sake!

WATSON: I'm not at all sure. I was just sitting in the study correcting a few pages for my next edition, and I heard this buzzing against the window pane. I came in to have a look, opened the window and the next thing I knew everything went black. Then, about two minutes ago, I woke up, opened my eyes and everything was still black. I started banging my elbows against the door, and then you came.

LESTRADE: Did you get a look at 'im, Watson?

WATSON: Not a glimpse, I'm afraid.

HOLMES: *(Who has already gone to the window to inspect)* This, no doubt, was the visitor at the window.

LESTRADE: That? Why that's just a dead worm, isn't it?

HOLMES: A hornet actually, a vespa crabro if I'm not mistaken, ingeniously glued to the outside of the window. You see it's actually stung the glass.

WATSON: A hornet?

HOLMES: Yes you may recall, Watson, we were given notice of a hornet's sting some short while ago in an unpublished piece of light verse.

LESTRADE: *(Looks to* WATSON*)* What's that all about?

HOLMES: Nothing important, Lestrade. *(To* WATSON*)* Go on, Watson.

WATSON: Well, there's nothing more to tell. I opened the window and then . . .

HOLMES: And then whoever it was who arranged the hornet's sting placed chloroform over your face, tied you hand and foot and bundled you into that closet leaving the way he got in—across the window ledge to the drainpipe and down to the pavement. You can just smell the faint whiffs of the chloroform on your lapel.

(LESTRADE *bends over and sniffs* WATSON's *lapel.)*

WATSON: But who in Heaven's name would want to . . .

HOLMES: *(Noticing letter pinned to his lapel.)* May I, Watson? I think this will contain the answers to all our questions.

LESTRADE: A letter! Pinned to his jacket. Like a baby! What's it say, Mr. Holmes?

HOLMES: It's addressed to myself.

LESTRADE: But what's it say?

HOLMES: Nothing concerning you, old chap.

LESTRADE: *(Fuming)* For Gawd's sake, Holmes, I've got a perfect right . . .

HOLMES: To stick your nose wherever you please, Lestrade, but not into my personal post. *(Folds it up.)* And now, Lestrade, I must insist you call off your bulldogs at once. Immediately. If this bumptious boy feels he has succeeded in rattling my composure and involving the formidable troops of Scotland Yard, it will only inspire him to new and more outrageous pranks—whereas if we do nothing at all, he will eventually desist.

LESTRADE: It could work in reverse, Mr. Holmes. If we paid him no mind, he might become even wilder in his schemes.

HOLMES: I can assure you, Lestrade, that within 48 hours the entire matter will be cleared up and Simeon Moriarty in your custody. You must give me your word, Lestrade.

LESTRADE: *(Protesting)* Mr. Holmes, I can't . . .

HOLMES: As an Inspector!

LESTRADE: I can't possibly . . .

HOLMES: As an Englishman!

LESTRADE: It would be far too . . .

HOLMES: As a servant of the Queen!!!

(LESTRADE *immediately comes to attention.*)

Good man, Lestrade. Now hurry along and walk out the front door as if nothing at all is amiss. Try whistling as you stroll down the pavement.

LESTRADE: If I do, I'll have a dozen bobbies at my heels within seconds.

HOLMES: Quite right. Just hum quietly to yourself.

LESTRADE: I don't know how to hum.

HOLMES: Then just make your way down the street looking blank. Everything must appear to be normal.

LESTRADE: *(About to protest)* Mr. Holmes . . .

HOLMES: *(Barking)* Dismissed!

(LESTRADE *snaps to attention, scowls at* WATSON, *plunks on his hat and trudges out.*)

HOLMES: Are you quite all right, old chap?

WATSON: Yes. A little the worse for wear. It's not very cozy in that wardrobe.

HOLMES: Still, it was not a very long ordeal. You weren't out more than ten minutes.

WATSON: How do you know that, Holmes?

HOLMES: By the residue of the chloroform, which was only barely evident.

WATSON: But what's in that letter, Holmes?

HOLMES: An accomplished scribe, this young Moriarty. One feels had he turned to literature rather than crime, he would have fared much better.*(Reads)* "As you can see, Mr. Holmes, I can penetrate your inner sanctum whenever I choose. Take this little encounter with Dr. Watson as a preamble to what is in store for yourself. Although you will not get off quite so lightly as your addle-brained stooge. Signed, Simeon." Hm, already on first-name terms.

WATSON: "Addle-brained stooge"! The little brat, I've a good mind to . . .

HOLMES: Don't you see, Watson. His entire purpose is to try to rattle us with these undergraduate high-jinks. Boorishness parading as wit —could anything be more British?

WATSON: Holmes, this fellow may be a mewling youth as far as you're concerned, but he *is* a Moriarty and therefore there's no telling what he might do.

HOLMES: Piffle.

WATSON: Holmes, you're taking this much too . . .

(The doorbell sounds. WATSON *stops in his tracks and looks fearfully to* HOLMES. *A pause. The doorbell sounds again.)*

HOLMES: I realize you may still be a bit shaky, Watson, but surely you recognize the sound of the front doorbell.

WATSON: Shall I answer it?

WATSON: Why not?

WATSON: What if it's . . .

HOLMES: Anyone who takes the trouble to scale the narrow ledge of a third-floor window in order to glue a hornet to the glass is not going to be so uncomplicated as to stroll through the front door. Or would you like me to attend to it myself?

WATSON: I'm going . . . I'm going . . .

(WATSON *exits.* HOLMES *picks up rope, puts salt and pepper on it, holds it by his ear, twists it and listens as one would listen with a cigar.)*

Not a sign of anyone. Just this parcel left outside your door. What do you say to that, Holmes?

(WATSON *hands parcel to* HOLMES *who unwraps it to reveal a gravestone.)*

HOLMES: A rather conventional piece of stone-cutting—not remarkable either for shape or texture.

WATSON: Read it, Holmes, read what it says.

HOLMES: *(Squinting through magnifying glass)* "In Memory of Sherlock Holmes Who Was Rash Enough to Believe He Could Outwit The Son Even as he Under-Estimated The Father"*(Craning forward for the small print)* Born June 1846—Died September 1897. *(Looks to* WATSON)

WATSON: And there is only one more week left in September.

HOLMES: What a bloody cheek!

WATSON: Eh?

HOLMES: Diabolical audacity!

WATSON: Don't let it upset you, Holmes.

HOLMES: Outrageous gall!

WATSON: It's a joke in very poor taste, I must say.

HOLMES: Making me out to be fifty-one when I'm not a day over forty-three!

WATSON: *(Confused) Eh?*

HOLMES: Watson, I want you to muster every atom of scientific objectivity you possess and answer me as truthfully as you know how: Do I look fifty-one!

WATSON: Holmes, I don't think that . . .

HOLMES: Don't hedge, dammit, and don't stammer. Do I give the appearance of being a man well into middle-age, on the lower rungs of fifty?

WATSON: Don't fret, Holmes, I'm sure he simply got his facts wrong.

HOLMES: It's all very well for a man of your advanced age telling me not to fret. You will never see sixty again.

WATSON: Come, come, Holmes.

HOLMES: It's quite another thing for a man in the very prime of life to have a gauche youth proclaim—in print—that I have one foot in the grave.

WATSON: What is much more important than the print on this morbid stone is the fiendish implication. The boy clearly means to do you in —whatever his sister may say.

HOLMES: *(Inspecting himself in glass)* There's very little weather in this face. No inroads to speak of: no hairpin bends. Even my smile is remarkably wrinkle-free. Wouldn't you say?*(Smiles)*

WATSON: It's a damn striking face, Holmes.

HOLMES: There is no frost threatening the temples. The back is straight and firm. A goodly frame, wouldn't you say?

WATSON: Olympic caliber.

HOLMES: The lustre in the eyes is bright. The voice, lubricious and resonant—winningly musical, when it chooses to be.

WATSON: Covent Garden standard, no one would dispute it.

HOLMES: And yet, this snivelling, green-gilled boy dares to insinuate a chronology of fifty-one years.

WATSON: Holmes, what are you going to do about this threat on your life?

HOLMES: *(Composing himself)* Do, Watson? We will do nothing at all. Using the dirigible of our wider perspective and the helium of our lofty breeding, we shall rise above it.

WATSON: What about Liza Moriarty?

HOLMES: Her description of her wayward brother's character appears to be quite accurate. We have made a proposal to her, and we shall stick to it.

WATSON: Holmes, I know you very well and if there is anyone who can get round you, it's a pale-skinned, fine-boned woman with red hair—which perfectly fits the description you've given me of Miss Moriarty.

HOLMES: Balderdash.

WATSON: Will you stand there and deny that you have a weakness for a woman of Miss Moriarty's appearance?

HOLMES: My curiosity for Simeon Moriarty grows daily. I shall quite relish the encounter, when it takes place. And now, I think I shall have a little smoke.

WATSON: *(Uptight)* I see. In that case I'll be getting along. But I do wish you would take this a bit more seriously, Holmes.

HOLMES: Matters of life and death are just flotsam and jetsam, but a full pipe, my dear Watson, is a good smoke.

WATSON: Who said that?

HOLMES: I did. Is your hearing defective?

WATSON: I'll look in tomorrow.

HOLMES: Do so.

WATSON: And be careful.

(WATSON *exits front door.*)

(HOLMES *who has already started packing his pipe with the mysterious substance, lights up and puffs languidly. Goes to looking-glass, inspects himself. Discovers a gray hair, pulls it out by the root, regards it scornfully, withdraws a black make-up stick from breast pocket, rubs it over hairline. Stops, scrutinizes face again.*)

HOLMES: *(Scornfully)* Fifty-one! I shall not rest till I have his testicles in the palm of my hand.

(*A pigeon flies through the window with a note tied to its foot and lands in the palm of* HOLMES' *hand. He removes the note, reads it, then tosses the bird towards the window, through which it blithely flies out. Then, with his magnifying glass he examines the droppings in the palm of his hand, looks up reflectively and the lights black out.*)

Scene 4

Lights up.

A dank cellar. A chair Center, draped with a musty sheet. A closet to the Right—Another, Left. Murky.

WATSON: *(With lantern)* Holmes, this is absolutely insane. Let me ring up Lestrade—at least tell him where we are.

HOLMES: *(With lantern)* That is expressly contrary to the instructions, Watson, and I do not wish to appear uncavalier. *(Finding lights)* Lantern, Watson.

WATSON: *(Realizing, involuntarily snuffing it)* But you know nothing about her, Holmes. And this Simeon, this crazy brother of hers— who's to say he hasn't arranged the whole thing as a trap? Who's to say they aren't both in it together?

HOLMES: My dear Watson, don't you think I've taken all the necessary precautions?

WATSON: What precautions?

HOLMES: Every detail of Liza Moriarty's story has been checked. The old mill in Dorset does have an antechamber, with a small piano installed against one of the walls. Moriarty's wife, this charming girl's mother, did die in the manner described on the date in question, as this Times clipping clearly reports. The character of Simeon Moriarty's hand does suggest an unstable personality with marked proclivity towards rash action. The P's and Q's are precisely those of a man consumed with revenge whereas the I's and O's of Miss Moriarty's hand in this letter informing us of this tryst, so conveniently received by carrier pigeon, are those of an honest and straightforward person with unblemished character. So far, the pieces fit together quite correctly.

WATSON: But look at this place . . . who's to say that this man, the man who wrote that letter, hasn't lured you here to wreak that very revenge you say is burning in his bosom? I beg you, Holmes, let me ring Lestrade. If anything should happen . . .

HOLMES: Yes, Watson?

WATSON: Well, need I spell it out, Holmes? Not a soul in the world knows where we are, and if this Moriarty girl has been leading you up the garden path, we may be in grave danger.

HOLMES: When Professor Moriarty left this vale of tears, all real danger left with him. Now that he is gone, there is no one, no thief, no

assassin, no confidence-trickster so deadly he cannot be disarmed by
my superior intelligence. One may well call that arrogance . . .

WATSON: Indeed one may . . .

HOLMES: But, like all my other observations, it is founded on verifiable
fact.

WATSON: But where are we, anyway? And why did we have to come
such a roundabout route? We'll never find our way back.

HOLMES: Like his father, the boy has a flair for the melodramatic. This
is the only place he would agree to meet his sister.

WATSON: *If* what she's said is true. But what if it isn't? What if the two
of them are . . .

HOLMES: Will it put your heart at ease if I tell you that the meeting
was set for 11:00 p.m.?

WATSON: Eleven! But it's only 7:30.

HOLMES: Exactly. I wanted to be here well in advance of either Miss
Moriarty or her brother. If indeed there is a worm, which I doubt,
the early bird, I am led to believe, has the odds-on chance of catching
it.

WATSON: *(Relieved)* Thank God you're still ticking away up there,
Holmes. I had a terrible fear that girl had turned your head. Well,
shall we go?

HOLMES: Certainly not.

WATSON: But they won't be here till close on midnight.

HOLMES: Exactly, and therefore no traps can be devised.

WATSON: Damn it, Holmes, I really don't know where I am with you.
One moment you say there's nothing to fear—the girl is honest, and
the next you're talking about traps being set.

HOLMES: The only way to deal with a woman, Watson, is to speak to her as if she were an angel and assume she is a serpent. *(Removes cover from chair)* Let's see, what have we here?

WATSON: It's some kind of barber chair, is it?

HOLMES: Or a dentist's chair—somesuch.

WATSON: Check the floor, Holmes. Make sure there are no trap doors or anything.

HOLMES: Quite solid. I tested it with my hollow-heel boot a moment ago.

WATSON: What about the exits?

HOLMES: There's only this winding staircase coming from the street above. I examined the door when we entered and it seems perfectly sound.

WATSON: It's terribly dank in here. Why couldn't we just meet at a pub or something? What's this here, Holmes?

HOLMES: A broom closet, I expect. Firmly locked from the outside. *(He withdraws stethoscope from inside his coat)*

WATSON: What have you got there, Holmes?

HOLMES: A stethoscope, my dear Watson. Surely *you* are familiar with the breed. However, in the highly sophisticated form you see before you, capable of discerning the sound of human breathing at a distance of twenty feet. *(Listens to door)* No. Quite, quite still.

WATSON: I say, Holmes, I've never seen one of those.

HOLMES: It is not a standard piece of equipment at St. Bart's, I should imagine, having invented it myself only six weeks ago. *(Packs it away)* Good. We are quite alone at the moment, and so long as we remain until the Moriarties appear, there is no chance of any unexpected arrivals.

WATSON: Holmes, what if this boy gets out of hand?

HOLMES: Out of hand, Watson?

WATSON: Yes, what if he becomes incensed and tries to do the job right here and now. How will you ward him off?

HOLMES: You are fiendishly inquisitive, Watson.

WATSON: I'm not made of iron like you, Holmes. I'm quite mortal, and quite frightened.

HOLMES: If the boy does attempt a sudden lunge of any sort, I think my own ju-jitsu training will be equal to the situation. Should it not be, this ring will do the trick.

WATSON: Hit him with that? Good God, Holmes, it would barely scratch him.

HOLMES: Not hit him with it, Watson. Spray him with it. *(He demonstrates)* A carefully prepared solution of sodium-sulphate and spirit of ammonia issues from a tiny spout in the heart of this ingenious ring causing severe blindness and temporary impotence.

WATSON: Holmes, I am continually amazed by your knowledge of chemicals. How in Heaven's name do you come by it?

HOLMES: They are easily prepared from simple solutions available from any chemist's shop without prescription. It's simply a matter of knowing how to mix them. But, Watson, you're dealing with chemicals all day long. Surely you know how simple a matter it is.

WATSON: Confound it, Holmes, I'm dealing with sophisticated compounds, not ordinary penny-farthing oils and ointments.

HOLMES: The characteristic of great minds, Watson, is the ability to transform the ordinary into the extraordinary. *(Sits)* A bit like changing water into wine.

WATSON: What's this?

HOLMES: What's what, Watson?

WATSON: Here on this chair . . . some . . . lever . . .

HOLMES: Lever?

(Pushes levers. Chair suddenly closes up around HOLMES, *clamping down* HOLMES' *arms and legs.)*

Well, I'll be damned! I haven't seen one of these for years. It's a La Frontenac Chair.

WATSON: La Frontenac?

HOLMES: Developed by a demented French dentist in the early sixties. His aim being to seduce a young girl who had consistently rejected his advances. When he sat her down, ostensibly to fill her cavity, it closed up on her, just as this one does, tipped back, and then to the best of my recollection, he proceeded to ravish the girl mercilessly.

WATSON: Good God!

HOLMES: An amazing replica; if replica it is. Well, I must say, that does put a slightly different complexion on the charming Miss Moriarty and this whole business. I'm afraid your own fears were, in this instance, a bit more prudential than my own. Now, how to get out of this thing?

WATSON: But is that possible, Holmes?

HOLMES: *(Looking for ways to extricate himself)* Is what possible?

WATSON: What you just said.

HOLMES: What did I just say?

WATSON: About my own fears being, in this instance, more prudential than your own. I mean, that's never happened before; that I should have reached some kind of conclusion which was correct, before yourself. Or, as it is in this case, by means of a completely original deduction.

HOLMES: I don't wish to be rude, dear boy, but perhaps we could continue the analysis a little later.

WATSON: But it's really quite astounding, if it's true. I mean, deductions are, always have been, your own special province, your speciality, one might say. I can usually recognize them after the event, but never beforehand. That is quite out of character.

HOLMES: Watson, these straps are rather tight . . .

WATSON: I know. I made them so that they would just pinch your skin enough to produce discomfort but not outright pain.

(Long pause as HOLMES *regards* WATSON. *Then* WATSON *gingerly slips* HOLMES' *ring off his finger and removes a revolver from his inside pocket.)*

Yes, you were quite right—yet again, my dear Holmes. Spot on. It is the La Frontenac Chair, recently part of a medical exhibition at St. Bart's, and a very popular item it was, too. Not that anyone would miss it now as it's already gone back to Birmingham—or so the officials believe. And you're quite right. It does tip back. *(Tips it back)* And, as you see, it is quite binding.

HOLMES: Since everything has an explanation, I assume this . . . action . . . has one as well.

WATSON: Undoubtedly, my dear Holmes, but isn't it curious, it's one that has not occurred to you? Why is that, I wonder? Well, I shall tell you and perhaps you will find it elementary, my dear Holmes, because for me, for whom so many things have been elementary, this is the most elementary thing of all.

You consider yourself quite a sleuth, dear Sherlock—quite observant. Very good at uncovering clues, sifting evidence, observing details. How is it that in all your many exploits, or should I say 'our exploits,' you never noticed one recurring symptom. A trait which was present at every single case with which you dealt. I refer to—a wince. A slight, infinitesimal shiver which ran through my nervous system every time you asked me to corroborate some brilliant discovery of your own. A wince which punctuated every deft comment you ever uttered in correcting the muggy little obscurities and confusions of my own pathetic mind. A wince which, if it could speak, would have said: You arrogant, supercilious, egocentric, narcissistic, smug and self-congratulatory bastard. How you enjoy lording it over your bumbly, slow-witted, treacle-minded aide-de-camp. Your selfless, fawning, ever-faithful Boswell for whose benefit you paraded your brilliance and your ingenuity.

God, I can just imagine how insufferable Johnson was to *his* faithful recorder. Slowing down to make sure he caught every word of the telling epigram; every nuance of the well-turned phrase.

It starts very slowly, you know; very gradually, the way all great vendettas begin. A slight here, a sarcasm there, the ego first rubbed the wrong way, then bruised, then battered, then seething with convulsions of rage and dark dreams of revenge. A chance remark to Lestrade the point of which is—you noticed, I didn't. A passing remark to a mutual friend the inference of which is certain minds can grasp the innuendo, other minds cannot. And then gradually, taking your superiority for granted; taking equally for granted my doziness, my backwardness, my innate lack of perception. But who am I? Did you ever ask the question? Or did you ever answer it further than by saying, my lackey, my shadow, my faithful lapdog.

I am a Doctor of Medicine. I trained. I studied. I was honored at University. I received certificates. I won awards. When I walked down a hospital corridor, then I was no flunky, no lapdog but a respected member of the medical profession with a flair for literature and an enviable intellect. But later, after you had insinuated yourself on my personality and into the minds of everyone who knew me, I was those things no longer. I was poor bumbly Watson, you know, the good-natured stooge of that detective fellow. No, not Holmes—Watson's the other one, the dull chap who never gets it quite right.

(Slowly subsides before the next.)

Are you beginning to understand, my dear Sherlock, the enormity of your crime? Beside it, everything Moriarty ever conceived or executed pales. And nothing can redeem it; nothing but the supreme penalty.

HOLMES: You don't seem to have learned very much, Watson, from your years of, what I suppose you would call 'servitude'! Do you really believe you will get away with whatever preposterous action you are contemplating?

WATSON: I'm sure of it, my dear Holmes, because I have learned from the master.

HOLMES: When Liza Moriarty gets here and finds that . . .

WATSON: Liza Moriarty? *(Laughs)* You really are priceless, my dear Sherlock. Liza Moriarty! *(Laughs)* Bertha Walmsley! You don't know the name? Why should you? A poor out-of-work actress grateful for any role that affords some small remuneration, even if only playing a fictitious character named Liza Moriarty for a bumbly old Doctor Watson given to playing practical jokes on his dear old friend Sherlock Holmes. Obviously very underrated as an actress for she took you in very well. But then *I* rehearsed her and so, I suppose, the credit is really mine. It took a little while finding a pale, fine-boned redhead, but then I did so want to choose the kind of girl I knew you would fancy. I did take pains, you know.

HOLMES: But that old mill in Dorset . . .

WATSON: Is two miles from a Medical Institute I visit every summer. Six months ago I arranged for an upright piano to be stored in its ante-chamber.

HOLMES: But I read that article in The Times.

WATSON: Which I never doubted you would. It refers to an absolutely true incident at which an unfortunate contralto was the subject of a rather grotesque accident. That part of the story is entirely true, but I'm afraid the other details of her background are my own, somewhat melodramatic, invention.

HOLMES: And that letter from Simeon . . . ?

WATSON: Was, as you so aptly put it, the work of a man consumed with revenge. Knowing full well you would use your expert powers to analyze that scrawl, and since my scheme called for just such a character, I took it upon myself to write the letter in longhand. It was bravado, I grant you, but you see, I banked on the fact that through all these years, you have been so consumed with your own affairs and so oblivious of mine that never, in a thousand years, would you have recognized my handwriting. After all, Holmes, handwriting, as you yourself have taught me, is something very personal to a human being, and since you have never in all these years recognized me as a human being, there was little danger you would recognize my hand. No, Holmes, the reason I would always be the very last suspect on your list is because I am for you an invisible man. Like a doormat is invisible, until you need it to wipe your boots on.

HOLMES: And do you really think Miss Walmsley, or whatever her name is, will keep your little secret?

WATSON: Certainly not. Out-of-work actresses are as untrustworthy as . . . long-suffering general practitioners. It was important to select a performer who would not be around to stoke up any old coals. Miss Walmsley perfectly fitted the bill as she is suffering from acute consumption and has barely six weeks to live, a diagnosis I carefully carried out before recruiting her into my project. The sum of money I provided for her assistance has already enabled her to set sail for Australia, a country in which medical science is so backward, there is no chance of her obtaining proper treatment. In two weeks she will be coughing up blood. In four, she will be bedridden. In six, it will all be mercifully over.

(HOLMES *tries to wriggle out of the chair's grasp.*)

The straps on that thing are quite ingenious, I assure you. Almost as ingenious as my own knots when I tied and gagged myself in the closet and sprinkled a few drops of chloroform onto my lapel—where I knew, without fail, you would discover them. A bit extreme all that, but again, I knew it would appeal to your sense of melodrama. It took hours to train that bloody pigeon. A long, messy business too, and doctoring that cuckoo clock wasn't easy either.

(WATSON *goes to closet, unlocks it with his own key and removes a small trolley which contains a quantity of test-tubes, bunsen burner, etc. on which he proceeds to mix chemicals.* HOLMES *watches all of these actions coolly.)*

HOLMES: Watson, I think I have underrated you all these years.

WATSON: *(Exaggeratedly)* Oh thank you, Master. Praise from Sherlock Holmes is praise indeed.

HOLMES: In spite of everything you've said, I still harbor some affection for you and I would hate to think of you winding up in the dock charged with murder.

WATSON: So would I, dear Sherlock, and that's why I've taken all the necessary precautions to avoid such a fate.

HOLMES: Have you? And how will my . . . disappearance . . . be explained to others?

WATSON: The fact is, apart from other skills acquired in your service, I have become an expert calligrapher. I've got your own hand down to a T, and I, or rather you, have written the following letter which will be found in your Baker Street flat tomorrow morning, I expect. It reads as follows:

"Since the death of Professor Moriarty, I have felt no challenge in the art of detection. Each case has only been a repetition of former triumphs. Therefore, in my last communication to the world, I want it to be known that I intend to dismantle the personage that has become Sherlock Holmes, so this is the last you shall ever hear of him in that guise. I am going off to start a new life, in another land, with another name, and a new entirely unremarkable personality. For all future enquiries, I direct you to my trusty colleague Dr. Watson, without whom my entire career would have taken a quite other course."

I like that last touch, don't you?

HOLMES: And you honestly believe that will settle the matter? Why, there will be a tremendous search through every continent in the world to seek me out.

WATSON: Correct, my dear Holmes, and in every metropolis, there will be news of you. You will be found time and time again. In Hong Kong, in Sydney, in Innsbruck, in Minneapolis. It will always be Sherlock Holmes, and it will never be you.

HOLMES: And do you believe my friends will believe such a letter . . . ?

WATSON: What friends? Lestrade? Mrs. Hudson? You have no friends. Only clients from the past, and they're no longer interested in you. Your only friend is myself, and I shall see to it that your memory remains untarnished. I shall never deflate the myth of Sherlock Holmes, you can be sure of that.

By the way, all of this could have been avoided you know, if you'd heeded my prophetic little quatrain, "If you should know the hornet's sting, Seek the insect in his nest." And what other insect is there in your dishevelled nest, but myself; a hornet buzzing out your story to the world.

HOLMES: I suppose I never unravelled that puzzle because I could never think of you as a hornet. A worm, now that would have been a better clue.

WATSON: Do I sense the first little niggles of spite? I think I do. How welcome they are—

HOLMES: When Mrs. Hudson returns to London . . .

WATSON: You will have mysteriously disappeared and no one will be more forlorn and desperate than I. By then, of course, she will have discovered that letter about her dying grandfather to be a cruel hoax. Another of my ingenious literary inventions. But her capacity for lamentation will not be wasted. She'll have you to mourn and me to commiserate with. *(Beat)*

You must admit it is a grand design. Perhaps the Grandest Design ever concocted by the Mind of Man.

HOLMES: *(Cool)* You are quite mad. Quite, quite mad.

WATSON: *(Beat) (Grimly)* I know that. My own scientific objectivity tells me so. Quite, quite mad. But as with all madness, the first question the doctor must answer is whence came the disease. What is its root, and its cause? *You* are the root and cause of my madness. Your pride and arrogance, and when I realized that, although quite, quite mad, I was on the road to recovery, for I decided to pull out the roots of my disease where I found them.

(HOLMES *looks about, wriggles in his chair.)*

They're quite unbendable, those straps. Old La Frontenac took no chances. He was really set on buggering that girl, you know.

(Picks up a unique-looking, hand-crafted canister and proceeds to insert acid into it.)

Yes, only sophisticated chemicals in my laboratory, Sherlock. Like this ingenious mixture especially concocted by myself which kills in seconds and within a matter of hours, thoroughly, and efficiently, eradicates human flesh—leaving a whittled-down skeleton, like a chicken bone plucked clean. Of course, to do its job efficiently, it must not be diluted with oxygen, and so, my dear Sherlock, I took the precaution of turning this cellar into an airtight chamber, and when I leave, I will, using a wax especially designed for the purpose, seal the framework of that door, rendering this already dank and stuffy cellar, entirely airless. I doubt anyone will venture upon the place as it is condemned property due to be demolished in two or three years, by which time the chance discovery of a skeleton may create a small flurry of curiosity—although there will be nothing to connect those corroded bits of calcium to the Great Sherlock, and therefore no chance of any serious publicity. Sorry about that. I know how much you were looking forward to a posthumous notoriety.

(HOLMES *quietly digests everything he has heard.)*

HOLMES: I have listened very carefully to everything you have said, Watson.

WATSON: You couldn't very well do otherwise.

HOLMES: And I really must compliment you. You have devised what, in my professional opinion, is a perfect crime. Your preparations were meticulous; your choice of performers, the witting and the unwitting, expertly made. But in all your calculations, you seem to have lost sight of one rather important fact.

WATSON: Ah, here it comes. The ultimate coup-de-grace that makes fifty million readers tremble with delight and boggles the minds of criminologists from Peking to Peru.

HOLMES: You say you were an underling, and you say you resented it. And yet this, the most remarkable act of your life, could only have come about because of me. Because of my influence and my instruction.

WATSON: Because of your arrogance, and your conceit!

HOLMES: Call it what you will. Who made you remarkable? Who permitted you to stand out from the rest of your fellow men? It was I. It was proximity to myself that gave you whatever credence you had. Without that, you were nothing.

WATSON: So you say. So you believe!

HOLMES: You've said as much yourself. Without Sherlock Holmes, there is no Doctor Watson. If you kill me, you destroy the only thing that gives meaning to your life.

WATSON: On the contrary, your death is the only thing that can possibly restore meaning to my life. However, don't let me interrupt. Carry on; the acid is almost ready.

HOLMES: You think you're so unique; so especially exploited. But there are millions like you. You're the drones of the universe. There are only a handful like me. One sensibility like mine is worth fifty million of yours. Yours only has value in so much as it is touched by mine. Without my coat-tails, you drag in the gutter. Without my heightened sensibility, you remain a clod of earth. You should get down on your knees and thank God your paltry and pathetic span of time on earth was made remarkable by exposure to Sherlock Holmes.

WATSON: Carry on, carry on. This is the music I wanted to hear.

HOLMES: Yes, I ignored you, neglected you, took you for granted, spat upon you, shat upon you . . . What were you but a kind of sounding board for ideas you could never, in a thousand years, invent yourself?

WATSON: Go on, sing . . . sing . . .

HOLMES: Elementary, my dear Watson, is what you *always* were: composed of brute and basic elements. Earth, air, water . . . but never fire. That is one element you always lacked. *That* I gave you, or rather you sucked it up out of the conflagrations of my intellect. For years you have warmed yourself with my coals; read by the sparks of my flame, lived by the heat of my fire!

(WATSON *uncovers a wind-up gramophone and puts on a record. He tips back* HOLMES *in the chair and begins to spray him with the acid-filled canister.*)

WATSON: Dust we are, to dust we return. Elementary, is it not, Holmes? Very elementary.

(*As* HOLMES*struggles, in the background, a record of Boccherini's Minuet echoes scratchily from wind-up gramophone.*)

HOLMES: You cannot destroy essence. I am essence. I am the incarnation of life. You are dross. You are earth.

(*Grows weaker.*)

Clod.

Stule.

Dung . . .

Dust . . .

(After a few moments, HOLMES *is completely still.* WATSON *takes out his stethoscope and applies it to* HOLMES' *heart. Content that there are no signs of life, he packs it away, gathers together his belongings, does a little dance to the Minuet and exits.*

The lights fade on the inert and lifeless body of SHERLOCK HOLMES.*)*

Curtain

Act 2

Scene 1

Lights up.

HOLMES' lodging in Baker Street. Conspicuous addition of wall telephone. WATSON is seated in HOLMES' easy chair puffing on HOLMES' pipe and reading through the morning mail. Suddenly he discovers a letter that gives him a start. He reads it agitatedly, then stands to attention imagining some strange honor. As he laughs with immense satisfaction, MRS. HUDSON enters.

MRS. HUDSON: A bit more tea, Dr. Watson?

WATSON: No thank you, Mrs. Hudson, I've had two cups already and am just wolfing down the fourth of your delectable muffins. Fit for a king. And while we're on the subject, I shall now read you the contents of one of the letters you were kind enough to deliver to me this morning.

MRS. HUDSON: Is it about Mr. Holmes? Have they found something?

WATSON: Patience, patience. *(showing the letter)* You see the seal?

MRS. HUDSON: *(Aghast)* Is it . . . ?

WATSON: None other.

MRS. HUDSON: But could it really be from . . .

WATSON: Attend: *(Reads)* "In respect of the magnificent work conducted by Mr. Sherlock Holmes through his eventful career both here and abroad and the invaluable participation of his trusted aide-de-camp (referring to me of course), Her Majesty the Queen wishes you to accept a knighthood in the next birthday honors list so that the world will be able to witness the esteem in which the Monarch holds the memory of this great sleuth and his conscientious collaborator. (That of course is me again). We will be contacting you in due course to organize details. Signed, Lord Privy Seal for Victoria Regina."

MRS. HUDSON: *(Awestruck)* Gods 'strewth, is it true?

WATSON: It seems pretty authentic to me, Mrs. Hudson.

MRS. HUDSON: Does it really mean that from now on . . . you're to be . . . good Lord!

WATSON: Lordships are a step or two ahead, Mrs. Hudson, but yes, it does mean *Sir* John Watson.

MRS. HUDSON: Oh dear. *(Wistful)* What would Mr. Holmes say, I wonder, if he was here now?

WATSON: Something rather cutting, I suspect.

MRS. HUDSON: Oh, but I do miss him, Dr. Watson. I keep thinkin' one day I'll hear his tread on the stair, he'll swing open the door and shout out like he always did: "Wipe me boots, you slovenly old cow!" D'you remember?

WATSON: An endearing harshness of manner that concealed a heart as big as a bun. But life must go on, as indeed it has for these past fourteen months and I must say, Mrs. Hudson, you've been a brick through it all.

MRS. HUDSON: I know that's what Mr. Holmes would have wanted. To soldier on here at Baker Street no matter what. Wasn't it wicked that fellow from Bognor pretending to be Mr. Holmes and getting our hopes up like that.

WATSON: A thoroughpac'd scoundrel. I knew in a trice he couldn't be Holmes.

MRS. HUDSON: But 'e looked the spittin' image, didn't he, Dr.? Got the voice down pat—and even the clothes.

WATSON: Yes, but when he offered to take us all to the Cafe Royal and pick up the check himself, he showed his hand.

MRS. HUDSON: And then that hussy from Margate getting herself into man's clothing to pass herself off as Mr. Holmes. The cheek of the hussy.

WATSON: An outrageous sally which, thanks to my well-kept anatomical records, was quickly exposed for the fraud it was.

MRS. HUDSON: I just can't figure the number of wicked people in the world, Dr. Watson. Like whoever it was that wrote that letter about my dyin' grandfather and when I got there I found he was a hale and hearty 90-year-old who'd just married a 16-year-old bride. If he hadn't had a stroke three weeks later, the whole trip would have been a waste. Who could have thought up such a wicked thing?

WATSON: Some warped and embittered individual, Mrs. Hudson, with some great imaginary grievance.

MRS. HUDSON *(Emotional)* Oh Dr. Watson, you do think he's still alive, don't you? He will come back one day, won't he?

WATSON: Of course he will, Mrs. Hudson. You know what they say about bad pennies.

(MRS. HUDSON *bursts into tears.)*

Oh please, Mrs. Hudson, you must learn to restrain yourself. If every mention of the poor chap's name is going to . . .

MRS. HUDSON: It's not that, Dr. Watson. It's the ceremony.

WATSON: The ceremony?

MRS. HUDSON: I haven't a frock to be going to the Palace with.

WATSON: I'm sure we can stretch the housekeeping far enough to purchase an appropriate gown for the Queen.

MRS. HUDSON: Do you really think so?

WATSON: It isn't every day we're summoned to Buckingham Palace.

MRS. HUDSON: Should it be white, do you think and a little off the shoulder?

WATSON: Since it's Victoria, I think gray and high at the neck might be more appropriate.

(The telephone rings. MRS. HUDSON *starts for the door.)*

It's the telephone, Mrs. Hudson, not the door.

*(*MRS. HUDSON *stares hypnotically at the telephone which continues to ring.)*

Probably the Palace. Go on. Go on. It won't bite you.

*(*MRS. HUDSON *warily approaches the telephone, lifts the receiver, bows involuntarily before she says:)*

MRS. HUDSON: The Holmes residence, your Highness.—Who?— Oh it's you! *(To* WATSON) It's Inspector Lestrade.

WATSON: *(Taking receiver, anticipating congratulations.)* Good morning, I suppose you've heard on the grapevine, eh? No doubt your own time will come. There's no reason—*(Stopped in his tracks)* Found him? You've found him . . . But, Lestrade, we've been through this many times before. How can you be sure that . . . Amnesia? . . . Bombay? . . . Really, Inspector, I think we're wasting a lot of time over . . . Well of course, if you think it's urgent, I'll come over to . . . You've brought him here!? Downstairs? Do you think that's . . . I see. Test him on his home ground, quite right—Well, I certainly hope this isn't another wild goose chase, Inspector. Fine . . . fine . . . Goodbye.

MRS. HUDSON: *(Incredulous)* They've found him! He's back!

WATSON: Come, come, Mrs. Hudson, we've been through this many times before and have always been bitterly disappointed.

MRS. HUDSON: But Lestrade, he's never brought any of them over here —to the flat.

WATSON: If we keep our wits about us, we'll be able to deal with the imposter.

MRS. HUDSON: But what if it ain't no imposter. What if it's Mr. Holmes?

WATSON: *(Beat)* Well, in that case, of course, I'll be delighted. We both will, but what I mean is it's best to remain sceptical for the moment —to avoid a disappointment afterward.

(The doorbell rings. MRS. HUDSON looks constipated.)

Mrs. Hudson, it would be best if you made yourself scarce for the moment. This is going to be a rather delicate interview.

MRS. HUDSON: Of course, Dr. Watson.

(She leaves for another part of the flat. WATSON opens the door and INSPECTOR LESTRADE enters.)

LESTRADE: So glad you could accommodate us, Dr. Watson. He's just outside.

WATSON: These false alarms are becoming very trying, Inspector. Must we really waste time on every single . . . ?

LESTRADE: I tell you, Dr. Watson, the man is the spittin' image of 'olmes. I've been took in three times before so I'm not about wastin' my time with all that lot, but I tell you, this resemblance is positively uncanny.

WATSON: That's what you said the last time when that fellow's false nose began to wilt in the gas light. He too was a 'spitting image.'

LESTRADE: But 'e got the manner, the walk, the tone of voice, even if 'e is a bit scruffy. 'E's told me things about me'self and the Yard that even the wife doesn't know.

WATSON: A few months of intensive research and almost any tubercular chap with a hook nose can pass himself off as Sherlock Holmes.

LESTRADE: Well that's just what I thought, so I says to m'self, don't play around with it. Give 'im the old Watson Test straight off.

WATSON: I have a great many pressing things on my calendar, Inspector.

LESTRADE: The thing is, Doctor, I wouldn't be doin' my job if I didn't investigate all these chaps. Just imagine that 'olmes did come back and 'e was just shunted aside, didn't get a look-in as it were. That wouldn't go down very well with the Superintendent—*or* the British Public, I 'spect.

WATSON: *(Beat)* Very well, Lestrade. Show the 'gentleman' in.

LESTRADE: Many thanks, Doctor. I do really appreciate it.

(LESTRADE *goes to the door, opens it to announce* HOLMES *and the* HOLMES LOOK-ALIKE *comes wheeling in.)*

May I introduce . . .

HOLMES: *(Pumping* DR. WATSON's *hand)* Watson, old man. How good to see you after so many months. What an escapade. You'll never believe it when I tell you. I can barely believe it myself. I say, the place looks as ever. Is Mrs. Hudson about? I've actually been looking forward to seeing the old biddy. First time that's ever happened as far as I can recall. I say is that my pipe?

WATSON: *(Removing it quickly)* Do have a seat.

LESTRADE: Well, Dr. Watson, this is the gentleman of whom I spoke. He has a very interestin' story to relate and I told him it would be best if he told it himself.

WATSON: Quite.

(Turns to HOLMES.*)*

HOLMES: Come along, old chap. There's no need for all this standing on ceremony. Surely I haven't changed all that much. You certainly look the same. A little better fed perhaps. I hear 'the firm' has been getting on splendidly without me. Much trade?

WATSON: Before we become too deeply enmeshed, 'Mr. Holmes', may I remind you that you are not the first person to try to pass himself off as *the* Sherlock Holmes.

HOLMES: Oh bother it, Watson. We both know all those others were sheer adventurers.

WATSON: I should point out to you that although there is a striking resemblance to the man whose name you claim to bear, that has happened before—to no avail. You are aware, no doubt, that modern science has recently perfected the art of skin-grafting to the point where almost anyone who can afford it can have whatever face he chooses.

HOLMES: Is that really the case?

WATSON: It is.

HOLMES: *(To* LESTRADE*)* I say, Lestrade, that means there's still hope for you.

LESTRADE: The point at issue here is your mug, not mine.

WATSON: And not only, as Lestrade puts it, your 'mug,' but a great many other things. And therefore, 'Mr. Holmes,' I wonder if I might put a few questions to you. No doubt, you will come up with perfectly good answers.

HOLMES: Holmes interrogated! That's quite a switch.

WATSON: Perhaps, Inspector, you would be good enough to wait outside. There is a sofa in the hall.

LESTRADE: If you like, Dr. Watson, but wouldn't it be . . .

WATSON: I think that would be the most convenient.

(LESTRADE *eyes* HOLMES *suspiciously and then nods to* WATSON, *as if to say, 'If I'm needed, I'll be nearby,' then exits.*)

HOLMES: Lestrade has been behaving very peculiarly for the past twelve hours. If I wasn't certain of his gender, I'd say he's showing the first signs of menopause. I do hope, Watson, that *we* won't take too long to break the ice.

WATSON: I certainly hope not, 'Mr. Holmes.'

HOLMES: Come, come, old man. Surely we can drop the formality.

WATSON: I should like to retain it a little while longer if I may.

HOLMES: As you like.

WATSON: I understand you had some sort of 'encounter at sea,' is that correct?

HOLMES: It was the damned awfullest thing you could imagine. I was standing by Wapping Stairs when a gray Sikh in a striped jellaba hit me on the head with a yard-arm and tossed me into a ship bound for Bombay. When I woke, I had a bump on my head the size of the Blarney Stone and no idea whatsoever of who or where I was. The blighter had gone through my pockets and taken not only my miniscule bankroll but all my papers of identification as well. The Captain concluded I was a stowaway and put me to work in the galley— shaving potatoes and plucking cabbage leaves. I'd be there still if the ship's doctor hadn't recognized me and begun putting all kinds of questions about Baker Street, Baskerville and Speckled Bands. I thought the chap was barmy. When he asked me down to his cabin to try on some clothes he'd gathered in port, I grew quite alarmed. I fully expected corsets and frilly underwear but found, instead, a half-caped greatcoat and a deerstalker. When I donned the garments, he clapped his hands and cried: 'Eureka, I've found him.' The next thing I knew I was scuttled off the ship, brought to England and placed in the dubious custody of a man they called Lestrade.

I can't say I'm entirely back to normal—whatever that may be—but I am now quite prepared to believe I am Sherlock Holmes of 221B Baker Street and that you are my friend and companion, John Watson.

WATSON: Whether I or anyone else is prepared to believe it remains a moot point. Well perhaps we can verify that.

HOLMES: How so?

WATSON: I've drawn up a short questionnaire which has been useful in the past in trying to determine the identity of would-be Sherlock Holmes. I wonder if you'd be good enough to submit yourself to a few questions.

HOLMES: Is it like an examination?

WATSON: Yes, you could call it that. A kind of 'legitimacy test.'

HOLMES: But is this very reliable, Watson?

WATSON: So far it has never failed in exposing imposters. Not that you, 'Mr. Holmes,' are one.

HOLMES: It sounds very ingenious, Watson. One of your creations?

WATSON: Yes, I'm proud to say, it is.

HOLMES: I am all expectation.

(WATSON *takes a clipboard, adjusts his spectacles, and formally begins.*)

WATSON: Given all the information readily available on Holmes' background and characteristics, it would not be too difficult for someone to acquire all the facts they might need, therefore, these questions are in no way concerned with the statistics of Holmes'—your—past life but rather his—your—character and personal idiosyncrasies—information rather more difficult to come by. You are game, I take it?

HOLMES: Perfectly.

WATSON: Excellent. *(Prepares)* Sitting comfortably? Good. "If you were on your deathbed receiving the last rites with only one minute left to live, what would you ask for?"

HOLMES: A second opinion.

WATSON: "If you were about to be immortalized in print for all time to come, what would you demand of your biographer?"

HOLMES: 50% of the royalties.

WATSON: "If a fairy godmother appeared and offered to grant you three wishes, what would you ask for first?"

HOLMES: Her credentials.

WATSON: *(After a study)* "Let us assume you have a five-pound note in one pocket and a half-crown in the other and a starving woman accosts you on the street begging for help. What would you give her?"

HOLMES: Is she plain or fair?

WATSON: What?

HOLMES: This beggar woman, is she plain or fair?

WATSON: What difference does that make?

HOLMES: If she were plain, I'd give her the half-crown.

WATSON: And if she were fair?

HOLMES: Make her earn the fiver.

(WATSON *scrutinizes* HOLMES *carefully.*)

WATSON: Complete this sentence. "A friend in need . . ."

HOLMES: Is an insufferable bore.

WATSON: A bird in the hand is . . .

HOLMES: Inviting a bit of a mess.

WATSON: A rolling stone gathers . . .

HOLMES: Rather more than I'm doing from all these daft questions.

WATSON: I would appreciate it, 'Mr. Holmes', if you fastened your attention to the matters at hand.

HOLMES: Sorry, old chap.

WATSON: *(Very harried, decides to abandon this tack)* I'm going to give you some words and I would appreciate it if you answered me with the very first word that comes into your head. Understand?

HOLMES: Beeswax.

WATSON: I haven't started yet!

HOLMES: Sorry.

(WATSON *fumes inwardly and proceeds.*)

WATSON: Windy.

HOLMES: Mackintosh.

WATSON: Waterloo.

HOLMES: Napoleon.

WATSON: Rainstorm.

HOLMES: Wellingtons.

WATSON: Africa.

HOLMES: Gumboots.

WATSON: Siberia.

HOLMES: Coconuts.

(WATSON *pauses for a moment trying to interpret the import of the exchange, then, without warning, blitzes him with the next.*)

WATSON: Danger.

HOLMES: Banana.

WATSON: Kidnap.

HOLMES: Sleeping goat.

WATSON: Strangulation.

HOLMES: Underpants.

WATSON: Imposter.

HOLMES: Prove it.

WATSON: Poison.

HOLMES: English cooking.

WATSON: Embezzlement.

HOLMES: Coconuts.

(WATSON *pauses again, circling* HOLMES *warily then suddenly machine-guns out the next.*)

WATSON: Women.

HOLMES: Crocodiles.

WATSON: Marriage.

HOLMES: Quicksand.

WATSON: Honeymoon.

HOLMES: Whale blubber.

WATSON: Mother-in-law.

HOLMES: Elephants.

WATSON: Corsets.

HOLMES: Coconuts.

(WATSON *mops his brow for a moment, then takes the next exchange much more slowly and warily.*)

WATSON: Fame.

HOLMES: Money.

WATSON: Poverty.

HOLMES: Fame.

WATSON: Money.

HOLMES: Poverty.

WATSON: *(Speeding up)* Success.

HOLMES: Kippers.

WATSON: Celebrity.

HOLMES: Canteloupes.

WATSON: Securities.

HOLMES: Pussycats.

WATSON: Bullion.

HOLMES: Hollyhocks.

WATSON: Posterity.

HOLMES: Coconuts.

WATSON: Emeralds.

HOLMES: Coconuts.

WATSON: Balderdash!

(Throws away clipboard.)

HOLMES: Haemorrhoids.

WATSON: Enough!

HOLMES: Catapults.

WATSON: *(Exasperated)* It's finished.

HOLMES: Succatush.

WATSON: *(Desperately)* The test is over, Mr. Holmes. No more words.

HOLMES: *(Back to earth)* Oh sorry.

WATSON: *(Mopping brow)* Would you care for some tea?

HOLMES: Don't mind if I do.

WATSON: Milk and sugar?

HOLMES: No thank you.

(He takes a tiny vial out of his pocket and pours it into the teacup, then stirs and sips. Euphorically.)

A little delicacy from Morocco *(Sips tea)* They call it 'happy syrup.'

WATSON: *(Fearfully)* Would you care for a smoke?

HOLMES: Very decent of you.

(Takes his pipe from WATSON's *pocket, moves to coal scuttle. Finding no pouch there, he removes one of his own from inside pocket and proceeds to stuff a pinch of its contents into the bowl. Then puffs contentedly.)*

It's been so long since I've had a really good smoke.

*(*WATSON *steps back, drops the match and stands aghast.)*

WATSON: *(Eyes bulging)* Holmes, it really is *you!*

*(*HOLMES *smiles and puffs.)*

I just couldn't bring myself to believe it. There've been so many dashed hopes.

HOLMES: Quite understandable, Watson, and your scepticism does you credit.

WATSON: We heard rumors of you from Madagascar, Calcutta, St. Tropez, Brisbane, but they all came to naught.

HOLMES: No doubt. The Let's-Have-a-Go-At-Being-Sherlock-Holmes Industry has prospered greatly these past months. But how have you managed the cases without me?

WATSON: Inadequately, of course. Our clients knew they would never receive first-class service with the Master gone, but they felt—or hoped leastways—that some of your genius might have rubbed off on me over the years.

HOLMES: Gratifying, gratifying.

WATSON: Everything was going swimmingly until about two weeks ago, in fact.

HOLMES: Oh?

WATSON: An extraordinary case. This middle-aged lady from Cheltenham who tried to reach the spirit of her recently deceased husband through a medium. When she made contact, the spirit told her to give all her savings to the medium. Of course, it looked like a hoax, but the medium refused to touch a penny of it. His reward, he said, would be in heaven. It completely flummoxed us.

HOLMES: You mean the medium actually refused the gift.

WATSON: Wouldn't accept a penny.

HOLMES: And the lady?

WATSON: Determined to honor the word of her departed husband, she insisted the money be handed over—hoax or no hoax. But the medium flatly refused to accept it—no matter what. Not knowing which way to turn, the lady came here to seek advice.

HOLMES: I say, that is a bit of a pickle. Certainly foxes me. What would you suggest, Watson?

WATSON: Could you excuse me for one moment.

HOLMES: Certainly.

(WATSON *goes to door, opens it and calls out.*)

WATSON: Lestrade, would you come in!

(LESTRADE *runs in quickly.*)

Put your cuffs on the fellow at once. He's an impostor!

HOLMES: I say, what's the meaning of . . .

LESTRADE: Are you sure, Dr. Watson?

(LESTRADE *crosses to* HOLMES *and cuffs him.*)

WATSON: Not a shadow of a doubt.

HOLMES: Now, Watson, I don't think . . .

WATSON: *Doctor* Watson to you, and no, you *don't* think—certainly not very well—whoever you may be. Your replies to my questions were quite ingenious. Coconuts, indeed! But a moment ago, you dropped the fatal clanger. When I told you about our latest case and you turned to me and said: "What would you suggest, Watson?" you showed yourself up in your true colors. *Sherlock Holmes would never in a million years have solicited my opinion!* That was your fatal mistake!

(HOLMES *about to protest, begins to cringe and sob.*)

HOLMES: *(Cockney accent)* 'Ave a bit'a pity can't you? I'm only a poor entertainer. A Quick Change Artist and Impersonator with the Kit Karno Travellin' Circus. We've been tryin' t'find a spot in the halls for over two years, but nobody wants Quick Change Artists no more.

LESTRADE: Do you mean to tell me you're an actor!?

HOLMES: I thought if I could pull it off, I'd 'ave enough for me and the missus to go steerage to Australia. I didn't mean no 'arm. 'Ave a bit o'pity. I'm just 'ungry.

LESTRADE: You'll be more than 'ungry when I get through with you.*(Turns to* WATSON) I am so terribly sorry, Dr. Watson, I really thought . . .

WATSON: No harm done, Lestrade. All part of the day's work.

HOLMES: *(To* LESTRADE) Couldn't you just turn the other way 'n let me bugger off. I h'aint done no one no 'arm.

LESTRADE: Misrepresentation, False Credentials and Imitatin' a British Institution without a warrant. I hope they boil you in oil.

HOLMES: What about me wife and kids?

LESTRADE: I hope they throw them into the same pot. Good day, Dr. Watson.

WATSON: Good day, Inspector.

HOLMES: *(Being carried off)* Don't mean no 'arm. *(Suddenly bitter)* God blast you both. I 'ope the ghost of Sherlock 'Olmes 'aunts you t'yer dyin' day.*(Pleading)* 'Ave a little thought, Inspector, I'm a family man.

(The door closes on both of them. WATSON, *visibly shaken, absent-mindedly raises* HOLMES' *teacup, the one into which he had poured his 'happy syrup.' Just as he is about to take a sip, he remembers its contents and slaps the cup back into saucer.* MRS. HUDSON *enters.)*

MRS. HUDSON: *(Entering)* What is it, Dr. Watson? I heard all the racket from downstairs.

WATSON: *(Trying to compose himself)* Another false alarm, Mrs. Hudson.

MRS. HUDSON: *(Incredulous)* No!

WATSON: I told you not to get your hopes up. A theatrical impersonator of some sort. Down on his luck.

Frank Langella and Donal Donnelly

Donal Donnelly and Frank Langella

Frank Langella and Melinda Mullins

Pat McNamara, Donal Donnelly and Frank Langella

MRS. HUDSON: What a wicked world it is.

WATSON: Full of wicked, wicked people, Mrs. Hudson. *(Rises and puts on coat)* However, life goes on and I've a rather important errand to run.

MRS. HUDSON: But I've almost got the supper ready.

WATSON: It's rather urgent that I confirm the whereabouts of an old friend, Mrs. Hudson, and I'm sure I won't be able to consume a mouthful until I'm certain he is where I think he is.*(Almost at exit)* If the Palace rings, take down the number and say I'll get back to them directly.

(Exits.)

MRS. HUDSON: *(Thinking of the hoax)* Wicked, wicked.

(Shaking her head and muttering to herself, MRS. HUDSON *slumps into the seat beside the table and absent-mindedly begins sipping the tea into which* HOLMES *has poured his 'happy syrup.' Admonishingly.)*

Wicked, wicked, wicked, such wickedness.

(After a few more sips, the brew gets to her. She settles more comfortably into the seat, her eyes glowing and incandescent, her entire body afloat, transported by the 'high'. She suddenly jumps up and starts singing as she dances to exit.)

You take the high road and I'll take the low road and I'll get to Scotland afore you. For me and my true love will never meet again. On the bonny, bonny banks of loch Lomond.

(She exists into the closet.)

Blackout

Scene 2

Pitch black. A lantern switched on from above momentarily blinds the audience. It roams for a while around the room revealing the dank cellar from Act 1. We then see WATSON light a lantern and move into the interior of the cellar. Slowly, he raises the lantern and approaches the La Frontenac chair. He tips up chair and we see a skeleton wearing the tatters of HOLMES' Act 1 outfit. WATSON then approaches the skeleton, takes out a magnifying glass and inspects its wrists nodding approvingly as he discovers the last vestiges of the clamp marks he expected to find. He then steps back and contemplates the skeleton.

WATSON: Sorry, Holmes—just checking. Nothing like being absolutely certain. You taught me that.

(Returns magnifying glass to pocket, raises lantern. It mysteriously snuffs out.)

VOICE IN DARKNESS: Highly unreliable.

(WATSON strikes a match and looks about trying to determine if he did or didn't hear a voice in the darkness. The match burns his fingers and he drops it.)

WATSON: Blast!

VOICE IN DARKNESS: Temper, temper.

(WATSON re-lights the lantern and frantically surveys the entire cellar.)

WATSON: Who's there? Who is it?

VOICE IN DARKNESS: An old friend.

WATSON: I've a pistol. You'd better show yourself.

VOICE IN DARKNESS: *(Laughing)* Pistols hold no fear for me. They never did.

(WATSON *turns to skeleton. Fires at it. The bones crumble into a thousand pieces causing the tattered clothing to slouch to the floor.)*

A bit redundant that, don't you think?

(WATSON *turns round from side to side trying to discover the source of the* VOICE. *The record of the Boccherini Minuet begins to play. He shoots it and it comes to a screeching halt. He then spies the side-closet and slowly approaches it. After a moment's hesitation, he whips it open and from the gloom, a* FIGURE *dressed in a half-caped topcoat and deerstalker appears.*

WATSON *shrieks and backs away, across the room. Instinctively, he turns round to discover another* FIGURE *also wearing the half-cape coat and deerstalker coming down the stairs. It knocks the pistol out of his hand.* WATSON *now caught between* BOTH FIGURES, *tries to escape. They both bear down on him, forcing him towards the Center of the stage. As they swoop down on him, he falls to the floor and begins blubbering like a baby.)*

WATSON: Mercy! Mercy! I had to remove you, Sherlock. I couldn't live otherwise. I had to do it, I had to do it.

(One figure suddenly removes its top-coat and deerstalker. It is revealed to be INSPECTOR LESTRADE. *The other with a like motion, does the same. He is revealed to be* SHERLOCK HOLMES. WATSON,*stupefied, stares boggle-eyed at the two men.)*

HOLMES: You've made a note of the exact words of the confession, Lestrade, I take it?

LESTRADE: *(Grimly)* No fear, Mr. Holmes. I've got it all down.

WATSON: *(Looking to* LESTRADE, *then to* HOLMES) But . . . but . . .

HOLMES: Come, come, Watson. You didn't really think, in your heart of hearts, you could outwit me, did you?

WATSON: *(Looking at remains of skeleton)* But I thought . . .

HOLMES: Precisely what I'd have you think, old man. Same height; similar bone curvatures and, of course, the mark of the clamps applied to the wrist, which I was sure you would examine straight off.

WATSON: *(After a pause, turns to* LESTRADE*)* You knew—all the time.

LESTRADE: Not until last week when Holmes came to me with the most incredible story I ever heard. One that I couldn't for the life of me believe. That you had plotted to murder your good old friend. It was because I wouldn't believe it that we went to all that fuss to obtain your confession, pretending to find that music-hall entertainer, exposin' him, making you think everything was just like you left it.

WATSON: (To HOLMES) That quick-change artist, you!?

HOLMES: The cockney was a little rusty, I'm afraid. But I knew the only way to drive you back to the scene of the crime was to plant that seed of doubt.

WATSON: But where . . . where?

HOLMES: Everywhere they said I was, old chap. Madagascar, Calcutta, St. Tropez—particularly St. Tropez. I knew very well the longer I stayed away, the more complacent you'd become.

WATSON: *(Stupefied)* I mixed that gas myself . . . I listened with my own ears . . . There was no heartbeat.

HOLMES: A Tibetan Yoga exercise, Watson, which suspends respiration and deadens the pulse. Had you used my hypersensitive stethoscope instead of your own standard model you might have discerned the faintest of hums.

WATSON: But you were rooted to that chair. You couldn't escape! There was no way . . .

HOLMES: There was one way, Watson, and I would have thought being a man of science you would have hit upon it. Although your deadly vapor began to do its job quite efficiently and you were thoughtful enough to seal up any chink of air in the cellar, you neglected to withdraw my pipe.*(Whips it out and holds it aloft. The next all in one breath.)* In which, thanks to a fortuitous wad of badly-packed tobacco, there was an air-block between the stem and the bowl. After you left, I managed to squirm the thing into my mouth and that gave me just about forty-five seconds of oxygen. Enough time to topple myself to the floor and stick the stem of my pipe through a knothole in the timber *(Kicks it out with his heel)* below which flowed enough air to combat the lethal fumes. Although the gas had no immediate ill effect upon me, it did, as is the nature of toxic matter on rawhide, expand the leather clamps on the chair, thereby enabling me to wriggle out of their grasp.

LESTRADE: After all these years, Dr. Watson, to do such a thing to a good, unselfish man who gave you everything. It just turns my gut. I've lost all faith in human nature, y'know. That's what you've done to me.

HOLMES: We shall endeavor to restore it, Lestrade, and towards that end, I wonder if you would be good enough to leave the Doctor and me alone for a while.

LESTRADE: What!? Leave you alone with that homicidal maniac!

HOLMES: As you can see, Lestrade, Watson is quite helpless now. It took all the gumption he could muster for his one great gamble. That having failed, I really don't think we need ever worry about him again. *(To* WATSON) Do we, Watson?

(WATSON *remains silent.)*

Go along, Lestrade.

LESTRADE: *(Pocketing* WATSON's *pistol, looks to* HOLMES *then to* WATSON) You should be ashamed of yourself, Dr. Watson.*(Muttering as he goes)* I'll never be the same again, y'know. You've shattered me. *(Exits)*

HOLMES: A touching fellow, Lestrade—despite his Neanderthal brain.

WATSON: *(Now gathering himself together)* Let's get on with it, Holmes. We have nothing to say to each other. I made my play and I failed. I'm ready to take the consequences. Even life in prison would be a blessing, since I'd be free of you once and for all.

HOLMES: Not strictly speaking, Watson.

WATSON: All I want is the oblivion I so richly deserve.

HOLMES: But would it be oblivion, old man? Within a matter of weeks the more jaundiced of the yellow-journalists would be on to you for your memoirs. You'd be hounded to the grave telling and re-telling the plots you laid and mislaid, recounting your envy, ventilating your disgust, becoming more and more predictable and cantankerous in each succeeding Sunday edition. It would be pathetic, Watson, pathetic.

(WATSON *peers at* HOLMES.)

WATSON: Why are you trying to wring the last drops of blood out of me, Holmes? Isn't it enough that you turned me into a criminal and now, a life-long convict?

HOLMES: It would be such a fiendish waste, Watson. All your years of commendable medical achievement, banished at a stroke.

WATSON: Does your spite know no bounds?

HOLMES: You're not catching my drift at all. What I am saying, old man, is that your life-long incarceration serves no purpose whatsoever. It will make you even more miserable than you are at this very moment and it won't do me a blind bit of good.

WATSON: *(After a pause)* What are you proposing?

HOLMES: Just this, Watson, and I think it's a rather charitable offer.

WATSON: *(Beat)* What 'charitable offer'?

HOLMES: I will take you back.

WATSON: *(After a pause)* Back?

HOLMES: Back . . . to Baker Street. Back to the firm. Back to the fold. You will continue to chronicle the events—although you won't figure in them as prominently as you did.*(Beat)* Of course, I couldn't possibly let you out of my sight. That would be far too hazardous, so I'll prepare a little room for you in the basement of 221B. It used to be the maid's actually. A bit cramped and windowless, but once you've made it your own, put up some of your bottles and charts, you'll find it quite jolly I'm sure. To the outside world, Holmes will have returned and the old partnership of Holmes and Watson lovingly restored. We would know the truth, but the public need not.

WATSON: *(After a longish pause)* You are suggesting the life of the walking dead. A fate far worse than imprisonment. Total and abject captivity to that man in the world whom I despise above all other men.

HOLMES: *(Lightly)* That's about the size of it, old chap.

WATSON: You must be mad to imagine I would consider such a thing.

HOLMES: The alternatives are rather grisly. No more club. No more pub. No dinners at the Ritz. No more hansoms. No more vacations in the Highlands. No more notoriety. No more esteem—self, social or otherwise. And, of course, no honors.

WATSON: Honors?

HOLMES: You haven't forgotten Her Majesty's gracious offer.

WATSON: You mean . . . you would let me . . .

HOLMES: Let you? I would insist, old chap. It would be Sir John for all time to come. Sir John Watson, M.D., P.H.D., C.B.E., D.U.D.—whatever!

WATSON: *(Reflectively)* I must admit no matter how contemptible it sounds, when I was informed of that honor, it was the first real flicker of happiness I've had in fifty years.

HOLMES: Then why deny it to yourself? After all you've been through, no man deserves it more. And how the old bosom would swell with pride as you knelt before the heaving monarch surrounded by a crowd of admiring colleagues and the royal saber tapped gently on the shoulders of your rented morning suit: 'Arise, Sir John Watson.'

WATSON: *(Who has been empathizing* HOLMES' *description)* No, no, never never! I despise you, abhor you! To rid myself of you, I have destroyed the best part of myself. I have risked ruin and degradation. It would make a mockery of everything to return now . . . to be your serf, your slave, your hireling—even more debased than before. I won't do it, Holmes, do you hear? I won't do it, and you can't make me. You can't!

(WATSON *overturns a stool in his passion and* LESTRADE *comes rushing in.)*

LESTRADE: Is everything all right?

HOLMES: *(Coolly)* Yes, Inspector, everything is quite all right. I think Dr. Watson is ready for you now.*(To* WATSON) Am I right?

(WATSON *sets his jaw and looks straight ahead indicating 'Yes.'* HOLMES *picks up the lantern, surveys the dark cellar for one last time and then briskly snuffs out the light.)*

Blackout

Scene 3

The Baker Street flat—now tidy and resplendent with new curtains, tablecloth, etc.

On LIGHTS UP, a strange man dressed in the attire of a Victorian youth stands before the open window with his back to the audience and a revolver in his hand. He stands furtively for a moment, then, as soon as voices are heard in the hall, he steps onto the window sill, deftly closes the window behind him and disappears.

*Enter WATSON, decked out in his morning suit; MRS. HUDSON in her
new frock; HOLMES in his usual grubby dressing gown. All are holding
up drinks for a toast.*

MRS. HUDSON: To Sir John! May he live a long and prosperous life and
always remember this lovely day. Bottoms up.*(They all drink)*

(Euphorically) It was just so lovely. There's no words for it. I've
never been inside the Palace before. Wasn't it lovely, and didn't the
Queen look lovely?

HOLMES: A fine figure of a woman; a bit dwarfish, but the lifts do
wonders.

MRS. HUDSON: *(Atmosphere soured)* I didn't notice any lifts.

HOLMES: The royal hem had been sewn especially to conceal them, but
there's a telltale list in the monarch's stance which gives it away. *(To
WATSON)* Did you notice as she began the dubbing, she was so far
forward on her toes, she almost tapped you with the hilt.

WATSON: I was rather preoccupied myself at the time.

MRS. HUDSON: *(To WATSON)* And I've never seen you look as hand-
some as you did today.

WATSON: Thank you, Mrs. Hudson, and might I say that in that gown,
you too were quite enchanting.

MRS. HUDSON: I managed to borrow it from my sister-in-law. She wore
it for the Coronation and we're still almost the same size.

HOLMES: It was my understanding, Mrs. Hudson, the extra six shil-
lings in last week's wage packet was specifically for new apparel for
this gala occasion. I assume we can subtract the unspent amount
from your next week's pay.

MRS. HUDSON: *(Piqued)* I was going to buy a dress, Mr. Holmes, when
my sister-in-law kindly offered.

HOLMES: Very generous too. The most practical solution all round.

(Sound of what could be gunshots are heard in the distance. DR. WAT-
SON *jumps;* MRS. HUDSON *runs to the window.)*

MRS. HUDSON: Good Gawd!

HOLMES: No need for alarm, Mrs. Hudson. I expect those are the first
volleys of the Guy Fawkes celebration. We can expect fireworks well
until dawn.

MRS. HUDSON: Ought to be banned—all that bother over a bounder
like that!

HOLMES: On the contrary, Guy Fawkes is the only explosive politician
Britain ever produced.

MRS. HUDSON: And it's only just tea time. They start earlier each year.
But I still can't understand why you declined your knighthood, Mr.
Holmes.

HOLMES: Didn't want to steal your thunder, old chap.

WATSON: Do you really mean, Holmes, it was an entirely selfless gesture?

HOLMES: I wouldn't go so far as to say that.

MRS HUDSON: Then why in Heaven's name did you . . .

HOLMES: The fact is, if you must know, I have it on the authority of
the Lord Chamberlain that in the next Lists, it is even money I shall
be awarded a Life Peerage and proclaimed Lord Holmes, Baron of
Baker Street and, as I have every hope of a long and active life, I
thought it more prudent simply to 'pass' this year.

MRS. HUDSON: *(Aghast) Lord* Holmes, God!

HOLMES: I did in fact investigate the possibility of the latter title but
was informed the Monarch is not empowered to confer deific status
on anyone, alas.

WATSON: Well of course, it's just a piece of piffle, but I must say, I feel quite honored.

MRS. HUDSON: It'll up my station as well, Dr. Watson. When I go to market now shopping for Sir John's table, I won't be fobbed off with no pigs'-trotters or scrawny pork chops. It'll be prime cuts from now on or I'll know the reason why. But, Dr. Watson, are you really sure you want to live down in that pokey little room in the basement? I can't for the life of me see why . . .

HOLMES: Watson is a grown man, Mrs. Hudson, and if he prefers the intimacy of a small and frugal abode in our basement to the sumptuous salons of Harley Street, it is not for us to question it.

MRS. HUDSON: It's so dark and musty down there. I don't mind the extra chores, Doctor, but why in heaven's name would anyone want to . . .

HOLMES: *(Changing the subject)* Now that the regal excitement has subsided and the cucumber sandwiches have been fully digested, do you think we might return to more mundane matters?

MRS. HUDSON: It isn't every day we have a knighthood, y'know.

HOLMES: No, but it *is* every day that the hall carpet needs brushing and the pantry cleaning—neither of which has been done today, I believe.

MRS. HUDSON: You're as soft-hearted as always, aren't you, Mr. Holmes? I thought after your time away, you might have mellowed a little.

HOLMES: Wine mellows with age, Mrs. Hudson, but people exposed to the same process only grow sour. And speaking of wine, perhaps you would be good enough to cork this and replace it in the larder.

(MRS. HUDSON *takes the bottle, glasses and tray and exits pointedly.)*

Dear Mrs. Hudson. She looks exactly like an overstuffed saddlebag. When she walked into the Palace grounds, I half-feared the Horse Guards would lead her straight to the stables.

(There is a strained moment of silence between WATSON *and* HOLMES, *then . . .)*

WATSON: Sherlock, about that room in the basement . . .

HOLMES: Yes, Watson.

WATSON: It's really rather cramped—and both of the windows seem to have been bricked over.

HOLMES: There's a perfectly adequate candlestick.

WATSON: Yes, I know but . . . it's unrelievedly dark and dingy down there—and very little air.

HOLMES: Yes. Very like a place I've known myself.

*(*HOLMES *and* WATSON *share a moment in which* WATSON *decidedly gets the point.)*

We shall see, Watson. Perhaps in nine or ten months, we can consider the whole question of renovation. Perhaps one of the windows could be restored. The smaller one.

*(*WATSON, *not wishing to push the matter further, silently defers. The outside bell rings, and rings again, and again.)*

Where in Heaven's name is that tiresome old woman?! She really will be the death of me.

WATSON: Shall I . . .

HOLMES: No, I'll see to it. *(He exits.)*

(As WATSON *admires his medallion and tries to console himself with his new honor, a* FIGURE *appears at the window behind him. Stealthily, he*

opens the window and creeps in-unseen by WATSON. *Then, sensing his presence,* WATSON *turns and confronts the* FIGURE—A YOUNG MAN *with mustachios who holds a pistol in his hand. As* HOLMES *re-enters the room, the* MAN *motions for* WATSON *to be quiet as he slips behind the curtain.)*

HOLMES: Must be those wretched Baker Street Irregulars again. They're always playing silly buggers with the doorbell. Nothing would please me more than to take them by the scruff of the neck and . . . *(He notices* WATSON *looking petrified.)* I say, Watson, what . . . ?

*(*WATSON *turns towards the curtains. The* YOUNG MAN *steps out from behind the curtains and trains his revolver on both of them.)*

MAN: The doorbell was a device of my own, Mr. Holmes—to enable me to make my entry without obstruction. Mrs. Hudson has been summoned on a fool's errand which, by my calculation, should take her about twenty minutes.

HOLMES: *(After a study)* And to what do we owe the honor of this . . .

MAN: Before we proceed too far, I wonder if you'd be good enough to drop your pistol—the indentation of which is quite visible under your waistcoat. (HOLMES *does so)* Many thanks. And now if you'd be good enough to oblige me by sitting in that armchair and you, Dr. Watson, over there.

*(*HOLMES *and* WATSON *do as they are told.)*

HOLMES: Since it is unlikely you are an autograph seeker, I wonder just who you are and what the object of your visit might be.

MAN: I can answer both questions at once, Mr. Holmes. My name is— Damion Moriarty. You were both closely acquainted with my father, I believe.

*(*HOLMES *looks to* WATSON *and gradually explodes with anger and exasperation.)*

HOLMES: Really, Watson, this is too much!

WATSON: But, Holmes, I . . .

HOLMES: A joke is a joke, but this is an appalling display of poor taste.

WATSON: I assure you, Holmes, I have absolutely nothing to do with . . .

HOLMES: We've already dispensed with the whole of this pointless far-rago—your Lizas and your Simeons—and if you think for a moment . . .

WATSON: I tell you, Holmes, I have . . .

DAMION: *(Firmly)* Would you both please oblige me by shutting your mouths!

HOLMES: My dear fellow, I don't know who you are or why you've felt it necessary to play out this preposterous charade, but I can assure you we've had our fill of this Moriarty nonsense and have no desire to . . .

(DAMION *shoots* HOLMES, *wounding him in the shoulder.* HOLMES *doubles up, clutches his arm which spurts blood through his shirt.)*

DAMION: That was the first bullet, Mr. Holmes, of three that will be fired this afternoon. Shots that, I've no doubt, will be heard round the world—although today, on Guy Fawkes' Day, they will not be particularly audible.

WATSON: *(Aghast at what he has seen)* Who are you??!

DAMION: You already have my name. My father was well known to both of you. Throughout his life, you stalked him from one city to another and, at the Reichenbach Falls, finally hounded him to his death. On the day I received the news, I knew I would never rest until I avenged his death. When you were miraculously rediscovered, I knew that God had restored me to my mission. And that is why I am here today.

(WATSON *is astonished. He turns slowly to* HOLMES, *his face racked with perplexity.*)

WATSON: Holmes, is it possible?

HOLMES: Fact imitating fiction, Watson? Happens every day. The real world is so impoverished of original ideas, it rifles art at every turn.

(Turns to DAMION)

No doubt it bolsters your self-esteem to pretend to be the son of the arch-criminal of the age but, as you know, there is no record whatsoever of a Moriarty offspring.

DAMION: I'm not obliged to prove anything to you, Mr. Holmes—but to satisfy your curiosity, I shall tell you that I, myself, was unaware of my identity until about five years ago when my father, piqued by some inexplicable paternal sentiment, sought me out and personally revealed it to me.

HOLMES: No doubt your father furnished proof of his identity.

DAMION: You yourself know that Professor Moriarty had only one distinguishing physical characteristic.

HOLMES: And that was?

DAMION: An ingrown toenail on the small digit of the left foot. The very feature which I have inherited from him. *(Suddenly extends foot)* You'll have to take my word for it, I'm afraid.

HOLMES: *(To* WATSON) You see what all this damned, biographical tampering has wrought—a full-blown, diabolical incongruity!

DAMION: Don't you call me an 'incongruity!' I've had all the palaver I'm going to take from you.

(Training his own pistol on HOLMES, *he takes up* HOLMES' *weapon in his free hand, expertly empties five cartridges out of the chamber, locks the remaining one in place, then puts pistol on table.)*

There is now one cartridge in that pistol. That is the bullet that will end your life, Dr. Watson, and you, Mr. Holmes, will be responsible for discharging it. That done, I will dispatch you as promptly as possible. *(Checks watch)* But I'm on a very tight schedule. Time is of the essence. Therefore, I must ask you, with no further ado, to dispatch your colleague. *(He raises his pistol threateningly to* HOLMES*)*

HOLMES: Do you honestly believe that . . .

DAMION: If you don't, I *shall*—and rather more brutally than yourself. Take your choice. Pick up that pistol.

(HOLMES *turns to* WATSON. WATSON *receives his distressed look. Reluctantly* HOLMES *stoops and picks up the pistol.)*

WATSON: *(Philosophically)* There's nothing for it, Holmes. It's providential it should end like this.

HOLMES: My dear Watson . . .

WATSON: It's all right, Holmes. Just Fate having the last laugh. On both of us. I've been half expecting this ever since I first made my insane resolution to eliminate you. But, Holmes—before I—I want you to know this. Those fourteen months without you were the longest in my life. I hated you! I loathed you! I wanted to be free of you —I was certain of that, but the fact remains, during those fourteen months, I was quietly and inconsolably miserable. Perhaps when one hates someone as intensely as I did you, it turns into some perverse kind of love; I don't know. All I do know is this seems quite inevitable, and quite just.

HOLMES: *(Visibly touched)* Watson, when I realized in that contemptible little cellar that you were truly intending to take my life, I vowed, with every atom of my being, that I would outwit you and survive. And often, during those long months on the run, when I thought back to your treachery, I felt I could happily rid myself of you forever. But now . . . like this . . . *(Choked up)* I find that . . .

DAMION: All of this would be very touching, if I had the slightest idea what you were talking about, but the fact is, time's a'wasting. Holmes, I will give you a count of five to pull that trigger—or else, you shall go first.

HOLMES: *(Tortured by choice)* You bastard, you really *are* a Moriarty, aren't you?!

DAMION: (DAMION *raises pistol)* Pull that trigger, Holmes, for if you don't as God is my witness, I shall blow you to smithereens. One!

WATSON: *(Looking plaintively at* HOLMES) It's all right. I don't mind.

DAMION: Two!

WATSON: This is the retribution I deserve . . .

DAMION: Three!

WATSON: It's been marvellous, Holmes. All of it.

DAMION: Four!

WATSON: I wouldn't have traded it for a barrelful of honors.

DAMION: FIVE!!

(HOLMES *pulls the trigger,* WATSON *sensing the gunshot, moans, clutches his body and topples over in a heap.)*

HOLMES: *(Removing sponge with red paint from inside the shoulder of his jacket)* Get up, Watson, you're quite all right.

(DAMION *pulls off moustache, wig, eyebrows, etc., and steps out of his costume revealing himself to be* BERTHA WALMSLEY *in a plain, feminine frock.)*

Bravo, Miss Walmsley. A trifle overplayed perhaps; a bit melodramatic here and there, but on the whole, quite convincing.

BERTHA: I didn't think much of *your* performance, Holmes. That fall to the floor was like something out of a third-rate rep.

HOLMES: But life *is* like a third-rate rep, Miss Walmsley. The old exploding bloodsack worked a treat. *(Removing it)*

BERTHA: Standard equipment at Ipswich or Hackesfield.

HOLMES: Very lifelike. *(Sniffs the bandage)* But a horrible smell. I hope it doesn't stain.

BERTHA: A little soap and water 'clears us of the deed.'

(WATSON, *who has watched the transformation boggle-eyed, is speechless, He stares at* LIZA MORIARTY-*cum*-BERTHA WALMSLEY *and cannot bring himself to speak a word.)*

Bedridden and spitting blood in the charity wards of Australia, is that what you hoped for?! Sorry to disappoint you, Dr. Watson, but I am quite alive—no thanks to you. I daresay my consumption would have thoroughly consumed me by now if Mr. Holmes hadn't sought me out in the slums of Brisbane and whisked me off to an American specialist—but some gentlemen really *are* gentlemen. *(She extends her hand to* HOLMES *who gallantly kisses it)* Got a clean bill of health now and resuming my career, thanks to a certain benefactor. *(Smiles at* HOLMES) Begin a tour of *Uncle Tom's Cabin* in a fortnight's time. It's only the role of Little Topsy but I *am* understudying the lead, who, I understand is accident prone, so, who can tell.

(WATSON, *still boggle-eyed, turns to* HOLMES, *then back to* BERTHA. *Still pulverized by events, he turns again to* HOLMES, *his eyes pleading for a word of explanation.)*

HOLMES: You've only yourself to blame, Watson. You can't play fast-and-loose with people and not expect them to feel a touch vindictive. Anyway, it's all over now. Miss Walmsley's had her satisfaction and you're none the worse for wear. I must admit, I was quite touched by your remorse. Almost brought a tear to my eye. Well, let's all kiss and make up. Do tell the girl she's forgiven.

(WATSON, *shattered and impotent, rises shakily, still looking from* HOLMES *to* BERTHA *and then back again to* HOLMES. *When he speaks, it is with a voice we have never heard before.*)

WATSON: May I retire to my room?

HOLMES: Why, old chap, of course you can. You're not a prisoner here, you know.

(WATSON *looks at the clothing and make-up piled on the floor, again to* BERTHA *and to* HOLMES, *and then walks slowly toward the door.*)

May I say, Miss Walmsley, without meaning to flatter, you are almost as fetching as a boy as you are a girl. In some ways even more so.

BERTHA: Thank you, Mr. Holmes. I wonder if I may ask you one question?

HOLMES: Most certainly.

BERTHA: I *was* very bitter when I heard what Watson had planned for me, and I am grateful you allowed me to get my own back. But was that the only reason you went to such lengths?

HOLMES: Not entirely, Miss Walmsley. You see, I had to hear from Watson's own lips that he harbored a genuine affection for me—which I always suspected he did. Now that that's been confirmed, he and I are quite safe under the same roof for the duration of our natural lives. For, as you know, Miss Walmsley, to be the subject of a genuine affection always puts you one-up in any personal relationship.

(BERTHA *smiles, quietly interpreting this remark for herself.*)

BERTHA: I must confess, despite all his wickedness, I feel a little sorry for him.

HOLMES: And not for me?

BERTHA: You? I would have thought, Mr. Holmes, in the whole wide
world, you are the person least in need of pity.

HOLMES: Which shows how poorly you have considered the matter.
Just think: when a conflict reaches unbearable proportions, it is Sherlock Holmes who is turned to, and when the murder is solved, the
missing person found, the stolen property recovered, it is Sherlock
Holmes who is immediately banished from one's thoughts—a dis-
turbing reminder of troubled times. Nor am I able to fraternize like
other men. Who would want as a bridge-partner or a drinking-com-
panion, a man of searing intellect and unbearable perceptions. It
makes people nervous, and so, I am reserved exclusively for professional ministrations. You see how even with Watson, it was impossi-
ble to sustain anything like a reciprocal relationship. No, my dear
Miss Walmsley, *(coming dangerously close to her)* no one is able to
appreciate the exquisite isolation that sets the superior being apart
from his fellow men. Envied by all, befriended by none, soaring too
high for the amity of creatures that inhabit the lower stratospheres. It
may seem like a blessing to the amateur sleuth or the penny-dreadful
enthusiast, but to Sherlock Holmes *(turning pitiably away from her)*,
it is a curse.

*(There is a poignant moment of pain. Bertha is just about to move to him
to offer solace when he immediately revives.)*

And now, I think this performance deserves a toast.

(HOLMES goes for the bottle.)

BERTHA: *(Hurrying to recover her aplomb)* Is that your Chateauneuf-
de-Pape 1794 'for very special occasions'?

HOLMES: You remembered.

BERTHA: Ingenues are trained to have good memories, Mr. Holmes.

HOLMES: Yet another of your thoroughly enchanting attributes.

*(They crook arms and glasses and drink, looking seriously into each
other's eyes. In the background, we hear the faint thud of what may be a*

gunshot. BERTHA, *alarmed, turns in the direction of the sound, the same direction* WATSON *has exited.)*

(Calmly explaining) Guy Fawkes' Day—the fireworks have started very early this year.

(HOLMES *looks steadily into* BERTHA's *somewhat alarmed eyes. As she slowly lowers her glass . . .)*

The curtain falls

Characters

MATT	early 40s
LUEEN	late 30s
TAD SIMMONDS	40s
LAURA	aged 12
MOTHER	60s

Ah, Sweet Mystery of Life! was first presented at the Pioneer Square Theater in Seattle, Washington on Wednesday, August 12th 1981. The play was directed by the author and designed by John Zagone with costumes by Jean Bloch. The cast was as follows:

MATTHEW	Doug Marney
LUEEN	Lori Doe
SIMMONDS	Ed Baron
LAURA	Jessica DeLeers
MOTHER	Pamela Peters

Ah, Sweet Mystery of Life!

Act 1

Living Room of a well-furnished apartment in North London.

MATTHEW, early 40s, constitutionally meek and unassuming, is busying himself for what is clearly an important arrival.

He transfers roses from one bowl to another, pricking his fingers in the process, accidentally emptying the water from the vase over his trousers. He dusts frantically, polishes surfaces that are already glistening, puffs up pillows so strenuously that the feathers fly out of them, and he has to scramble about the floor to recapture them. In the midst of all this, the DOORBELL SOUNDS.

He drops everything, stands stock still, transfixed.

The bell sounds again. And again. The third time it activates him and he scrambles to the door.

LUEEN: Didn't you hear me?

(LUEEN *is a very well-preserved blonde in her late thirties.*)

MATT: You're looking marvellous.

LUEEN: *(Inspecting it)* I think I've split my nail on that bloody bell.

MATT: Do you want a file?

LUEEN: I want a drink.

MATT: You're looking marvellous.

LUEEN: The cases.

(MATT *pops outside, to return instantaneously with two over-sized valises and two large hat boxes, all of which he balances with great difficulty.*)

MATT: I tried to fix up the place. It's been a pigsty for days. I couldn't get a new cleaning lady. Bronwyn gave notice, you know.

LUEEN: You let Bronwyn go?

MATT: *(Mildly defensive, still struggling with the cases)* I didn't *let* her go. She just gave notice.

LUEEN: After ten years?

MATT: She said the dust was getting into her lungs. She'd contracted pneumoconiosis.

LUEEN: Only miners get that.

MATT: She kept coughing up wads of black cottonwool. Just like a cat.

LUEEN: You probably offended her.

MATT: Really, dear—it was her health. She showed me the X-rays. They looked like bramble-bushes.

LUEEN: Bronwyn has never been sick a day in her life. You probably said something.

MATT: I offered her a rise. Even health cover. I even said I'd do it half the week myself, but she just unplugged the Hoover and left.

LUEEN: I hope you didn't pay her in advance.

MATT: I thought she deserved a bonus after all that time.

LUEEN: She walks out and you hand her a bonus!

MATT: She said she was going to a health farm. It was the least I could do.

LUEEN: As gullible as ever. Bronwyn in a health farm, really! She's probably sunning herself in Southend.

MATT: There hasn't been any sun in Southend for thirteen years.

LUEEN: Under a sun-lamp, then. As argumentative as always, I see!

MATT: I was trying to explain about Bronwyn.

LUEEN: Cottonwool, my eye. *(Facetiously)* Well, I must say, I'm really enjoying that drink.

MATT: *(Realizing)* Oh God, yes. Is it vodka and lemonade?

LUEEN: Isn't it always? Watch those hatboxes. They're Schiaparellis.

MATT: *(Pouring)* Vodka and tonic, coming up.

LUEEN: I said lemonade.

MATT: *(Fearful)* I'm afraid the lemonade's run out.

LUEEN: A fine welcome home.

MATT: It never does—so I never thought to check.

LUEEN: But it did today.

MATT: The tonic is . . .

LUEEN: Not lemonade! Oh, let's leave it.

(She swigs down a bit, unbuttons an expensive coat, sits and begins to fumble for a cigaret.

MATT *goes immediately to light it. The cigaret lighter doesn't work. He fumbles for a matchbox which turns out to be empty. He smiles lamely and runs into the kitchen, returning after a moment with a flaming piece of newspaper which he places so close to* LUEEN's *nose that she practically jumps out of the chair.*

After burning his fingers on the flaming remains, he stomps out the smoldering ashes and tries to compose himself.)

MATT: You look marvellous. Really great.

LUEEN: Have you been sleeping all right?

MATT: What do you mean?

LUEEN: You're a funny color.

MATT: Well, of course, I'm heavily on the pills.

LUEEN: As weak-willed as ever.

MATT: *(Genial)* It's a matter of sleep, Lueen. I just don't sleep without them.

LUEEN: Why don't you exercise? That always tired you out.

MATT: Oh, I jog every day. Sometimes three or four miles.

LUEEN: *(Sceptically)* You? In the park?

MATT: Oh, no. In the house. I run up and down the stairs sometimes thirty or forty times with this clock-o-meter round my neck. It clocks all the miles, you see. I tried jogging in the bridle path, but the horses kept forcing me into the ditch. They're really aggressive at eight in the morning.

LUEEN: Nothing's changed, I see.

MATT: I have, Lueen.

LUEEN: Really?

MATT: You'd never recognize me now. I've been through an almost complete personality-transformation.

LUEEN: It doesn't show.

MATT: You just walked in.

LUEEN: Is there any ice?

MATT: Oh, of course.

(He races out, returns immediately with ice and plops a few cubes into her drink, causing it to splash.)

I've been to three different shrinks since I last talked to you and enrolled with the Mata Shara for daily lessons.

LUEEN: The Mata what?

MATT: He's marvellous. He's a Freudian Mystic. He's been a real help. Better than the shrinks. I had to give them up, I kept falling asleep on the couch—depressions make you awfully dozy—but worse than that, when I woke up, I found the shrink asleep. I thought, what's the point of paying twenty-five quid an hour for both of us to have a kip.

LUEEN: You probably bored him to death.

MATT: *(Self-deprecatingly) And* myself.

LUEEN: And yourself?

MATT: That's why I gave it up. But the Mata Shara really works. He's made me realize just how selfish and stupid I've been. Especially in regard to you.

LUEEN: He sounds like a miracle worker.

MATT: Oh he is, Lueen. He doesn't just deal with the symptoms, you see. He gets right down to the underbelly of the problem. Like, in my case, it's "arrested development in the infantile stage". I keep turning women into my mother. It's all her fault.

LUEEN: So it's all your mother's fault. How convenient!

MATT: Not her fault—but her doing. I've found out so many things, Lueen, it's been a real eye-opener. Like the clothes. She kept me in swaddling clothes long after I was able to walk around. I kept tripping over myself for years and I never knew why. It was those woolly straitjackets. She had no right to do that.

LUEEN: So it all goes back to your swaddling clothes. How useful to have your own personal Mata Hari to get you off the hook.

MATT: Mata Shara—and it doesn't get me off the hook at all. It forces me to acknowledge the terrible things in my personality.

LUEEN: I could've told you about them for nothing.

MATT: I realize now how terrible I've been; how it's all been my fault. That's why I'm so happy you've come back. To give me a chance to make it all up to you.

LUEEN: Now listen, Matt, let's have all this clear from the start. This is a *trial* reconciliation—not a reconciliation. There are no promises.

MATT: I know that, Lueen, and I've no right to ask for any. I'm grateful you're even talking to me.

LUEEN: You should be.

MATT: I am.

LUEEN: I don't know why I got talked into this in the first place.

MATT: Don't think I don't appreciate it.

LUEEN: It wasn't at all convenient leaving L.A.

MATT: I really appreciate it.

LUEEN: There are very few women who would even have considered it.

MATT: My gratitude is unending.

LUEEN: *(After a beat)* Are you sending me up?

MATT: Of course not. I'm absolutely sincere. I know I've been beastly and I want to make it up to you. I've lived only for these weeks. I've dreamed about your coming back. Planned for it.

LUEEN: That's why there's no lemonade.

MATT: *(Up)* Should I run out and get a crate?

LUEEN: It's too late now. Sit down.

MATT: I've rehearsed this moment a thousand times. What I would say. How it would be—and now it's going all wrong.

LUEEN: Doesn't it always?

MATT: But that's the whole point, Lueen. Things aren't the way they were any more. I've been, I suppose, you might say, reborn. And this is sort of the christening.

LUEEN: Bet there's no champagne either.

MATT: You see. I don't even mind your sarcasm anymore. I'm a changed man.

LUEEN: Well, you can't blame me for being a little narked. What you put me through!

MATT: It wasn't me, Lueen. It was the devil inside of me. But he's been exorcised. You see, I'm completely even-tempered. I don't raise my voice. I'm loving, gentle, considerate, warm.

LUEEN: *(After a moment)* Are you on anything?

MATT: What?

LUEEN: Are you on some kind of drugs . . . ?

MATT: Only sleeping pills. Why?

LUEEN: I don't know . . . Don't look at me so funny . . . It takes a little getting used to. I haven't seen you for twelve months.

MATT: Thirteen months six days.

LUEEN: I'm surprised you haven't got it down to the hour.

MATT: It hasn't been an hour. *(Checks watch)* Seven minutes . . . I wish you'd written.

LUEEN: You seemed to be writing enough for the two of us. The postman thought you were barmy. Six letters a day, every day, without fail.

MATT: I had to communicate. I had things on my mind. You never 'phoned.

LUEEN: I told you our conversations were too upsetting. We always talked when you called.

MATT: You know what my telephone bill was this last year?

LUEEN: Nobody asked you to ring.

MATT: Three thousand, two hundred and twenty pounds. I got a congratulations note from the 'phone company. It was more than the whole Department of the Environment account for the same period.

LUEEN: I told you it would be expensive.

MATT: I developed a cauliflower ear from holding the receiver so long. I couldn't make normal conversation without cupping my hand over it. People thought I was an acoustic folk singer.

LUEEN: Stop exaggerating.

MATT: Why couldn't we have a few chats?

LUEEN: If your bill was three thousand and two hundred and twenty pounds, we must have had some marathons.

MATT: But I did all the talking.

LUEEN: Didn't you always?

MATT: We never interacted. That's what the Mata Shara said.

LUEEN: You were too busy over-reacting.

MATT: He said it was a transmission failure.

LUEEN: Maybe you need a tune-up.

MATT: He said your sarcasm was a castration-ploy.

LUEEN: Charming.

MATT: Oh, he didn't mean anything by that. You didn't realize it.

LUEEN: Thanks.

MATT: It's like a transference.

LUEEN: You've learned a lot of fancy new words.

MATT: You can't be blamed—but what you were really doing was emasculating me out of penis envy.

LUEEN: *(Rising)* I think I've heard quite enough.

MATT: What's the matter?

LUEEN: First I'm accused of wanting to cut off yours, and then of wanting one of my own. And I haven't been back fifteen minutes.

MATT: You're distorting all this.

LUEEN: And you're reborn, are you? Loving, gentle, considerate and warm!

MATT: I am. I am.

LUEEN: Twisted, cruel, selfish and stupid is closer to the truth.

MATT: I've fantasized these two weeks for thirteen months. You can't do this!

LUEEN: *I* can't?!

MATT: We're blocking; double-binding; we're not psychically 'clear'.

LUEEN: You're not clear. Why don't you talk English?

MATT: Let me pour you a drink. (LUEEN *subsides with effort.*) There may be a little lemonade if I really look.

LUEEN: I see, so you haven't really looked!

MATT: There wasn't any, but there may be.

LUEEN: How come there wasn't a minute ago?

MATT: There may be. I have to look.

LUEEN: Holding out on the lousy lemonade. What a welcome home!

MATT: Promise me an open wave-length.

LUEEN: What?

MATT: That you'll keep all the cables of communication open.

LUEEN: You sound like a TV repair man.

MATT: I've dreamed about this day for thirteen months.

LUEEN: Go find the lemonade.

MATT: Thank you. *(He goes.)*

(She gets out of her coat, looks through the curtains of the window and inspects the room.)

MATT: How about barley-water?

LUEEN: *(Plunking down glass)* Never mind. I'm not thirsty.

MATT: I can pick up the lemonade. It's only six miles to the supermarket.

LUEEN: Sit down, Matthew. Please.

MATT: *(On his guard)* You're being friendly.

LUEEN: Just sit down, will you?

MATT: I don't know why I have this feeling that I'm about to be executed.

LUEEN: Because you're so full of Jewish guilt, Matt. That's always been your trouble. You carry your own wailing wall around with you wherever you go. Now sit and listen.

(MATT *has sat and is listening.*)

Before we got married . . .

MATT: If you're going to start as far back as that, *I'll* need a drink.

LUEEN: You should've thought of that while you were up. Now be quiet. *(Starts again)* Before we got married, I was a happy, carefree, fun-loving girl with a lot of prospects. Six months with you changed all that.

MATT: Did it only last six months?

LUEEN: I'm making a generous estimate. When I think back it feels like six days.

MATT: But I was deliriously happy for thirteen years.

LUEEN: Deliriously, Matt, is the operative word. You weren't happy—
you were delirious. I, on the other hand, was miserable. You were
grouchy, broody, moody and rude.

MATT: It sounds like a law firm.

LUEEN: And unfunny—in precisely *that* way with boring, pointless and
irrelevant jokes when I was trying to talk sense to you . . . which is
what I'm trying to do now.

MATT: I'm sorry.

LUEEN: *And* full of apologies.

MATT: I'm *really* sorry.

LUEEN: Exaggerated apologies!

(MATT *about to say something, says nothing.*)

You made our marriage a dungeon and appointed yourself the resident warden. You worked at it with diligence and delight.

MATT: Diligence, maybe, Lueen . . . but never delight.

LUEEN: No, I suppose you never delighted in anything . . . not even
my misery. But that's only because you were incapable of delight—
which is another one of your endearing traits.

MATT: Is this going to take much longer? It's beginning to feel like my
analysis.

LUEEN: I haven't even started yet. I'm trying to fill in the background
of this trial reconciliation . . . just in case you've forgotten what's
happened the past thirteen years.

MATT: If this is the reconciliation, what will the divorce be like?

LUEEN: You may well find that out very soon, Matt.

MATT: *(Stung)* Don't say that, Lueen. You know I don't want that. I've hung on a thread for thirteen months because I want us to make it up. I've been through wholesale personality-transformations, bankrupted myself on the long-distance telephone, fantasized a whole new life for us. I've had more sleeping-pills than I've had cornflakes. I've got pains in my chest and a ruptured retina. I have nightmares every night and have even started to pray again . . . even though I know He sees right through me. So please don't talk about divorce. It's like a knife in the heart.

LUEEN: And have you noticed what you haven't asked me all this time?

MATT: What?

LUEEN: Have you noticed a subject you haven't brought up?

MATT: Your ulcer?

LUEEN: No, not my ulcer, thank you very much.

MATT: Is it all right?

LUEEN: When it perforates, I'll let you know. Otherwise, just take it that I'm in constant and unendurable agony.

MATT: I knew there was a reason I didn't ask.

LUEEN: Of course, you could never bear to hear about anyone else's suffering. It crabbed your act. No, Matt, not my ulcer.

MATT: Then what?

LUEEN: Your daughter, Matt. Or, should I say, my daughter, since you've never shown any kind of fatherly feeling for her.

MATT: It was on the tip of my tongue.

LUEEN: Just behind the tip, Matt. On the actual tip was your selfishness.

MATT: I'm sorry. How is Laura?

LUEEN: *Now* you want to know!

MATT: You asked me to ask.

LUEEN: Wrong, Matt. I said you hadn't asked.

MATT: Well, I'm asking.

LUEEN: *Now* you're asking.

MATT: Is this an Abbott and Costello routine?

LUEEN: Your whole life is an Abbott and Costello routine, and you know how rum they were.

MATT: How is my daughter?

LUEEN: Fine, thank you!

MATT: All that for this.

LUEEN: Fine, because away from you. Happy, because no longer in your line of fire. She may even grow up to be normal. The shrink gives her a fifty-fifty chance.

MATT: The shrink? You put a twelve-year-old girl on the couch?

LUEEN: Where'd you expect her to have analysis—in the sandbox?

MATT: A twelve-year-old girl with a shrink!

LUEEN: You've had dozens.

MATT: I'm in a mid-life crisis, a marital bind and a stress-situation. Laura is still licking lollipops.

LUEEN: How dare you say that about my daughter!

MATT: What?

LUEEN: I read all your horrible innuendoes.

MATT: What innuendoes?

LUEEN: And why did I have to take her to an analyst?! Did you ever ask yourself that?

MATT: *(Subsides)* Because of me.

LUEEN: Right the first time.

MATT: I messed her up. I gave her infantile traumas. I didn't toilet train her.

LUEEN: *(Wincing)* You never trained yourself!

MATT: There is no law, Lueen, that says the toilet seat must always be in a recumbent position.

LUEEN: I am not going to discuss this. You know I don't approve of that word.

MATT: What word?

LUEEN: You know very well.

MATT: They don't call it "lavatory training". They call it toilet training.

LUEEN: I don't care what they call it. I am not here to discuss personal amenities.

MATT: You mean toilets?

LUEEN: I don't wish to hear that word in this house. And you're only saying it to irritate me. Is this what you brought me back for—to cover me with filth?!

MATT: We are losing our heads.

LUEEN: *We?*

MATT: All right. I am losing my head. I am giving in to pent-up bitterness and repressed hostilities.

LUEEN: You talk like a textbook.

MATT: Why shouldn't I? . . . I'm a textbook case! Anyway, I'm
sorry. Truly sorry. No, I didn't ask you come here to discuss . . .
(Looks for euphemism) . . . water-closets. I asked you because I
love you and I want to try and get it all together again.

LUEEN: You'd better start with yourself.

MATT: I'm trying. That's why I need you.

LUEEN: Do you ever listen to yourself?

MATT: Sometimes I think I'm the only one who does.

LUEEN: Now listen, Matthew. I've come 6,000 miles, and so you'd
better listen. I've had time to do a lot of thinking, and if there's to be
any kind of future, there have got to be some changes made. Do you
agree?

MATT: Absolutely. Exactly what I feel. I've changed, so now it can all
change. You always said it would have to change.

LUEEN: So you agree to changes?

MATT: Absolutely.

LUEEN: Good. I'm glad that's all settled.

MATT: *(After a beat)* What's all settled?

LUEEN: That it will have to change. That you agree.

MATT: I agree it has to change—but what's all settled?

LUEEN: There are lots of things. For instance: I think it would be best for Laura if you didn't visit her. It only upsets her and we have to consider what's best for her.

MATT: You mean never?

LUEEN: If you see her at all, you'll only undo the good of not seeing her. Don't you see that?

MATT: I guess that's logical.

LUEEN: Of course it is. If you want the child to get over something, it's better if it's a clean break. The sooner she forgets all about you, the better it will be all round.

MATT: I suppose that's so.

LUEEN: Of course it's so. There's no point in torturing the child—and tormenting yourself, and that's all you'd be doing. It would be best all round.

MATT: Couldn't I see her two or three times a year? Christmas, Easter —that kind of thing?

LUEEN: Is that fair? To shatter the child during what should be the happiest times of her year?

MATT: No, I suppose you're right.

LUEEN: Of course I am.

MATT: Perhaps I could see her without her seeing me.

LUEEN: What do you mean?

MATT: From a distance, maybe. Through a high-powered telescopic lens . . . just watching her development from afar.

LUEEN: Well, we could consider that at a later date. And then there's the property.

MATT: The property?

LUEEN: I think we had better have the house and the car. Laura will need a home and I can't be expected to travel on public transportation.

MATT: Is this a reconciliation or a property settlement?

LUEEN: We have to be practical, Matt. If the reconciliation doesn't work out, we should have all these things decided.

MATT: Oh, I see. This is just in case the reconciliation doesn't work out.

LUEEN: Of course. It's just looking ahead.

MATT: To the time the reconciliation doesn't work out.

LUEEN: *If* it doesn't work out.

MATT: But you think it will?

LUEEN: It's in the lap of the gods, isn't it? I have come back, haven't I? That's what you wanted, isn't it?

MATT: Yes, that's true. But I don't know, I somehow thought we might . . . kind of . . . make a different sort of effort.

LUEEN: We will, Matthew, but we have to be practical just in case things don't work out.

MATT: Provide for the future.

LUEEN: Exactly.

MATT: But in the meantime, we could pick up the marriage and live like man and wife, right?

LUEEN: Naturally.

MATT: Great.

LUEEN: Then there's the financial arrangements.

MATT: The what?

LUEEN: After all, Matt, I do have a child to bring up. You can't expect me to take in washing. There'll have to be some kind of allowance.

MATT: Of course . . . of course.

LUEEN: I only want what's fair, Matt. I think we should agree some monthly sum that will keep Laura and me to the standard to which we've become accustomed. After all, I did give you the best years of my life—and I'm not exactly a chicken any longer.

MATT: This is in case the reconciliation doesn't work out?

LUEEN: Haven't you been listening to me?

MATT: I thought that's what you said.

LUEEN: Of course it is! But we don't want to leave all these things for the last minute . . .

MATT: You mean if there *is* a last minute?

LUEEN: Exactly.

MATT: That makes sense.

LUEEN: You were never any good with practical matters, Matt. You must admit that was never your strong point.

MATT: Actually, when I think back, I can't remember any strong points at all.

LUEEN: It's too late to start brooding on that now. Anyway, I thought if we can agree all this, as we seem to be able to, the best thing is to get it all cleared up and out of the way—which is why I asked Mr. Simmonds to come along.

MATT: Mr. Simmonds?

LUEEN: My private solicitor. He's outside in the car.

MATT: Your solicitor is outside in the car?

LUEEN: Well, I didn't want to haul him in here before we had a chance to talk. What kind of person do you think I am?

MATT: Quite right. Very considerate.

LUEEN: *(Going to window and motioning)* He's just outside, and since we're discussing these things, it might be best to get everything cleared up.

MATT: You mean if the reconciliation doesn't work out?

LUEEN: Of course. There'll be no need otherwise, will there?

MATT: You mean if we get together again—all this will be . . .

LUEEN: Totally irrelevant. This is just in case it doesn't. Surely you can grasp that, Matt. It's not higher calculus.

MATT: No . . . no . . . it's not that.

(There is a knock at the window.

LUEEN *motions the stranger around to the front—then opens the door for* MR. SIMMONDS, *who wears a hound-tooth jacket, a cravat around his neck and has the look of an affluent used-car salesman.)*

MR. SIMMONDS: Tad Simmonds—terribly glad to make your acquaintance. Vodka on the rocks would be spiffing; the inside of that Rover is like a blast furnace.

MATT: If I'd known you were there, I'd have brought it out to you.

MR. SIMMONDS: Bloody decent of you. Everything going well?

LUEEN: Yes, Tad. He is being very reasonable and we've agreed most of the main points.

MR. SIMMONDS: Delighted to hear it. I'm a firm believer, Mort, may I call you Mort—I can't stand first-name terms unless all the parties agree—bloody rude, otherwise.

MATT: Matt.

MR. SIMMONDS: Pardon?

LUEEN: It's Matt.

MR. SIMMONDS: Just as you like. I'm a firm believer . . . Matt?

MATT: That's right.

MR. SIMMONDS: Firm believer in negotiated settlements. There need never have been a Second World War if Chamberlain had understood that.

MATT: *(Inoffensively)* But I thought he did negotiate a settlement.

MR. SIMMONDS: It wasn't firm, Max, and that's why it didn't hold. Get all the small print clear between both parties. If there'd been a few more binding clauses and all the loopholes were closed up, we would have been spared the whole shooting match. Chamberlain just didn't understand the art of negotiation. Neither did Stalin or Roosevelt— none of them, and what's the consequence? Misunderstanding. Conflicting views. False constructions. "I thought you meant so-and-so" . . . "I thought it was such-and-such" . . . Result? World War. Bloody waste of time and all because of faulty negotiation.

MATT: That's certainly an original view of history.

MR. SIMMONDS: Is that my vodka on the rocks?

MATT: *(Who has been holding it)* Oh, sorry.

MR. SIMMONDS: Thanks, old man. I'm not usually so parched but in this weather, the inside of a Rover is like the ovens at Belsen.

LUEEN: I've touched all the main points.

MR. SIMMONDS: Good. May I sit down?

MATT: Certainly. Certainly. Would you like a footstool?

MR. SIMMONDS: Never touch the stuff. Straight vodka-man. Shall I get straight to the point?

MATT: What point?

MR. SIMMONDS: *(His aplomb suddenly wilted, turns to* LUEEN*)* But I thought . . .

LUEEN: We've just touched on the issues, Tad. Just gone through the preliminaries.

MR. SIMMONDS: *(Aplomb returned)* Good. The preliminaries are out of the way and we're ready for brass tacks. That's efficient procedure, Mort. Get the preliminaries done with—etch in the broad outline so all the parties have the gist of the thing—then get straight to the crux of the matter. Preliminaries. Gist. Crux. Follow those ABCs and you can't go wrong. *(Removes documents from briefcase)* Now I've got four copies. One for each of us. *(Hands them out)* Lueen . . . *(Hands her a copy)* Mort . . . *(Hands him copy)*

MATT: *(Correcting)* Matt.

MR. SIMMONDS: Sorry. Tad . . . *(Gives one to himself)* . . . and *(throws one back into briefcase)* . . . file-copy. That's another essential, Mort. Always have a file-copy of everything. I don't do a shopping list without a carbon. It's a principle with me. Never know when you're going to need a spare. Right. Now we're all settled in. The preliminaries are done; we've got the 'gist' of the thing; we're now ready for the . . .

MATT: *(As if giving a cue)* Crux.

MR. SIMMONDS: *(Admiringly)* Have you ever considered the Bar?

MATT: Only half-heartedly.

MR. SIMMONDS: You've got a firm grasp of procedures, Mort, and that's all a solicitor is—a man with a grip on procedures. Now, let us proceed. *(Mulls over documents)* The whole of this first page is a lot of legal jargon that's of no real consequence. Law is like one of those very talky foreign films that gets boiled down to a short, snappy subtitle, and that's what solicitors are for. The whole of this . . . *(Turns page)* . . . and this *(Turns page)* . . . and this . . . *(Turns page)* . . . simply means you agree to turn over the house to Lueen. God knows why there's so many subordinate clauses. All it needs is one simple declarative sentence really. "I Mort, agree to turn over the house to my wife, Lueen". But no, they've got to whereas-it and wherefore-it and all the rest of that malarkey. Anyway, that's clear, isn't it?

MATT: Yes. The house.

MR. SIMMONDS: Well, that's only fair, isn't it? Man's home is his castle and all the rest of it, but a woman's place is in the home, and there's an end to it. Now . . . as for Laura . . .

MATT: Um . . . is there anything there about me?

MR. SIMMONDS: *(After a beat)* How do you mean, old chap?

MATT: I mean, I understand about Lueen getting the home. That's completely clear. I've got the gist of it, the crux of it, everything. But is there anything there about me?

(SIMMONDS *looks blankly to* LUEEN.)

LUEEN: Don't start getting silly, Matt.

MATT: I was just sort of wondering where I would live?

MR. SIMMONDS: Well, that's the beauty of this thing, Mort. There's absolutely no restriction whatsoever on where you are to live.

MATT: I can live anywhere?

MR. SIMMONDS: You can go through this document with a fine tooth-comb and not find a single provision—not even a subordinate clause —that in any way restricts your choice of domicile. Brighton. Black-pool. South of France. You're free as a bird.

MATT: Well, that's a relief.

LUEEN: Now stop being silly, Matt. Tad hasn't got all day.

MATT: Sorry.

MR. SIMMONDS: Now as for custody of Laura—visiting rights, all that malarkey . . . this *(Turns page)* . . . and this . . . *(Turns page)* . . . and this *(Turns page)* simply means you relinquish all custody of your daughter to the child's mother, and that's an end to it.

MATT: Now could we discuss that one a little?

MR. SIMMONDS: *(Turns painfully to* LUEEN*)* I thought you'd taken care of all the preliminaries?

MATT: Oh, she gave me the 'gist' of it all right. It's just that we don't quite see eye to eye on this particular 'crux'. You see, I'd like to see my daughter—assuming, that is, that our reconciliation doesn't work and that my wife leaves me and takes my daughter—none of which is happening—is that right?

MR. SIMMONDS: Of course not, old chap. That's the beauty of these things. It's like the button on the Hydrogen Bomb. You don't push it till you have to—but, when you do, everything happens at once— exactly according to plan. Now, let's see if I have this right. You're wanting some kind of provision concerning access to your daughter?

MATT: That's it, Tod.

MR. SIMMONDS: Tad, old man.

MATT: Sorry.

MR. SIMMONDS: That seems to me, and I have to say this in front of my client, no matter what construction she may put on it, quite fair and reasonable. Do you agree?

LUEEN: No. Matt only upsets Laura and I think it would be best all round if he didn't see her.

MR. SIMMONDS: That, too, I must say, sounds fair and reasonable. *(Turns to* MATT) Wouldn't you say?

MATT: Well, the thing is, I still want it.

MR. SIMMONDS: That, I must say, sounds rather less fair and reasonable . . . but, and this is the beauty of the British Law, there is always a solution through compromise. And this again is where I come on. One inflexible position—another inflexible position—like two cliffs jutting out across an angry sea, and British Law delicately builds a bridge between them and everyone is happy.

LUEEN: I'm not happy. I don't want any bridges.

MR. SIMMONDS: Now be fair and reasonable, Lueen. That's the secret of a negotiated settlement. Fairness and reason will see us through the darkest hour. Now, what would you say, Mort, to this . . . *(Thinks for a moment)* Visiting rights and full powers of access every February 29th.

MATT: But that only comes round once every four years.

MR. SIMMONDS: Now be reasonable, Max. The whole point of a compromise is you don't get everything you want.

LUEEN: I thought you really had changed.

MATT: Once every four years! I'd have to introduce myself each time.

LUEEN: I thought we'd been through all this.

MATT: Was I here?

LUEEN: Apparently not.

MATT: *(The pacifist)* Look, since we're here to patch everything up, couldn't we leave these details till later? What's the point of discussing custody and all the rest of it, when we're trying to get together again?

MR. SIMMONDS: Ah, now, there's the point, old chap. Always work out the difficult bits when things are hunky-dory. Afterwards, nobody wants to know. Doors are shut. Telephones slammed down. Hard words. Bitter feelings.

LUEEN: I've explained all of that, Tad. He just won't listen.

MATT: *(Contrite)* No, I'm sorry. I'm just being selfish again. The Mata Shara says it always surfaces when I'm feeling wronged. You're right. Both of you. Accept my apology.

MR. SIMMONDS: That's awfully decent of you, Milt. You know, if Hitler or Mussolini had uttered those words in the dark days of '39, there would never have been a Flanders Field.

MATT: Wasn't that the First World War?

MR. SIMMONDS: Yes, but I daresay it was still there in the Second. That's the rub, isn't it, old scout? One calamity leads to another. The world never learns. *(Returns to legal documents)* Fine, so the custody's all settled. You see, we're getting on like a house on fire. Now, as for the allowance, nobody wants to be unreasonable and my client accepts that your earning-power has dwindled somewhat due to . . . due to . . . I can't recall what that *was* due to?

MATT: Due to your client, actually. I've been too depressed to work for a year and have had analysis five times a week, so I'm a little skint.

LUEEN: Lots of us have to get up in the morning and go to work no matter how we feel, Matt. It's not everyone who can lay about on couches all day.

MATT: I haven't been able to. I've wanted to, but I haven't been able to.

LUEEN: You were always lazy, Matthew. Sleeping at the analyst's is just par for the course.

MATT: I didn't go there to sleep. If I was going to sleep, I would have stayed in bed. It would have been cheaper. *(Turns to* MR. SIMMONDS*)* You understand, don't you?

MR. SIMMONDS: I'm the last person to ask, old boy. Got the temperament of a village vicar. Never depressed. Never blue. Start the day with a smile. End it with a contented yawn. A little booze. A little golf. A few pleasantries after dinner. Simple pleasures.

MATT: You're never depressed?

MR. SIMMONDS: Don't know the meaning of the word.

MATT: How do you explain that?

MR. SIMMONDS: Mediocrity.

MATT: *(Beat)* I don't follow.

MR. SIMMONDS: It's quite simple, old chap. Mediocrity—that's the ticket.

MATT: *(Looks about)* Could you enlarge on that?

MR. SIMMONDS: Most people have a low opinion of it. They tend to sneer—particularly the intellectual bods. You know, so-and-so's so ordinary; nothing very special; run-of-the-mill, you've heard it a thousand times. But the fact is, mediocrity's a kind of boon if you're into day-to-day comfort. Never take up any challenges—ergo, less chance of failure, ergo, even a fair-to-middling showing looks quite impressive. You don't get riled by passions or convictions—nothing troublesome like that. My natural reaction to any burning issue is to let it all subside in its own sweet time—which it always does—one way or another. No strong opinions of any sort. If there's no wine, I'll take beer. No beer, lemonade.

LUEEN: You'll be lucky to get lemonade in this house.

MR. SIMMONDS: The point is—never feel anything very strongly. Let life just wash over you. Not too extreme one way or the other. Except for moderation, of course; that *must* be taken to the extreme. Oh, I grant you, it doesn't make for dynamic personalities. God knows, if you were button-holed in a corner with me at a cocktail party, I'd probably bore you to tears. Nevertheless, when the party was over, you'd go to your bed troubled and churned up and I'd sleep like a babe without a thought in my head. It's not fashionable, I'll give you that, being a mediocrity, but it's a damned comfort in this world where almost everyone else is constantly on the go, in a sweat, round the bend, up a gumtree—you follow?

MATT: And it doesn't bother you at all? Being a . . . ? *(Hesitates to use the word)*

MR. SIMMONDS: Mediocrity? Gadzooks, man, it's a positive blessing. I thank my lucky stars. Do you suppose I'd be any kind of a solicitor if I weren't? Wouldn't change things for all the tea in China. There, that's what you'd call, I suppose, a mediocre turn of phrase; very ordinary, but oh, it's so comforting to hear phrases you've grown up with since you were a child. Fit as a fiddle. Safe as houses. Big as a bear. Tea in China. Dear old friends. Sometimes brings the tears to my eyes.

(A wistful moment.)

LUEEN: *(Bringing him back)* Tad . . .

MR. SIMMONDS: Right! Financial settlement. Suggest two-thirds of your total income . . . reducing to half after three years to be entirely withdrawn in the event of a remarriage.

MATT: Two-thirds? That leaves me only a third. Can I live on a third?

MR. SIMMONDS: If you were a Vietnamese peasant, my boy, you'd be grateful for a bowl of rice a day.

MATT: But I'm not a Vietnamese peasant.

MR. SIMMONDS: Precisely. Therefore a third of your income is a positive treasure trove.

MATT: Could we sort of negotiate on that?

MR. SIMMONDS: I'd have to take advice from my client.

MATT: Well, she's right here.

MR. SIMMONDS: Lueen?

LUEEN: I can't stand discussing money matters, Tad, it's so sordid. Let's call it three-quarters and leave it at that.

MATT: But three-quarters is even more!

LUEEN: I'm not going to start horse-trading.

MATT: At three-quarters, I'd have no horse to trade. Not even the hay.

MR. SIMMONDS: Let's not quibble, old man. After all, it's only money.

MATT: But it's my money.

MR. SIMMONDS: Only temporarily. Let's say fifty-fifty with a twenty-per-cent increase for inflation in yearly increments.

MATT: What does all that mean in money?

MR. SIMMONDS: Let the accountants work that out, old fellow. That's their job.

MATT: Still, it'd be nice to know beforehand.

LUEEN: *(Aside)* As paranoid as ever.

MR. SIMMONDS: I say, old man, I hope you don't think anyone's trying to diddle you.

MATT: Well, I don't know. I mean, I haven't had a chance to consult a solicitor. It's all come as a bit of a surprise. I mean, this was supposed to be a reconciliation.

MR. SIMMONDS: As I understand it, that's precisely what it is. *(To* LUEEN*)* Is it not?

LUEEN: I've told him a dozen times. He just refuses to understand. I don't think he wants it.

MATT: Oh, I do, Lueen. Really I do. I'm just not prepared for all this now. Couldn't we leave it till tomorrow? We haven't even unpacked the bags. It all sounds fine. I'm sure we'll be able to work out something as you say 'fair and reasonable'. I am a little worried about Laura.

LUEEN: Well, I think you'd better talk with the child, Matt. After all, we have to take her own feelings into consideration. Shall I get her?

MATT: Is she here?

LUEEN: In the car.

MATT: *(Beat)* What have you got out there, a charabanc? Why didn't you bring her in?

LUEEN: I wasn't going to have her upset by you the minute we walked through the door. Laura's a sensitive child and she's been through a lot.

MATT: Of course, of course. I don't want to upset her.

LUEEN: It's a wonder she's normal at all, given what she's been through.

MATT: I'm sure, I'm sure.

LUEEN: You'd better have a chat with her before she goes up to Mother's.

MATT: Isn't she staying with us?

LUEEN: I thought it would be best if she stayed at Mother's. It's not fair, inflicting our problems on an innocent child.

MATT: No, I suppose not. How long is she staying at your mother's?

LUEEN: We can decide that afterwards. Depending on how things go. Do you want to have a talk with her or not?

MATT: Oh, yes . . . yes, I do.

LUEEN: We'll make ourselves scarce. Now, I don't want any scenes, Matthew. Remember, she's a sensitive girl and she's been living in the States for over a year now so she's lost some of your quaint English ways. Don't churn her up.

MATT: No, no . . . certainly not.

LUEEN: What do you think, Tad. Should we risk it?

MR. SIMMONDS: Are you asking my advice as a solicitor or as a family counsellor?

LUEEN: Whichever.

MR. SIMMONDS: Well, as a solicitor I'm bound to say there's no bar to the father seeing the child at this stage of the proceedings. As a family counsellor, however, I have no qualifications whatsoever, so I'd better reserve judgement. But on purely humanitarian grounds, I would suggest we get the child out of that Rover as soon as possible, or she'll burn to cinders.

(LUEEN *taps on window and motions* LAURA *in.*)

Lovely place you have here. Always thought of northwest London as a kind of ghetto. Washing on the lines; old people with whiskers and skull-caps; that sort of thing. It looks quite civilized.

MATT: This is the fashionable end. A few blocks down they still butcher cows in the street and use open drains.

(LAURA *enters, aged 12, wearing dungarees, tight-fitting American T-shirt. She speaks through the corner of her mouth—like a Chicago gangster.*)

LUEEN: Laura, you remember Matthew. He's your father.

LAURA: Hi, dad.

MATT: *(After a beat)* Very transatlantic, isn't she?

LUEEN: Laura's on the football team, aren't you, Laura?

LAURA: Cheerleading squad.

LUEEN: Well, it's the same thing, isn't it *(Looks to* MR. SIMMONDS) Well, Tad and I are going to pick up a few things at the chemists while you have a little visit with Matthew. Is there anything you'd like us to get you?

LAURA: Chocolate chip cone—double-scoop—Haagen-Daz.

LUEEN: You've already had ice cream today, Laura, at breakfast—remember?

LAURA: That was a long time ago.

LUEEN: Then again at lunch.

LAURA: *(Threateningly)* Are you trying to hold out on my Haagen-Daz?

(LUEEN *looks painfully to* MR. SIMMONDS)

MR. SIMMONDS: Now, now, if little Laura wants ice cream—that seems quite fair and reasonable to me.

LUEEN: Again?

MR. SIMMONDS: This is a special occasion. It isn't every day she sees her father. Right then. We'll be off to . . . um . . . pick up a few things and be back in, say . . . *(Checks watch)* . . . twenty minutes, um?

(MATT *nodds weakly.*

LUEEN *and* MR. SIMMONDS *exit with* LUEEN *doing a last-minute straightening of her daughter's clothes.*

MATT *studies the child, trying to find an entrance-route to a conversation.*

LAURA *is remote, her eyes swivelling in her head, preoccupied with other things.)*

MATT: *(After too long a pause)* Well, this is nice, isn't it?

LAURA: Depends.

MATT: *(Pause continues)* Would you like some potato chips or a coke?

LAURA: No thanks. *(Takes out a packet)* Want some toot?

MATT: Some what?

LAURA: It's coke, but not in bottles.

MATT: *(Oblivious)* No thanks, I'm not into sweets before dinner.

LAURA: *(After inspection)* Hasn't changed much.

MATT: The old place—No, no . . . not much. And how about you? Are you enjoying America?

LAURA: I'm in L.A.

MATT: *(Corrected)* Oh, of course. And what do you do there?

LAURA: I watch the Z-channel a lot.

MATT: Oh, I see.

LAURA: You want to know my favorites? *(Launches right in)* George Raft. James Cagney. Edward G. Robinson. Jack la Rue. Paul Muni—when he's being tough—not wet. Humphrey Bogart. Al Capone. Bugsy Siegel. Pretty Boy Floyd. Baby Face Nelson and Legs Diamond.

MATT: I see.

LAURA: I seen those pictures, maybe twenty times each. I know all the lines by heart. I memorized 'em instead of Hiawatha. "Mother of God. Is this the end of Rico?" I woulda liked to be a gun-moll, but I'm too short.

MATT: Maybe when you grow up.

LAURA: Nah. Gun-molls are born, not made. I lost my chance on account'a I'm such a dwarf. Did'ja ever pack a 45?

MATT: Um . . . no.

LAURA: Me neither. I snuck a Saturdaynight Special into my pencil-box once, but the principal took if off'a me. Somebody in Geography finked on me.

MATT: You can't trust anyone nowadays.

LAURA: I got my own back. I put an eel into her gym suit. She did the mile in half a minute. She's on the track-team now—but without the eel, she's nowhere.

MATT: *(A beat to recover, and then)* And how's the cheerleading coming along?

LAURA: I don't do that no more.

MATT: Outgrew it, eh?

LAURA: Got kicked off the squad.

MATT: Oh?

LAURA: Don't tell Mom. She thinks I go to practise three nights a week.

MATT: But you don't . . . ?

LAURA: Uh uh.

MATT: Where do you go?

LAURA: *(After a beat)* Can I trust you?

MATT: I am your father, Laura.

LAURA: That's why I'm asking.

MATT: Of course you can trust me, Laura. We've always been pals, haven't we? We've always had our little secrets, and I never let you down, did I?

LAURA: No, you was pretty up-front most of the time.

MATT: So?

LAURA: I got a boyfriend. I go to his place.

MATT: *(Beat)* Well, I don't think mother would object to that.

LAURA: He's a Nigerian.

MATT: Oh—I see—well, I guess . . .

LAURA: A little older than you.

MATT: Oh. A rather mature companion for a girl your age, still . . . What's he like? What're his interests?

LAURA: He's into sixty-nine a lot.

MATT: *(After a beat)* Into . . . ?

LAURA: Head's all he ever thinks about. It's real boring.

MATT: *(After a longish, thoughtful pause)* Now, let's just see if I've got all this straight, Laura. You're seeing some Nigerian fellow . . .

LAURA: His brother's worse. He keeps dressin' me up all the time.

MATT: His brother? What's his brother got to do with . . . ?

LAURA: They live together. I kinda go with both of 'em.

MATT: *(After a pause)* Now, let's just make sure we don't have any crossed wires here, Laura. You're saying that you're seeing these two Nigerian brothers and that you're . . . having some kind of . . . liaison or something with them?

LAURA: Gee, I hope Mom hurries up with that ice cream. I'm parched.

MATT: Now look, Laura. I don't think I've ever come on heavy with you—Big Bad Dad, or any of that kind of thing, have I?

LAURA: No, you're pretty neat.

MATT: Right. All right, so if I'm 'pretty neat', I'd like you to just clarify a few things about this relationship of yours with . . . what's his name?

LAURA: Aguba.

MATT: Which one is that?

LAURA: He's the one into head. Arimba's into the cheerleader outfits.

MATT: He makes you dress up as a cheerleader?

LAURA: Might as well. I ain't on the squad no more.

MATT: What then?

LAURA: Huh?

MATT: What happens after you get dressed up as a cheerleader?

LAURA: Oh, he's real boring . . . grunts and groans—a real heavy number. And when Aguba gets into the act, it just goes on for an ice-age.

MATT: Together! You're with both of them?

LAURA: They're brothers!

MATT: *(Getting riled)* What's that got to do with it? You've got a whole football team out there, you're not together with all of them for an ice-age!

LAURA: Not all together. Who do you think I am? Wonder-woman?

MATT: *(Stunned, but resolved)* When you say, Laura, 'not all together' —are you trying to imply that individually, that is—on a one-to-one basis, you've . . .

LAURA: They're all kids. They don't even know what to do. That's why I went with Aguba. He's real mature.

MATT: If he's a little older than me, he's more than mature . . . he's pensionable. What exactly does he do?

(LAURA *looks slyly at him.)*

I don't mean that! What's his work?

LAURA: He's visiting prof. at U.S.C. Social Studies 103. 'Ethnic Drives and the Coming Man'. Sometimes he sneaks me into his lectures—

even though I still got three years to go before I graduate high school. He thinks I'm pretty big for 12.

MATT: How nice.

LAURA: *(Under)* He's pretty big, too.

MATT: How long has all this been going on, Laura?

LAURA: Since I dropped out of Home Ec. About three terms.

MATT: Have you told Lueen about any of this?

LAURA: Nah, and you better not, either. I'm not goin'a stay cooped up in the apartment every night.

MATT: *(Sits her down)* Now listen, Laura. It's been quite some time since we last saw each other, and I know California is a go-ahead sort of place, and everyone's into swinging life-styles and all of that—but do you really think you're ready for an adult relationship at your age?

LAURA: What's an adult relationship?

MATT: What you're doing three nights a week with those . . . Ethnics.

LAURA: I got no relationship with 'em. That's just sex. You don't think I go steady with either of those apes. What do you take me for?

MATT: *(Swigs down a drink)* Laura, in many ways I've failed you as a father. I know that and I regret it deeply. And it may be too late to remedy matters. I should have laid down some moral precepts a long time ago. But Lueen was . . . well, anyway, there's no point in hashing up the past. The point now is . . . what in Heaven's name are you doing . . . ?

LAURA: *(Sniffing coke)* Want some?

MATT: *(Examines it with horror)* Is that what I think it is?

LAURA: I dunno—what do you think it is?

MATT: Is that a drug of some sort?

LAURA: It's just coke.

(MATT *takes it from her and rushes into the toilet with it—flushes it down.*)

Hey—that stuff's expensive!

MATT: Now listen, Laura. I'm not sure what is the best way to get this across to you. Maybe I'm not the best person to lay down the moral law, but a girl of twelve is . . .

LAURA: Aintcha comin' back to L.A. with us?

MATT: *(Beat)* Is that what you want to do—go back to L.A.?

LAURA: It's pretty neat.

MATT: And England?

LAURA: That's pretty neat, too—sometimes—but awful wet.

MATT: *(Boiling, irrational)* We know all about the foul atmospheric conditions of the British Isles, Laura, compared to the idyllic beaches and perpetual sunshine of America's West Coast, and if life was all fluctuations of Fahrenheit, there'd be nothing to choose between. But social values, cultural heritage and just simple, old-fashioned virtues like tolerable conversation with people who aren't being lobotomized or sticking hypodermic needles into their veins, still play some part. So the fact that it may be 'awful wet', Laura, darling, is not in itself an unimpeachable condemnation of an entire society.

LAURA: You sound just like Aguba sometimes—only his voice is a lot lower.

MATT: Everything about him sounds low. Laura, wouldn't you like to live together with Lueen and me, the way we used to?

LAURA: But you're split, aintcha?

MATT: Splits can be spliced.

LAURA: *(Knowing)* Oh?

MATT: Don't you think?

LAURA: Um. *(Meaning "maybe")*

MATT: Or do you think our splits are unspliceable?

LAURA: What do I know? I'm only twelve years old.

MATT: God help us when you're sixteen!

LAURA: Mom says you're not all there.

MATT: Oh. Really?

LAURA: I don't take sides. I'm like Switzerland. But Tad's a real creep.
I'd rather have you than him anyday.

MATT: What's Tad got to do with all of this?

LAURA: He's knocking her off, ain't he?

MATT: Knocking who off?

LAURA: *(Beat)* I think I just blew it.

MATT: Tad? That pompous, jargonizing jack-ass sleeping with your
mother?

LAURA: Don't you mean your wife?

MATT: What evidence do you have for that preposterous slander?

LAURA: I dunno.

MATT: What do you mean you 'dunno'? You seem to know about everything else.

LAURA: I'm neutral. I'm not takin' any sides.

MATT: *(Persuading himself)* I can easily see where a girl of your tender years might misconstrue a perfectly harmless relationship in which . . . *(Suddenly)* Have you seen anything or heard anything?

(LAURA *puts hands over eye and then ears, and then mouth.*)

You may think you're very clever, Laura, but I find all that clowning around very undergraduate.

LAURA: But I'm not even an undergraduate. I've still got six years to go.

MATT: Don't be smart, young lady. You're not too old to be put over my knee and given a good spanking.

LAURA: Arimba does that all the time. He gets a real charge out of it. It's real boring.

MATT: *(Agonized)* I don't want to hear another word about it. Those apes ought to be in custody.

LAURA: *(Inspecting drinks cabinet)* They was, but the Civil Rights lawyer sprung 'em.

(LUEEN *and* MR. SIMMONDS *enter.*)

LUEEN: Everything's shut. Bloody half-day closing! I keep forgetting how primitive it is out here.

MR. SIMMONDS: *(Handing* LAURA *the cone)* Here's your ice cream—double-scoop. Now what do you say?

LAURA: You forgot the nut-sprinkles.

MR. SIMMONDS: They didn't have any nut-sprinkles.

LAURA: *(Under her breath)* Alibis . . . alibis . . .

(MR. SIMMONDS *looks vexedly at* LAURA, *who gives him a sour expression and then turns to* MATT.)

LUEEN: Had a nice chat, then?

MATT: Lovely. Well, your room is all made up, Lueen. I suppose you'll want to unpack and I've arranged a special dinner for tonight. Turkey-stew and pumpkin-pie . . . all your favorites *(To* MR. SIMMONDS) Thanks very much for putting me into the picture, Tad. I'll study all those papers as soon as I get a minute.

(MR. SIMMONDS, *consternated, turns to* LUEEN)

LUEEN: Since there was so much to go through, I've asked Tad to stay a few days. I mean, there's no point his coming all the way from . . . where is it?

MR. SIMMONDS: Saffron Walden.

LUEEN: Without getting everything sorted out.

MATT: Stay? You mean stay here!

LUEEN: There *is* a guest room, Matthew. You make it sound as if I was asking him to share our bed. *(To* MR. SIMMONDS) You won't mind staying in the guest room, will you, Tad?

MR. SIMMONDS: Not at all. Delighted.

(MATT *looks painfully to* MR. SIMMONDS, *then to* LAURA *who gives him an 'I-told-you-so' look.)*

MATT: Excuse me. *(Taking* LUEEN *out of* MR. SIMMONDS' *earshot)* Look, Lueen, if we're going to try and patch things up, we don't really want strangers around.

LUEEN: Tad is no stranger. He's my private solicitor. It was only as a courtesy to you that he came down in the first place—because you have such a bad head for business. I thought you'd appreciate the help—getting all the papers sorted out.

MATT: You mean if we should need them.

LUEEN: Of course.

MATT: But we don't need 'papers sorting-out' for a reconciliation.

LUEEN: Of course not!

MATT: Then what's the point of having him here sorting out all the papers.

LUEEN: Just in case things don't work—like you said.

MATT: Did I say that?

LUEEN: Not half an hour ago!

MATT: But if a stranger is here with us—even if he is your private solicitor—it might not help things work out the way they would if we were working it out together.

LUEEN: Don't be silly, Matt. Que sera, sera.

MATT: What does that mean?

LUEEN: "Here today, Gone tomorrow!"

MATT: You do want us to get together again, don't you?

LUEEN: Why did I come 6,000 miles—will you tell me that?

MATT: Of course, of course.

LUEEN: Now stop being paranoid, Matt. Tad will go up to the guest room and make himself invisible and we'll get on as if there's only the three of us . . . until Momma comes for Laura, that is. You'll like that, won't you?

MATT: I think so.

LUEEN: Well, make up your mind. I didn't come 6,000 miles to hear 'I think so.'

MATT: You're right. I'm being paranoid. *(Suddenly)* Your mother is coming *here?*

LUEEN: This is where Laura is.

MATT: Of course.

LUEEN: I hope you have no objections to my mother dropping in. It is still my home, I believe.

MATT: No, of course not. I was just expecting there'd be the two of us.

LUEEN: And Laura farmed out with a nanny.

MATT: When I say the two of us, I'm including Laura.

LUEEN: You have a funny way of adding up.

MATT: *(Contrite)* I'm being paranoid—you're right.

LUEEN: Now try to be courteous to Tad. He's gone out of his way to help us work out all the details.

MATT: If we should need to.

LUEEN: Of course. There's no point otherwise, is there?

MATT: *(Thoroughly confused)* None.

LUEEN: Thank God that's settled. *(Turns to* MR. SIMMONDS) I'm sorry for being so rude, Tad—just a little domestic matter. Matt will be delighted if you'd stay for a few days. I'm sure you'll find the guest room comfortable. It's got a lovely sprung mattress, hasn't it, Matt?

MATT: I think so. It's been some time since I slept there.

MR. SIMMONDS: Anything'll be fine with me, old chap. When I was in Malaya, I slept in a hammock made out of grass and bamboo-sticks. Some of the sweetest slumbers in my life. On one occasion, actually had to share it with the company cook. Luckily, he was only five foot one and thoroughly dehydrated. Amazing time, Malaya. Were you ever in the Service?

MATT: No—I was defending the home front.

MR. SIMMONDS: Quite right, too. We all serve—even those who don't, eh? Think I'll freshen up a bit.

LUEEN: The bathroom is at the top of the stairs. Have a shower or something, Tad.

MR. SIMMONDS: *(To* MATT) I say, would that be all right? I do smell a little like a Bengal sewer.

MATT: Help yourself.

MR. SIMMONDS: Very decent of you, old top. I know that bathrooms are a little like private altars. Some people don't like strangers abluting all over them.

MATT: Ablute . . . ablute . . .

MR. SIMMONDS: Thanks, old scout.

(Exits upstairs.)

LUEEN: I've got to have a nap.

MATT: But you just got here.

LUEEN: I've got to have twenty minutes every afternoon. It allows the fluids to top up. Have you ever seen a Spaniard with a bad complexion? Of course not. That's because the siestas top up their fluids.

MATT: Couldn't you add it on to tonight's bedtime? I haven't seen you for thirteen months.

LUEEN: Just like you to ask me to risk my health for your convenience. You don't think I do this for fun, do you? I'm not one of those women who're going into middle-age with all their fluids dried up. Not for you or anyone! Tell Momma I'll ring her tonight, but under no circumstances wake me. If I'm only half-full, it can be dangerous.

MATT: If it's more than twenty minutes, might you overflow?

LUEEN: Don't be stupid, Matthew! Whoever heard of fluids overflowing.

MATT: Whoever heard of them being topped-up?

LUEEN: Marlene Dietrich, that's who! She tops herself up twice a day. Why do you think she looks like that at her age?

MATT: I haven't thought about it.

LUEEN: No, well you'd better start thinking about it. What kind of shape are you going to be in in ten years? *(Derisively)* Jogging up the stairs! All that does is give you cardiac arrest. You ought to spend that time taking wax baths to help soften your arteries.

MATT: Are there wax baths?

LUEEN: Don't be so stupid, Matthew. Wax baths are just like milk baths or mineral baths. You've heard of mineral baths, haven't you?

MATT: Is that like bathing in Schweppes?

LUEEN: I'm not going to continue this discussion. It's like talking to a two-year-old . . . except a two-year-old would be more intelligent. Tell Momma I'll call her later. Do not disturb me until . . . *(checks watch)* 5.45. *(Turns to LAURA, who is sniffing coke)*. Laura, stop sniffling and blow your nose. Go upstairs and put on a dress. Momma's coming to collect you any minute.

LAURA: I ain't got no dresses.

LUEEN: You've got that lovely white one with the pleats.

LAURA: That's a prom dress. Nobody wears a prom dress unless they're going to a prom.

LUEEN: Don't be argumentative, Laura. I'm not having you meet Mother in those railroad clothes. Put on that dress.

LAURA: I'll look like a hooker.

LUEEN: *(Alarmed)* Who taught you that word? *(Looks to MATT)*

MATT: I never said a thing. I don't even know what it means.

LUEEN: Get upstairs this instant, young lady, or you'll have cause for regret.

LAURA: *(Leaving—à la Bogart)* "You ain't heard the last of this, sweetheart."

LUEEN: That child is becoming more unmanageable every day.

MATT: Lueen, I don't mean to interfere in matters that don't directly concern me and, as you say, you've always been closer to Laura than I have, but do you think she's mixing in the right circles out there?

LUEEN: She's not mixing in any circles. She's just a child.

MATT: I mean her . . . classmates . . . and her schoolfriends.

LUEEN: Her classmates are exactly like her. They come along for ice cream and biscuits every Sunday, play disco-records and deafen all the neighbors. What are you getting at?

MATT: I'm not getting at anything.

LUEEN: She's been a lot more normal with me in L.A. than she ever was out here. In London, she didn't even get to school because the buses were on strike. When she did get there, she couldn't get in because the building-workers had walked out. When she finally did get in, all the teachers had started a go-slow and she had to come home again . . . walking all the way. I suppose that's your idea of how to bring up a child!

MATT: You don't think she's developed a hyper-active imagination, do you?

LUEEN: What are you on about?

MATT: She doesn't make things up, does she?

LUEEN: No, thank God, she hasn't started taking after her father yet.

MATT: I don't make things up. I stage-manage reality. That's what the Mata Shara calls it. It's quite normal.

LUEEN: Yes, and little white lies are just a lot of big black ones that have been sudsed down.

MATT: To avoid depressions, I invent attractive decor for my scenarios . . .

LUEEN: Do you have any idea what you're talking about?

MATT: It's a whole science, Lueen. I can't explain it in one day.

LUEEN: Don't imagine for a moment that I've travelled 6,000 miles to listen to a science lecture.

MATT: Why did you come?

LUEEN: Are we starting that one again?

MATT: You did come for us, didn't you?

LUEEN: I didn't come to be psychoanalyzed every other minute.

MATT: But you do want to give us a chance, don't you?

LUEEN: A trial reconciliation is just what the words imply.

MATT: Well, that's all I want—a chance.

LUEEN: Well, that's all you're getting. Now I'm going upstairs to unpack. Mother will be here any minute. She's enroute to a Tupperware Party so all she'll have time to do is collect Laura and leave. Try to be civil to her. You don't see her all that often.

MATT: I'm always civil to your mother.

LUEEN: That's what I mean. You're just civil to her. You never try to be warm—like a son-in-law should be.

MATT: You just asked me to be civil.

LUEEN: I'm asking you to be warm *and* civil.

MATT: *(Counting it out to himself)* Warm and civil. I've got it.

LUEEN: *(After a study)* Matthew, I sometimes wonder if all of this is going to be worth the trouble.

MATT: *(Frightened)* Warm and civil. Don't worry. I'll be fine.

LUEEN: Oh yes, and don't forget to set a place for Tad tonight.

MATT: Is he eating with us?

LUEEN: What do you expect him to do . . . send out for a Chinese take-away?

MATT: I just didn't expect it, that's all.

LUEEN: Try to be a little courteous, Matthew. I know it's an effort. You can't invite a person to sleep in your house and then send him out for fish 'n chips when you sit down to a three-course meal.

MATT: No, no, of course not. I'll run out and get some more food. I just wasn't expecting him.

LUEEN: Well, he's here now.

MATT: Right. Another place for dinner.

(LUEEN *goes upstairs.*

MATT *makes a few notes of supermarket items and, absentmindedly walks out the front door with sewing-basket, umbrella and squeegie-mop.*

After a moment, he returns the squeegie-mop and sewing-basket and picks up the shopping-basket hanging alongside it. He leaves.

After a moment, LAURA, *dressed in a typical American high-school white prom gown, comes down the stairs and into the living-room. Makes a bee-line for the drinks cabinet and mixes herself a stiff Martini. Settles back on the couch. Takes a little white pill from the locket around her neck and uses the drink to wash it down.*

MR. SIMMONDS, *wearing only a towel around his midriff, enters. His face is half-lathered.)*

MR. SIMMONDS: Blast, has Mort gone? I got half-way and then found I was out of razor blades.

LAURA: That's tough.

MR. SIMMONDS: Has Lueen, I wonder . . . ?

LAURA: Never uses the stuff. Strictly wax.

MR. SIMMONDS: Blast. I guess he's not out for long.

LAURA: You wanna shot?

MR. SIMMONDS: I say, old sport, should you be at the host's drinks like that?

LAURA: He ain't no host—he's my dad.

MR. SIMMONDS: Well, then—should you be having a drink at all at your age?

LAURA: How'd'ja like it if I said . . . should you be shavin' your whiskers at your age?

MR. SIMMONDS: That wouldn't make much sense.

LAURA: Right. Same with you. It's real borin' hearin' 'at your age' tacked on to everything. I heard it when I was eight . . . when I was ten . . . when I was eleven. I'm always a different age, but I keep hearin' the same line!

MR. SIMMONDS: You seem to be well versed in bartending . . .

LAURA: 'For a girl my age'.

MR. SIMMONDS: Well . . . um . . . yes.

LAURA: My first boyfriend was a bartender. He used to slip me double gin-fizzes in my Thermos. Nobody ever caught on until my classmate drank one by mistake and fell off the platform at an assembly period. Almost blew the whole gaff. You look kind'a cute with your pants off. You're knockin' off my mom, aintcha? *(Offers him a glass)*

MR. SIMMONDS: *(Hesitating, receiving the drink)* I must say, old girl, your trans-Atlantic sense of humor is a bit lost on a chap like me. Your mother and I are extremely good friends, who have recently come together on a professional basis.

LAURA: That's always the best, ain't it?

MR. SIMMONDS: What is?

LAURA: Comin' together. My boyfriends don't go for it, though. They like everyone to take turns.

MR. SIMMONDS: *(Swigs drink)* I think I'll postpone this shave. The lather's drying up in any case.

LAURA: Do you think I'm sexy?

MR. SIMMONDS: *(After a moment; not sure whether to drink or not)* You're a very attractive little person, Laura, and no doubt, you'll grow up to be a very lovely woman.

LAURA: Like my mom.

MR. SIMMONDS: Yes, I daresay . . . like your mother.

LAURA: But I ain't so attractive now?

MR. SIMMONDS: Well, I'm sure you are to some young fellow who's . . .

LAURA: 'My own age'.

MR. SIMMONDS: *(Flustered)* Well, yes. I'm sure there are many boys in your class who find you very agreeable. Or who will do in time.

LAURA: Does that mean sexy?

MR. SIMMONDS: Well, maybe not 'sexy' exactly, but attractive and charming in other ways.

LAURA: Sexy's all that counts.

MR. SIMMONDS: Where did you get that idea?

LAURA: I keep my eyes and ears open, old scout. Nobody's interested in the talkers. Everybody wants a little action—just like Judy Holliday says on The Z-Channel.

MR. SIMMONDS: I'm afraid I've never made the acquaintance of Miss Holliday, but I can assure you that . . .

LAURA: If you ain't got sex-appeal, you ain't got nothin'. Mr. Berenson gave me straight A's on account'a I let him feel me up in the locker room.

MR. SIMMONDS: *(Beat)* I don't know who this Mr. Berenson is, or what his intentions may be, but if that is true, he sounds to be a highly dubious type and someone you should stay right away from.

LAURA: Oh, I don't see 'im anymore. His wife got wind of it and dropped a pot plant on his head.

MR. SIMMONDS: Although one wishes ill to no man, I must say there is a certain poetic justice in that.

LAURA: Would you like to feel me up?

MR. SIMMONDS: Laura, my dear, I think you may have had just a little bit too much . . .

LAURA: I don't mind. We could go all the way except Mom might come in. We could do it in the car if you was fast.

MR. SIMMONDS: Laura, my dear, I don't know how to put this tactfully, but I'm afraid you're becoming rather wayward in the good old U.S. of A. Or else you're playing some fiendish little joke on me, which, I'm afraid to tell you, I haven't the imagination to appreciate. A fertile sense of humor was never my strong point.

(LAURA *has zeroed in on his towel.* MR. SIMMONDS *weaves away.)*

LAURA: I can do anything Mom can, y'know. I know all the positions. I didn't read the Kama Sutra, but I have seen all the drawings. But you have to keep your trap shut. I don't want nobody blowin' my cover. *(Tugs at* MR. SIMMONDS's *towel.)*

MR. SIMMONDS: laura . . . this is not funny!

MR. SIMMONDS *tries to escape towards the stairs and trips.* LAURA *tries to pull off his towel. He holds on for dear life.)*

LAURA: What'cha hidin', big boy?

MR. SIMMONDS: *(Struggling)* None of your bloody business!

(MR. SIMMONDS *darts away towards table.* LAURA *gives chase.)*

LAURA: Playin' hard to get's just a come-on.

MR. SIMMONDS: Stop this at once! Or I'll tell your mommy.

LAURA: You do, and I'll tell Daddy!

(Makes a grab for his towel and manages to pull it away.

Simultaneously, MR. SIMMONDS *covers his private parts with trembling fingers and* MATT *re-enters with the shopping.)*

MR. SIMMONDS: *(Now sprawled on table)* Sorry, old man . . . was just looking for a razor-blade.

(MATT *tries to stop* LAURA *ravishing* MR. SIMMONDS. *Pulls her from the couch into his arms while* MR. SIMMONDS, *shrieking, draws away.*

At that moment, MOTHER *appears at the door.)*

MOTHER: Matthew! Put that child down at once!

Curtain

Act 2

Scene: The Same.

MOTHER is played by the same actress as LUEEN, with wig, glasses and a padded dress in a slightly older cut. At LIGHTS UP, LAURA is sucking the last dregs out of a coke-bottle, making a deafening sound with her straw. After angling and re-angling the bottle to ensure maximum drainage, she empties the already empty bottle into her mouth. MOTHER has watched all this—mesmerized. Eventually, she snaps out of it and addresses LAURA:

MOTHER: Now tell me, Laura, what have you been learning in California?

LAURA: Surfing. Scuba-diving. Skate-boarding. I can do it with one leg up in the air.

MOTHER: You've obviously had a lot of practice, dear. And what about your studies, dear? Have you thought about what you might like to do when you leave school?

LAURA: Nah.

MOTHER: *(Wincing)* Nice girls say 'not really', dear. 'Nah' is a sound goats make.

LAURA: That's 'bah' ain't it?

MOTHER: There's not much in it. Have you thought of becoming a nurse?

LAURA: 'Not really'.

MOTHER: Or a vet, perhaps? It's very satisfying, dealing with dumb animals.

LAURA: 'Not really'.

MOTHER: How about social work? Relief work—that sort of thing?

LAURA: I do lotsa that already.

MOTHER: Don't be silly, Laura. What kind of relief work can a child your age do? I mean relieving persons who are suffering.

LAURA: Like relaxin' people who are all up-tight?

MOTHER: Well, in a way, yes.

LAURA: Yea, I do a lot of that already.

MOTHER: You ought to start thinking about those things, Laura. You're not a child anymore. What are you now?

LAURA: Twelve and a half.

MOTHER: That's getting on.

LAURA: I looked into some pension schemes, but my allowance don't cover the premiums.

(MATT *enters with small suitcase.*)

MATT: Here's all of Laura's things.

MOTHER: (*Coldly taking the bag, studiously avoiding* MATT, *turning again to* LAURA) Now I think it might be an idea to get into some travelling clothes, Laura dear. That dress is a little formal.

LAURA: It's my prom dress.

MOTHER: The proms are not for some time yet, and besides, I don't think the Albert Hall is a proper place for a 12-year-old. Do you have anything else?

LAURA: I got what I came in.

MOTHER: That will do fine. Change quickly, dear.

LAURA: Where we goin'?

MOTHER: I'm taking you on a little treat before we go home.

LAURA: *(Suspicious)* What kind'a treat?

MOTHER: You'll enjoy it.

LAURA: How d'you know?

MOTHER: Because all little girls enjoy treats. Then we'll go home.

LAURA: To L.A.?

MOTHER: No, not to L.A. To Golders Green.

LAURA: I don't wanna.

MOTHER: Don't be argumentative, Laura. Argumentative girls never marry well. We're going to spend a few days getting better acquainted. I've got some lovely strawbery yogurt for you in the fridge.

LAURA: I don't wanna.

MOTHER: Little girls don't always get what they want, Laura, dear. Sometimes they get what's good for them.

LAURA: *(Grim)* Will you get what's good for you someday—

MOTHER: I'm not going to argue with you, Laura. When you're all grown up, you can suck coke-bottles to your heart's content—till then you'll have strawberry yogurt. Now change quickly dear. Grandmother's got a pressing appointment. Don't dally.

(LAURA *looks sulkily at* MATT *then exits.*

MOTHER *then turns officiously towards* MATT.)

MOTHER: Now, Matthew, I have no intention of going into the incident that occurred a little while ago. I've always felt your influence on Laura has been deplorable, and everything I see only confirms me in that belief. Who was that semi-naked person?

MATT: He's a private solicitor.

MOTHER: Private solicitors don't go naked in public.

MATT: He was just having a bath.

MOTHER: With my grand-daughter!?

MATT: It didn't get that far.

MOTHER: Why wasn't he wearing trousers?

MATT: He ran out of razor blades.

MOTHER: What is the man doing in this house?

MATT: He belongs to Lueen.

MOTHER: To Lueen?

MATT: She brought him along to arrange the details of the divorce we're not having because of our trial reconciliation.

MOTHER: Where is my daughter?

MATT: She's topping up her fluids in the upstairs bedroom.

MOTHER: Don't be cheeky with me, Matthew!

MATT: She said she'd see you later. She's asleep.

MOTHER: If I didn't have a pressing social obligation . . .

MATT: A Tupperware Party.

MOTHER: Don't be insolent, Matthew. It never became you.

MATT: That's what Lueen said it was.

MOTHER: It's not *a* Tupperware Party—it's *the* Tupperware Party of
the Year, and I am officiating. It's just like Lueen to arrange things
with maximum inconvenience to me, and just like you to make snide
remarks and try to corrupt a 12-year-old child with naked solicitors
in bathtubs.

MATT: I don't think Laura is corruptible.

MOTHER: I should hope not! And let me tell you this, Matthew. I know
you've never liked me, and to be frank—a protracted conversation
with you has always been like an attack of the shingles. I was never in
favor of Lueen marrying you. It was a mis-match from the start. I
knew it the moment I saw you wearing gray-striped trousers and
plimsoles. Another thing. Lueen is profoundly Gemini and you are a
deadly Aquarian with unruly Scorpio influences in your ascendent. I
knew it would all come to a bad end, and, if you take my advice, you
will stop flogging a dead horse.

MATT: Are you referring to your daughter?

MOTHER: I am referring to what you've made of her. God knows
America is no Paradise, but I'd rather she was there than the Gulag
Archipelago you've made out of North Finchley. You were never able
to support her in the style to which I've become accustomed. Your
salary was always paltry—did you ever get that rise?

MATT: Yes, but then I got sacked. I've been unemployed for over a
year.

MOTHER: A devine retribution! All you Aquarians with Scorpio tendencies are a bad bunch.

MATT: I didn't choose the month I was born, Mother.

MOTHER: *(Under)* Excuses . . . excuses . . . And what you've put my daughter through . . . You're lucky you're not living in Sicily, or you'd have had your kneecaps shot off long ago. And let me tell you this. The sooner Laura is removed from your influence, the better it will be. And don't you try to get custody of the child because I'll fight it tooth and nail. And I've got powerful friends, Matthew. The Hadassah, Branch 303, The Tupperware Club of Greater London. And they're all behind me.

MATT: I know you wield a lot of influence south of the North Circular Road, but there isn't going to be any divorce. Lueen and I are trying to patch it up.

MOTHER: Patch up the Titanic, if you can. Patch up Vesuvius so it doesn't spout lava. *(Derisively)* Patch it up!

MATT: I know you find this hard to believe, Mother, but I love Lueen.

MOTHER: Like the wolf loves the lamb . . . like the spider loves the fly . . . and don't call me Mother.

MATT: Yes—mother-in-law.

MOTHER: And don't be so clever. Clever people are never on the invited list and you've never been on mine! The day you married my daughter was not only a black day, it was an eclipse. Why she came back I can't imagine.

MATT: Maybe she still loves me.

MOTHER: Then I will personally pay for the psychiatric treatment until she's fully recovered her senses. Look, Matthew, why don't you do us all a favor? Go away somewhere! I'm sure the Foreign Legion has an opening for a clever, middle-aged man with no future. *(Looks at watch, calls out)* Laura! I'm late. Australia is very nice this time of the year. Have you ever considered emigrating permanently?

MATT: Could I ask you a question?

MOTHER: Do you mean are you capable, or will I answer?

MATT: Will you answer?

MOTHER: Go on, Matthew, but be quick. I haven't got all day.

MATT: Don't you think after thirteen years you could understand the fact that Lueen is married and I'm your son-in-law?

MOTHER: I understand that perfectly.

MATT: Thank God!

MOTHER: I just don't accept it, that's all.

MATT: But it's a fact.

MOTHER: Don't give me all that nonsense about facts, Matthew. I've got along without facts for over sixty years, and don't need them now, thank you very much. Facts are just thrown up by people to keep other people from having their way. I see right through facts. The only fact that concerns me at the moment is that you're not the marrying kind.

MATT: But I am married!

MOTHER: Don't be silly, Matthew.

MATT: But . . .

MOTHER: You're the sort of man who should have a live-in house-keeper. There are lots of men like that. They need their trousers pressed and their buttons sewn—someone to make sure the fridge is stocked and the laundry is collected. Any little Swiss au pair can do that for you. But a wife is quite another thing. You haven't got the staying power that a husband requires.

MATT: What do you think I've been doing for thirteen years?

MOTHER: We'd all like to have the answer to that one, Matthew. You certainly haven't been acting like a husband. Have you ever brought your wife flowers?

MATT: She hasn't been here for over a year.

MOTHER: You could have wired them. It would have been a nice gesture. Or just kept them fresh till she got back.

MATT: I would've needed a hot-house for that.

MOTHER: No, just a little old-fashioned concern. Have you ever written her a sonnet?

MATT: A sonnet? I don't know how to write a sonnet.

MOTHER: A loving husband would have learned. Have you ever bought her a fur coat or a piece of property?

MATT: I can't afford those things.

MOTHER: Exactly—but a loving husband would have made a gesture.

MATT: I did buy her an angora wool sweater last Christmas.

MOTHER: And you think that makes up for the absence of a fur coat!? How would *you* like to go out on a winter's day wearing only an angora wool sweater? Couldn't you have bought her a plot of land to show you cared?

MATT: I made a deposit on a family vault.

MOTHER: Just like you. I'm talking about property development and you've already got my daughter six feet under. Don't you see how callous you are? How totally lacking in all charm and grace?

MATT: I thought it would be enough to love her.

MOTHER: Where have you been all this time, Matthew? Outer space? If you felt any love at all, you'd have have acquired some gilt-edged stocks in Lueen's name. Started an annuity or a trust fund. That's how normal people measure love, Matthew. Deeds—not words . . . property deeds, preferably.

MATT: I guess I didn't realize any of that.

MOTHER: How could you—not being an adult? How old *are* you now . . . No, don't tell me. It will only make me more depressed. Even a live-in housekeeper couldn't live with you. You probably need some form of welfare.

MATT: I wouldn't argue with that.

MOTHER: That's right. Be a drain on the exchequer, like all the rest of your Paki friends.

MATT: What Paki friends?

MOTHER: I know you visit some Eastern fellow every day and give him money.

MATT: He's a mystic. I'm learning from him.

MOTHER: How to live on the dole.

MATT: He's a moral teacher. He's giving me assistance.

MOTHER: And the government, no doubt, is giving *him* assistance— along with all the rest of his curry-swilling Paki mates.

MATT: He's not that kind of Indian.

MOTHER: The only good Indian is a dead Indian . . . as someone very sensibly said.

MATT: That was Custer, and he was talking about Red Indians.

MOTHER: Their color is irrelevant, Matthew, so long as it isn't white. And have you made a will?

MATT: What for?

MOTHER: That's right. Invite endless litigation, squabbles and counter-suits. Can't you even do the decent thing after you're dead?

MATT: But I'm not dead.

MOTHER: You will be one day, and then where will Lueen be? Out in the cold . . . wearing an angora sweater. That's your idea of being a good husband.

MATT: I'll get her a fur coat. I'll buy one next week.

MOTHER: In this weather? Are you out of your mind?

MATT: I'll reserve it for her. She can pick it up at Christmas. When-ever.

MOTHER: In my day, Matthew, there was still a little romance between people.

MATT: *(Interested)* Really?

MOTHER: Yes, really! When I was being courted, I remember dear sweet Alisdair, may he rest in peace, taking me to a quiet, tasteful, candle-lit bistro in Parson's Green with white tablecloths and discreet dark-skinned waiters who were always there with a match for your cigaret or a bowl for your fingers. I remember him taking my hand and telling me quietly and tenderly how, earlier that day, he'd taken out a comprehensive high-yield insurance policy in my name. Touch-ing. Generous. Unselfish. Men were gentlemen in those days. They not only held the door open for you, they threw down their vicuna coats for you to walk on. On our 20th wedding anniversary, he gave me an open cheque and urged me to write in whatever figure I wished. Beau geste? Not at all. A cavalier among men! He was gra-cious, courteous and gentle . . . even when the bank refused pay-ment.

MATT: Why did they do that?

MOTHER: *(Sour)* Because they were totally lacking in any kind of romantic spirit.

MATT: How much did you ask for?

MOTHER: None of your business, Matthew. The price is irrelevant. It's the thought that counts.

MATT: Was it more than he had?

MOTHER: Do you think I'm going to stand here and do audits with you on my married life?

MATT: I just wondered why they . . .

MOTHER: You're obviously incapable of grasping the point! The point, Matthew, is that *(Fervently)* the only true satisfaction a man can ever know is by *giving*— long and hard—without counting the cost— unstintingly!

MATT: And a woman?

MOTHER: By receiving, of course. One day you'll learn all these lessons —but it will be too late.

MATT: You may be right. It's quite possible.

MOTHER: *(After a study)* I sometimes wonder if you're all there, Matthew. I understand you're undergoing extensive mental treatment.

MATT: I've had some analysis. You make it sound like a lobotomy.

MOTHER: All in good time.

MATT: Mother-in-law, I wish one day we could sit down and have a reasonable discussion.

MOTHER: When you're recuperating perhaps, Matthew—in a rest home or wherever you wind up after all that treatment. Perhaps then you'll come round to seeing things the way everyone else sees them. I only hope it won't be too late. Assuming that is, it isn't already. *(Calls out)* Laura! I'm late!

(LAURA enters, again clad in T-shirt and dungarees.)

Tell Lueen to ring me tonight.

MATT: Yes, mother-in-law.

(MOTHER does a take on the words and begins straightening LAURA's attire. Suddenly noticing it.)

MOTHER: Is that the full range? Party dresses or railroad clothes?

LAURA: I got a bathing-suit, but no top.

MOTHER: While you're here, I'll get you a nice little dress so you'll look like a little lady.

LAURA: What little lady?

MOTHER: Don't be clever, Laura. *(Shoots a dirty look at MATTHEW)* Cleverness never got anyone anywhere. Ask your father.

(MATT comes over to kiss LAURA goodbye.)

MATT: Bye, bye, Laura. In case it's an ice-age before I see you, take this pin. I got it in school for a crossword competition. It's the only thing I ever won.

LAURA: Is it gold?

MATT: It is to me.

LAURA: *(Pins it on)* Thanks, Pop. Stay loose.

MOTHER: Remember to tell Lueen. I'll be waiting for her call.

MATT: Bye, bye, mother-in-law.

MOTHER: And remember. Absence makes the heart grow fonder . . .
So make it a nice long trip!

(MOTHER *grumps to herself, takes* LAURA *by the hand like the sweet
little girl she is not and, as the front door slams shut behind them,* MR.
SIMMONDS, *now clothed, appears on the landing.*)

MR. SIMMONDS: I say, old sock, I hope I didn't cause any grief there.

MATT: I explained it all.

MR. SIMMONDS: Little Laura has a rather West Coast sense of humor.
I'm afraid it slightly rattled me.

MATT: She's become a bit of a swinger. All part of the L.A. legacy.

MR. SIMMONDS: I hope, old man, I'm not too much of a burden. Could
just as easily slip into a motel overnight, but Lueen seemed so set
on . . .

MATT: Don't give it another thought, Ted.

MR. SIMMONDS: Tad.

MATT: You've obviously got a special relationship with my wife which
she seems to appreciate. Have you known her long?

MR. SIMMONDS: I helped her with a few legal transactions about a year
or two ago and, when I was out in California for a few weeks, I just
popped in to say hello. Great believer in client solidarity.

MATT: So you haven't known her for very long?

MR. SIMMONDS: Not really—although she makes it seem like donkeys'
years. Must say I feel just like one of the family now—barring your
own good self, of course. May I?

MATT: Do you have any views on adultery?

MR. SIMMONDS: Nothing very original, old tub, but as I explained, I've nothing very original to contribute on any subject really.

MATT: Any moral attitude to it?

MR. SIMMONDS: In a funny sort of way, morality doesn't come into it any more, does it, old bean? It's like padding the expense account or cheating the tax man, good clean fun for all the family.

MATT: I suppose you could look at it like that.

MR. SIMMONDS: Absolutely. Vices are just like fashions, you know. One year everyone's into incest; the next, coveting your neighbor's wife. 'Giving false witness' was very big in the Fifties—due for a comeback, I'd say.

MATT: Have you ever been married?

MR. SIMMONDS: Not what you'd call legally-notched, old fruit, but that's because of my intimate knowledge of the rules. Much too dangerous. Think you're going to the preacher's, but you're really going to the cleaner's. Get you by the nuptials, never let you go! No, I've made a kind of speciality of being the apex in triangular relationships. Marvellous position. Always there to have your shoulder cried on— soothe the ruffled wife—lip-serve the wronged hubby. Comfort and pleasure till 1 a.m. and then a prompt radio-taxi gives you complete access to your own double bed and spares you the morning post-mortems on performance or lack of it. It's a consummation devoutly to be wished, as another bachelor put it so eloquently.

MATT: And no little twinges of guilt?

MR. SIMMONDS: Good God, no. It's in the nature of a public service. Where can the tortured wife turn to if not the apex? Just think how many rows people like I defuse. If melancholy spouses couldn't comfort themselves with chaps like me, there'd be all that aggression knocking about the matrimonial home. As it is, I get the pleasure of their company and their husbands get the benefit of their restored good nature. Chaps like me are the pillars of matrimony. The edifice couldn't stand without us.

MATT: You've got a funny way of making things sound sensible.

MR. SIMMONDS: That's a by-product of the law again. Makes the un-palatable, palatable. Sows' ears, silk purses; water into wine.

MATT: Pearls before swine.

MR. SIMMONDS: You're getting the hang of it.

MATT: *(After a beat)* I'd be honored if you'd join my wife and myself to a little welcome-home dinner.

MR. SIMMONDS: Deucedly civil, old mole—are you sure?

MATT: Absolutely.

MR. SIMMONDS: Could just as easily pop out for a banger and mash. No cultured palate, mine.

MATT: Wouldn't hear of it.

MR. SIMMONDS: I'm all right with a Wimpy and a Strawberry Delight, you know.

MATT: Please be our guest.

MR. SIMMONDS: Well, that's very decent of you. The fact is I'm per-fectly ravenous. Of course, none of us is perfect but you catch my drift.

MATT: Why don't you wake Lueen while I set up the table?

MR. SIMMONDS: Do you think that would be quite correct?

MATT: Of course. One of the family—right?

MR. SIMMONDS: Yes, I suppose put that way . . . Is it left of the stair-case?

MATT: That's right. Just follow the scent. You can't miss her.

(MATT *in a bustle of activity rolls in the dining room table set for two and adds a third place—delicately placing silverware, arranging serviettes— all with a profound sense of meaningful ritual. He brings candles to the table and ceremoniously lights them. Having done so, he dims the lights and savors the effect.*

He then returns to the table and places his chair in the center with the remaining two on either side—then carefully reverses the fruit cocktail cups so that one is set before each place.

This done, he lights some incense and wafts it around the room before placing the taper on a side-table. Then he looks cautiously upstairs, dashes to the kitchen where we hear him clatter about some dishes—re-entering with a large serving dish which he places in the center of the table.

Another survey, and then he sits, contemplatively.

After a moment, he jumps up and places a record on the turntable. It is Nelson Eddy and Jeanette MacDonald singing Victor Herbert's "AH, SWEET MYSTERY OF LIFE!"

The sound of this provokes LUEEN's *cry from above.)*

LUEEN: *(Off-stage)* What the hell're you playing at, Matthew!

MATT: A little background music.

LUEEN: *(Off)* You know I can't stand that song!

MATT: Sorry, I thought it was one of your favorites.

LUEEN: *(Off)* It's one of *your* favorites. *I* can't bear it! Remember?

MATT: Sorry. I knew it was either one of your favorites or one of mine! *(Turns it down but it still plays softly in the background while* MATT *mimes the words passionately and performs it silently to himself— Pause)* Lueen—dinner's ready. *(Nothing.)* Lueen?

LUEEN: *(Off)* Just getting through a few things with Tad. Be right down.

MATT: *(Pause)* Because it's all ready. It's on the table.

LUEEN: *(Off)* This won't take very long.

MR. SIMMONDS: *(Off)* Down in a jiff, old scout. Just finishing off.

(MATT *sits, waits. Upstairs, faintly-discernible sound of shuffling bedsprings.* MATT *continues to sit patiently—impatiently.)*

MATT: It's on the table, Lueen. It's getting cold. *(Nothing.)* Lueen?

LUEEN: *(Strained)* Just coming.

(MATT *suspiciously looks upstairs then darts into the kitchen, returning with various condiments, seasons main dish, pokes in a finger, licks it studiously, sprinkles on a bit more, satisfies himself as to the taste, returns condiments.)*

LUEEN: *(Entering. Lights a cigaret)* What's all the fuss? You make it sound like a 5-alarm fire.

MATT: *(Smiling weakly)* It's all ready. Turkey stew, your favorite. Where's Tad?

LUEEN: He'll be right down. He's just showering.

MATT: But he just bathed half an hour ago.

LUEEN: Tad's from Saffron Walden. He's into personal hygiene. Is there anything wrong with that? Really, Matt, you make everything sound like a capital crime. What about the drinks?

MATT: The drinks?

LUEEN: Still no lemonade?

MATT: Oh, God, I knew I forgot something!

LUEEN: You're priceless—you really are.

MATT: How about a nice vermouth? A little brandy? Creme de menthe?

LUEEN: Sit down. The maitre d' bit doesn't really suit you. *(Sniffs)* What's that smell?

MATT: Essence of Jasmin.

LUEEN: Smells like the Mata Shara's underpants.

MATT: Do you remember how we got high in Torquay on the honeymoon?

LUEEN: Torquay? I've never been to Torquay.

MATT: We stopped there for three days on the way to the Lake District.

LUEEN: *We* did?

MATT: Stayed at that funny little bungalow with the Irish landlady who played the ukelele and did George Formby imitations.

LUEEN: I don't remember any Irish landlady, and I've never been to Torquay.

MATT: Don't you remember we went to some dance-hall—the Orpheum something—and didn't get back till five in the morning—missed breakfast and lunch. I tried to get us some food and all I could find was waffles and milkshakes.

LUEEN: I've never eaten waffles in my life, and loathe milkshakes. You're obviously mixing me up with one of your old flames!*(Derisively)* Torquay!

MATT: But we've got pictures standing outside the bungalow with you in a polka-dot bathing suit and me holding an umbrella.

LUEEN: You are thoroughly hallucinated. I never owned a polka-dot bathing suit, don't eat waffles and wouldn't be caught dead in Torquay.

MATT: But we were there for five days . . . an undersized double bed with pink, flower-patterned sheets . . .

LUEEN: Did you call me down to conjure up fantasies about non-existent seaside resorts or to have dinner?

(MR. SIMMONDS, *refreshed, enters in a dinner suit.*)

MR. SIMMONDS: Evening all.

(LUEEN *and* MATT *regard the full formal dinner suit, bow tie, tails.*)

I say, I hope you don't think this is too dressy. Never leave home without it. Can't resist dressing for dinner. Archaic custom, I know, but one I've always treasured. Always been a bit of a Romantic!

LUEEN: *(After a beat)* It's very nice, Tad.

MATT: *(Apologetic)* I'm afraid it's only turkey stew . . . and the wine's only supermarket plonk. It seems such a waste. *(Referring to the suit)*

MR. SIMMONDS: Not at all. Sometimes put it on for marshmallow-roasts. Nothing to do with the meal. Just a gesture to a bygone age. *(Suddenly apologetic)* Although I say, old bean, if it's in any way de trop, I can just as easily slip into some cavalry twills.

MATT: No, it's fine—just fine.

MR. SIMMONDS: Got a pair of faded denims and a jumper.

MATT: It's just fine.

MR. SIMMONDS: Shall I cut the tie?

LUEEN: You look lovely, Tad. Dressing for dinner is a lovely old custom. If my things weren't crumpled, I'd join you.

MATT: *(To* LUEEN) Should I put on a jacket?

LUEEN: You should have thought of that before—along with the lemonade.

MATT: *(To* MR. SIMMONDS) Well, if you don't mind.

MR. SIMMONDS: You look spiffing, old man. The casual look gives you something.

LUEEN: *(Dry)* Yes, a casual look. Now do you think we can actually start. I'm famished.

MATT: Oh, yes, of course. Now Todd, you sit here. Lueen, this is you here. We don't have to rush the fruit cup 'cause I've got one of those Chinese jiggers under the stew to keep it warm.

LUEEN: Then what was all the panic about coming down?

MATT: Well, I didn't want it to get soggy. Overcooked, you know—bad as underdone.

LUEEN: Quite the gourmet.

MATT: I've had lots of practise these last few months. Grills, roasts, deep-fried—I've spoilt almost every dish you can think of. *(To* MR. SIMMONDS) Of course, in the old days, it was just heaven when Lueen did all the cooking. Never really appreciated it.

LUEEN: *(Eating)* You can say that again. Tad, wouldn't you like a vodka with your meal?

MR. SIMMONDS: Well, I wouldn't want to put anyone to any . . .

LUEEN: Nonsense. Matthew, there's an unopened vodka bottle in the kitchen cupboard—would you bring it in for Tad?

MATT: I've bought this wine.

LUEEN: Don't be dreary, Matthew. The man would rather have a vodka. It's just next door.

MATT: Oh, certainly . . . vodka—coming right up. *(Dashes out . . . head pops back)* I'm afraid we're out of ice.

LUEEN: How can we be out of ice?

MATT: I forgot to make some.

(LUEEN *looks exasperatedly at* MR. SIMMONDS.)

MR. SIMMONDS: A little lemonade will be fine.

MATT: *(Stalling)* Umm . . .

LUEEN: Just bring the vodka and the tonic water, Matthew!

MATT: Vodka and tonic. Coming right up. *(Dashes out)*

LUEEN: There's too much spice in this thing.

MR. SIMMONDS: I'm so ravenous I can hardly tell.

(MATT *dashes back with vodka.*)

MATT: Vodka and tonic!

LUEEN: *(Notes its arrival: studiously turns back on* MATT*)* Anything interesting at the office?

MATT: I haven't been at work for over a year.

LUEEN: I was talking to Tad.

MATT: Oh, sorry. Sorry.

MR. SIMMONDS: Not really. Same old briefs as the Bishop said to the actress. *(Smiles)*

(Nothing from LUEEN *or* MATT *who just sit and stare at him.)*

I really must curb all those damp one-liners. The hardest thing for a mediocrity to realize is when he tries to add a breath of life, it's always the kiss of death. Father was exactly the same. One of his anecdotes could empty a dinner table in minutes flat. He once voided an entire banquet hall imitating Marie Lloyd delivering the Queen's Christmas speech. Good old Dad. Even the tombstone was a boner. The engraver put 'Rust in Peace' by mistake. Devil of a time chiselling it out.

MATT: Anyone like some bread rolls?

LUEEN: What happened to the Merry Widow case you were telling me about?

MR. SIMMONDS: Oh, she never did inherit. The mistress had the husband's last will and testament inked on a pair of lace knickers. They'd shrunk terribly—barely legible—but with the help of a forensic scientist and a brilliant photo-reproduction, they'd come up a treat. 'This is the genuine article,' said the magistrate holding them aloft in the courtroom, 'and it just goes to show, it pays to get it all down!' He meant 'in writing' of course, but the Clerk got the wrong end of the stick, started laughing uncontrollably and was summarily dismissed. The widow didn't get a farthing—although the mistress did offer her the offending knickers which I thought was deplorable bad taste.

LUEEN: The law is so fascinating. Never a dull moment.

MR. SIMMONDS: Well, they're all dull really. One giggle amidst a thousand squelched yawns—but I think that's only right. Don't want to turn judicial proceedings into a hootenanny. Attract all the wrong sort of people. As it is, anyone with an ordinary turn of mind and a stomach for unrelieved tedium can always find a haven at the Inns of Court. 'Swingers need not apply.' Great comfort, all those serried ranks of pukka faces dull as ditchwater, all emitting the same identical drone; a kind of tone-deaf Gilbert and Sullivan chorus. *(Sings flatly)* 'For now he's a judge and a good judge too!'—Oh, sorry. Have I been amusing again?

MATT: Not to worry. It didn't take. Do try the stew. It's been specially made.

MR. SIMMONDS: *(Eating)* Delectable.

MATT: *(To* LUEEN*)* It's still one of your favorites, isn't it?

LUEEN: *(Eating)* When it's not over-spiced.

MATT: Oh dear, I'm sorry.

LUEEN: *(To* MR. SIMMONDS*)* Perhaps after dinner, Tad, you and Matt can go into a corner and sign up all those papers.

MR. SIMMONDS: If you can spare the time, old toad. It would certainly facilitate things. Get it all wrapped up.

MATT: Just in case, you mean.

MR. SIMMONDS: Exactly. Stitch in time. Don't put off till tomorrow. In for a penny, in for a pound.

MATT: I'm sure we'll be able to work it all out. *(Beat)* Seconds?

MR. SIMMONDS: Don't mind if I do. Tummy like a billie goat tonight.

MATT: *(Offering)* Lueen?

(SHE *nods, but doesn't stop eating.)*

I don't suppose . . . *(Fishes for name for a moment)* Tad, isn't it?

MR. SIMMONDS: Got it in one!

MATT: I don't suppose you realize just what sort of occasion it is tonight. No reason why you should. But Lueen, you ought to know.

LUEEN: Occasion? Probably one of your imaginary occasions—like the Silver Anniversary of our first Torquay Paddle-Boat Ride.

MATT: Married thirteen years tomorrow!

MR. SIMMONDS: *(Impulsively)* I say, congratulations! Many happy returns!

(LUEEN *shoots him a look.)*

I s'pose.

MATT: Thank you, Tad. Thirteen years is a lifetime.

LUEEN: Would you pass the French dressing?

MATT: *(Automatically doing so)* You learn a lot about a person in thirteen years. All those private little things that only married people know. Where it tickles. Which side of the bed one lies on. How long to do the eggs. Pet peeves. Chewing gum. Whistling in the shower. Leaving the lid up.

LUEEN: I'm sure Tad is not interested in the details of our private life, Matthew, and I wouldn't have thought it was a very suitable topic for dinner table conversation.

MATT: I thought maybe as a contrast to the capers of Lincoln's Inn.

LUEEN: Is there any paprika?

MR. SIMMONDS: The stew is really scrumptious. Do you mind if I make a pig of myself?

MATT: *(Passing the paprika)* To thine own self be true.

MR. SIMMONDS: *(Helping himself)* Lovely.

MATT: And I've always thought they were good years. Ups and downs of course, but that's the only rhythm life knows. That's how it breathes—how it sleeps and wakes—how it procreates.

(LUEEN *plunks down her glass irately.* MATT *automatically fills it and continues unperturbed.*)

MATT: Up Down—In Out—Up Down—In Out—The Meta-physical Two Step.

MR. SIMMONDS: *(Eating ravenously)* Never mastered the art of tripping the light fantastic. Did a half-decent hokey-cokey in my college days, but only when pissed.

MATT: All in all—as marriages go—better than tolerable, I'd say. There were some knockdown rows, but just as many highs. Wouldn't you say, Lueen? There was never a spat that couldn't be cured with a Chinese take-away and a cuddle in front of the goggle-box. But when you left, it was like pulling the plug on my respirator. It was terribly disorienting being single again. Friends rang up and talked as if I'd got a terminal disease. I was offered everything from introductions to genial widows to bottles of plasma. I don't know why it is that separations are always treated like deaths in the family. But it was just a bump on the rocky road of matrimony. That's all I thought. I felt if I could sit it out, let you have your L.A. breather, we'd be better than ever. Of course, that's what you led me to believe which is why I believed it, I suppose. That, and the fact that I couldn't bear the idea of divorce! Good God! Being the unattached extra at the dinner party; a one-parent family without even a family. Easy prey for the computer dating services and the Singles Bar scavenger—Terrible prospect!

So, for thirteen months, fuelled by my bankrupting telephone calls, and your inconclusive answers to direct questions, I lived only for the day we would be reunited. Re-spliced. Re-stitched. Re-treaded. Husband and wife. Mom and Dad. Together again. I dreamt about it. I talked of nothing else to the shrinks. It was the daily obsession—to return to the unspeakable coziness of the marital womb—coffee-and-muffins in the A.M., cold cuts for lunch and midnight raids on the fridge to the accompaniment of shipping forecasts and Capitol Radio serenades. You see, I suppose, to put no finer point to it, I was in love.

LUEEN: What's for afters?

MATT: *(Lifting the lid on the chocolate mousse but continuing uninter-*
ruptedly) That in itself is not very remarkable. Love is commoner
than flu. Everyone catches it and everyone passes it on like the social
disease it is. No, what is remarkable and, Tad, as a self-confessed
mediocrity you should be able to appreciate this, the remarkable
thing is that one can love, live with, raise a family with, go to the
cinema with, row and make up with, spend most of one's waking
hours and all of one's sleep-time with someone totally . . . worth-
less. I mean, someone that, objectively speaking, has none of the
qualities one would attribute to an even semi-decent, quasi-human,
somewhat-being. A person whose snideness emanates from them like
the stench of rotten fish; whose selfishness deserves a whole chapter
in the Guinness Book of Records; whose entire manner belies the
cultural achievements of the past twelve centuries and leads one to
believe that Darwin must have got it all wrong—that we move not
from the bestial to the human but in precisely the opposite direction
and, conceivably, in a few generations, women like my wife will be
slithering on their bellies, darting out forked tongues and sucking
nourishment out of dust and stones, their leathery tails flicking on the
ground to ward off the stings of reptiles only slightly more developed
themselves.

(LUEEN *slowly looks to* MR. SIMMONDS *who has not been taking in*
MATT's *words, but eating obliviously.*

MR. SIMMONDS *looks up, smiles mechanically at* LUEEN, *who gives him a*
grim look.

Dimly conscious that something is going on but not quite sure what, MR.
SIMMONDS *looks up at* MATT, *who continues unperturbed.)*

It actually got to the point where I believed it was all my fault.
Spending thousands, supine on couches all over Harley Street, trying
to revive myself after being drained by a vampire with an insatiable
appetite for spouse-blood. I was being turned into one of the Walking
Dead—just like yourself—and the preliminary was laying horizontal
on all those couches, trying to retch your poison out of my system—
and I never put two and two together. I should have remembered.
Vampires are already dead, aren't they? They only give the appearance of life. I should have twigged when your looking glass gave back

no reflection. The window-curtains were always drawn tight against the full moon. I thought it was forties-style lipstick on your teeth—if I'd looked a little closer, I'd have recognized my own blood.

(*To* MR. SIMMONDS) You see, old groan, the great crime of women like Lueen is not so much that they destroy their husbands—which unquestionably they do—but that they whittle down almost to the point of vanishing entirely, the whole treasured notion of Romance— without which Man is just an illuminated digit on a cosmic computer. Because, if Man does not live by bread alone, and God knows he doesn't, it is Romance that spreads the jam and people like Lueen who make it evaporate—turning the warm, fresh, oven-baked staff of life into stale and twisted little cocktail-pretzels.

(MR. SIMMONDS, *not really sure of the gist of* MATT's *remarks, smiles lamely, turns towards* LUEEN, *who is looking even grimmer.*)

But, lest I make her sound ordinary, I hasten to add that Lueen was always a rare species. Past-mistress in the Art of Putdown; Grand Dragon of Derision—taught by the wisest of all the tribe's elders, the Guru of Golders Green; the woman who, if anyone could, almost justifies the genocides of Belsen and Buchenwald because, clearly, Hitler was motivated by women exactly like her. A *very* rare species. Through thirteen years, gradually but methodically grinding down a fairly pleasant, innocuous chap who was unfortunate enough to mistake a pirana for a loving spouse; spawning a daughter who turned into Sadie Thompson before she even had her wisdom teeth; whose only hobbies appear to be turning on and providing fellatio for Third World refugees. Then, adding insult to insult, taking as a lover a man beside whom the dullest yobbo and the dreariest bore, would loom like Oscar Wilde. A man who is the very incarnation of England's unparalleled genius for producing cultural vacuums that perambulate. And you have the nerve to have it off in our own bedroom while I am downstairs preparing the post-coital refreshment. But worse, much worse than all of this, you have the Jacobean gall to keep me alive with the prospect of restoring a marital state which, though once idyllic, has now acquired all the charm of the Grand Inquisition, and you seem to believe that I am still so besotted with you that I will sign away all my worldly possessions including my sanity and self-esteem, for the honor of remaining 'a married man', which, for thirteen months you have prevented me from being and which state, in any case, you have no intention of prolonging, which is perhaps the only mercy for which, when you come before Him, the Greatest Judge of All might find a little clemency. Assuming, of course, in your case there is a hearing at all and you're not automatically relegated to the Zone of Fire and Brimstone from which you unquestionably sprang.

(MATT, *having wound up, returns to earth and finally turns to his dinner-guests . . . both of whom have sat stunned for some minutes.*)

MR. SIMMONDS: I say old spouse, not what I'd call jolly after-dinner chat.

LUEEN: *(Measuredly)* Have you taken leave of your senses?

MATT: The ones you haven't already destroyed, you mean. *(To MR. SIMMONDS)* But, you must be asking yourself independently or together, what is the point of all these long-suffering grievances being aired, and aired at such an inauspicious moment—an elaborate clambake to celebrate a long-awaited return and thirteen years of dubious marital bliss. You may well wonder and, wondering, may realize that following any indictment, there must be a prosecution, a trial and a verdict. The prosecution, having shot its bolt, so to speak, rests. The trial is what I have been put through for thirteen years (or thirteen months, depending on your view of the statute of limitations) and the verdict is, of course, guilty. An appeal, given the unappealing character of the defendants, is certainly out of the question—which leaves only the sentence.

MR. SIMMONDS: I must say, whatever humor I may be lacking, I don't find this the least bit amusing.

LUEEN: *(Regarding him grimly)* I've seen it coming for a long time. Shrinks, meaningless jokes, three letters a day and telephone bills in five figures. You've finally snapped, Matt.

MATT: My patience certainly has. My mind has never been clearer. Nothing like a purged spleen to clear the head.

MR. SIMMONDS: Some of your innuendoes concerning your wife and myself are actionable, old fruit. I feel I should point that out.

MATT: Quite, and action *has* been taken. The sentence, so to speak, has already been carried out.

LUEEN: You always had the tendency and now you've finally flipped.

MR. SIMMONDS: What sentence?

MATT: Firm believer in punishment fitting the crime. Poetic justice is always the most terrible. Nothing in the tortures of the worst dictatorships to compare with Shakespeare's or Webster's. Oh, they really knew how to put the boot in in those days. A lost art, revenge.

LEUEEN: I'm not staying here another moment.

MR. SIMMONDS: *(Staring at* MATT*)* He's trying to tell us something, Lueen, and I don't like what I'm beginning to hear.

LUEEN: What are you talking about?

MR. SIMMONDS: What kind of sentence, Matt, old man?

MATT: Something fitting, old cock. Something lingering, old fruit. Something irreversible, old stew.

MR. SIMMONDS: *(After a beat)* Oh, my God! *(Looks in horror at plate)*

LUEEN: What's going on?

MR. SIMMONDS: *(Pushing plate away)* Oh, my God! My God! The stew!

LUEEN: Well, it *was* oversalted but nothing to make such a . . .

MR. SIMMONDS: *(Transformed, his social guise gone)* He's put something in the food, you blowsy cunt! Look, he hasn't touched his!

LUEEN: What do you mean—put something in the— *(To* MATT*)* What are you playing at, Matt? This is getting very unfunny.

MATT: Really? It's only just beginning to amuse me. Something fitting, old croak. I have had her toxins pumped into me for thirteen years—growing like a duck's egg in my craw—so it's only fitting that I return the favor. But I've been much more charitable. It won't take thirteen years for the corruption to take hold; thirteen minutes more like, and you should experience the first spasms. Thirteen hours and it will all be over.

LUEEN: Are you trying to tell me that . . . *(Looks at plate, realizes, shoves it to the floor)*

MR. SIMMONDS: *(Savage)* It's taken long enough for the penny to drop.

MATT: The heart rate should drop much faster.

LUEEN: *(Rises, staggers across the room, coughing, spluttering, ostensibly dying. Suddenly straightens up, recovered.)* I don't believe it. He hasn't got the guts. He hasn't!

MATT: Neither will you shortly—leastways none worth having.

MR. SIMMONDS: The phone! Get to the phone!

MATT: I'm afraid it's temporarily out of service. There's a box two streets down, but that's been out of order since some skinheads used it as the site for a rock concert three years ago.

MR. SIMMONDS: I'll see that you rot in jail for the rest of your days for this!

MATT: That threat is predicated on capture and conviction, old skull, and I think both are highly unlikely.

LUEEN: *(Coughing, spluttering, gagging)* You couldn't! You wouldn't have the heart!

MATT: It's been successfully ground to dust over the past year. Now we're even. I've got an empty sweet tin there—just like you.

(MR. SIMMONDS *is sticking fingers down his throat and retching.)*

LUEEN: What the hell are you doing?

MR. SIMMONDS: *(Desperate)* Trying to get it up! Trying to get it up!

MATT: You had no trouble before dinner.

MR. SIMMONDS: You rotten bastard!

MATT: Rotten is an unfortunate choice of word, old corpse. The only thing that's certainly rotting are your entrails.

LUEEN: *(To* MR. SIMMONDS*)* Stop that god-awful noise, can't you?!

MR. SIMMONDS: Don't tell *me* how to croak, you cow!

LUEEN: *(Straightening up)* I don't feel anything. Not inside. It may all be a hoax.

MR. SIMMONDS: A hoax—

LUEEN: Do you feel like you've been poisoned? It's just the *idea*—that may be all it is.

MR. SIMMONDS: *(Holding tummy)* I don't have any spasms—only a kind of grotty feeling inside.

MATT: It may all be the power of suggestion. Lueen has a point. Most of *her* poison was pumped into the mind before it trickled into the heart.

MR. SIMMONDS: *(Straightens up)* You bogus, feigning bastard!

MATT: *(Suddenly)* On the other hand, it may be just the first symptoms which are always faint and indistinct; the real agonies usually take about a quarter of an hour before they start pulverizing the system.

(MR. SIMMONDS, *as if on cue, suddenly doubles up in agony, as does* LUEEN.)

LUEEN: Matt, have you put something in that stew? You owe it to us to tell us that at least, you bastard!

MATT: I felt you owed it to me to say whether we were ever to be together again.

LUEEN: I came back, didn't I? That's what you wanted, wasn't it?

MATT: What I wanted was the restoration of contentment, the resolution of doubt, the latitude and longitude of domestic bliss. All I got was innuendo and horns.

LUEEN: You've got it all wrong. Tad is just a good friend. Tad, tell him!

MR. SIMMONDS: I'm not going to use my last breaths reassuring a psychopathic murderer about the state of his marriage. I'm going to get help while I can still crawl.

LUEEN: Wait . . . wait for me!

(They stagger, crawl, clamber toward the door. Halfway there, LUEEN, *consumed with loathing, turns to* MATT.)

If you've done this, may you rot in hell, Matthew. If you haven't, I'll strangle you with my own hands.

MATT: *(Mock-gentle)* Does that mean the trial reconciliation's a bust?

(LUEEN *glares fiercely at him and staggers toward the door.)*

LUEEN: Wait for me, you selfish bastard! (Crawling out) Serves you right for stuffing yourself with seconds! *(She is out)*

(MATT *looks toward the door for a moment, listening to* LUEEN's *and* MR. SIMMONDS's *groans fade away.*

He then climbs down from his exalted state and settles back in his seat. He regards the dinner table, looks again toward the door.

He picks up the stewpot, forks a few pieces of food, holds them in front of him for a moment, then drops them back again.

He then moves toward the drinks, examines them and opens a cupboard above. There he discovers a bottle of lemonade. Registers its unexpected presence and pours himself a drink.

He turns cautiously as he hears the sound of the door slowly creaking open.

MATT *looks toward it warily. When it opens fully,* LAURA *enters, dressed in a frilly child's dress—pink with bows.)*

LAURA: Hi.

MATT: What are you doing here?

LAURA: *(Inspecting)* The treat was all plastic, so I blew the coop.

MATT: Tupperware parties are always plastic. How did you do that?

LAURA: I said I was goin' for a pee, then climbed through the transom. It was just like lammin' out'a the pen—only no searchlights or loud-speakers.

MATT: Grandma will be upset.

LAURA: She'll live. Where's Mom and the creep?

MATT: *(A beat)* They're walking off their dinner.

LAURA: *(Looking at table)* They didn't eat much.

MATT: No, they didn't.

(LAURA *examines stew, poking it with a fork, while* MATT *studies her. After toying with it for a moment, she turns away and leaves it.)*

LAURA: Any cokes?

MATT: All out. But I did find some lemonade. *(Produces it)*

LAURA: No thanks. That's just rotgut. *(Mixes herself a very stiff highball and pops a pill)*

MATT: What are you eating?

LAURA: Purple hearts—you want one?

(MATT about to admonish, pauses and regards them for a moment, then impulsively takes them and swallows a handful.)

LAURA: Hey, take it easy. They ain't jelly-beans.

MATT: You shouldn't have these. I'm just confiscating them. When I was your age, I *was* on jelly-beans and very grateful, too. *(Swallows another handful)*

LAURA: You better cool it, Pop. If you OD on these, it's a real bad trip.

MATT: Life *is* a real bad trip. You should travel as painlessly as you can.

LAURA: You in the pits?

MATT: Bit of a downer, as you might say. You should be with grandma in Golders Green.

LAURA: That's a *real* downer.

MATT: You look quite nice.

LAURA: Feel like I've been gift-wrapped.

MATT: I don't think Lueen is coming back somehow.

LAURA: That's cool.

MATT: That doesn't bother you?

LAURA: Am I my mother's keeper?

MATT: Are you sure you want to stay here with me?

LAURA: You ain't gonna feed me no yogurt, are you?

MATT: No.

LAURA: Then I'll stay. *(Moves to record player)* Any Led Zeppelin?

MATT: I'm afraid not.

LAURA: That's cool. I'm into Monteverdi, anyway. How do you feel?

MATT: A little funny.

LAURA: After what *you* took, you oughta be hilarious. *(Inspects his eyes)* Your eyeballs are goin' like wagon-wheels.

MATT: *(Businesslike)* Good! Now! Tell me, Laura . . . *(Loses track for a moment. Static. Then recovers)* What do you want to be when you grow up?

LAURA: A godfather.

MATT: I think only Italians can be that.

LAURA: I'll convert.

MATT: *(Pills beginning to take effect)* You've watched too many Late Shows, do you know that? George Raft, James Cagney and Al Capone are no more. The great mobsters have been replaced by people like your mother. Murder Incorporated is now Matrimony Incorporated. Where're you going?

LAURA: *(Who has not moved)* Nowhere.

MATT: Then stop moving all over the place when I'm talking to you.

LAURA: *(After a beat)* Have you got any black coffee?

MATT: People's sights are set so low today. Why don't you want to be a saint or a Christian martyr?

LAURA: Can you have a Jewish Christian martyr?

MATT: You can convert.

LAURA: Maybe you should lay down awhile, Pop.

MATT: Will you sit still? I'm trying to talk to you. (LAURA *has not moved*) I'm trying to be a good father to you and you're hopping all over the place.

LAURA: You want I should get you a bringdown?

MATT: I've had enough bringdown to last me a lifetime. Laura, one day, who knows, perhaps *you'll* get married—some nice skinhead with a broken nose and a good future in the Mafia—if you do, promise you'll love him like blazes and make him feel like Mr. Big, no matter how penny-ante he really is. Because without love, baby, it's all downhill—even the cable car to the top of the jump. Promise, Laura.

LAURA: Sure, Pop. Have a snooze.

MATT: And stick to him, baby. Through thick and thin. Don't cop out, as you might say, when the going gets rough 'cause that's when it's really important to hold tight, hug hard and share the blankets—no matter how narrow the bed or how hard the mattress. Do you follow me, Laura?

LAURA: Sure, Pop. You wanna glass of water?

MATT: And Laura, there's something else I want to tell you and that's . . . *(Pause)*

(LAURA *waits.* MATT *is frozen in a state of suspended animation.*)

LAURA: *(After a moment)* Yeah?

(Nothing)

Pop?

(Nothing)

Should I . . . ?

MATT: *(Bursting into song)*
"Ah, Sweet mystery of life
At last I've found thee!"

(Pause. MATT *again frozen and immobile, suspended in time.)*

LAURA: *(After a moment)* Pop, should I . . . ?

MATT: *(Suddenly singing)* "Ah, at last I know the secret of it all."

(Pause. Nothing.

LAURA *about to speak,* MATT *suddenly resumes.)*

"Ah, the longing, seeking, striving, waiting, yearning,
The idle hopes, the joy and burning tears that fall . . ."

(Pause. MATT, *wobbly, rises and turns slowly toward* LAURA *who, at the same moment also rises and turns toward him.*

The stage is suddenly drenched in splendidly-colored, golden light.

The room disappears.

Everything is transformed into a magic landscape.

Slowly, MATT *and* LAURA *move toward each other like Nelson Eddy and Jeanette MacDonald on the brink of a lyrical outburst.*

MATT *opens his arms wide—*LAURA *strides into them, together making a stock romantic tableau. They embrace fondly and, as they do so, mime*

*the words of the voices of Nelson Eddy and Jeanette MacDonald which
fill the theater.)*

MATT/LAURA:
   "For tis love and love alone the world is seeking,
   And tis love and love alone I've waited for,
   And my heart has heard the answer to its calling,
   For it is Love that rules for evermore!"

*(The lights sparkle and explode around them as they look romantically
into each other's eyes until the fade-out of both music and lights.)*

Curtain

Characters

HAROLD   the houseboy, late 20's, rough and cockney

HANNAH   the housekeeper, late 40's or early 50's, working-class

INSPECTOR FARCUS mid 40's, cultivated cockney

POTTS   his Assistant, 30's, broad cockney

ALAN HOBBISS   50's, upper middle-class

BERENICE   his wife, played by a man

CHARLES APPLEY   50's, upper middle-class

LADY CALVARLEY   portly, mid 40's, attractive

THE COLONEL   60's, distinguished, very upper middle-class

The action takes place in an old country manor in rural England.

Clever Dick was given a staged reading at The New Mayfair Theater in Santa Monica, California on July 8, 1985. The cast was as follows:

HAROLD	Charles Shaughnessy
HANNAH	Diana Chesney
INSPECTOR FARCUS	Clive Revill
POTTS	Bernard Fox
ALAN HOBBISS	Alan Mandell
BERENICE	Jeanne Hepple
CHARLES APPLEY	Benjamin Stewart
LADY CALVARLEY	Carolyn Seymour
THE COLONEL	Basil Langton

Clever Dick

Act 1

COLONEL CALVARLEY, *a distinguished man in his sixties, is sitting in an easy chair inspecting a bottle of wine. He rises, moves to the window, draws the curtain and peers out for a moment. He then returns to the easy chair, pours himself a drink and knocks it back. For a moment, he relaxes in his chair savoring his drink. Suddenly his body constricts and a terrifying expression distorts his face. He clutches his throat, gasps, reels off the chair, staggers round the room and finally falls in a heap behind the easy chair.*

After a moment HANNAH, the housemaid, opens the front door and staggers in with a large bag of groceries piled almost to her nose. In her attempt to negotiate the blind walk to the kitchen, she stumbles over the elbows of COLONEL CALVARLEY jutting out from behind the chair.)

HANNAH: Oh damn!!!

(The grocery bag still masking her vision, she continues to negotiate her way through the room and into the kitchen.

After another moment HAROLD, the houseboy, wearing a striped servant's waistcoat, enters from another door carrying a load of firewood piled high, obliterating his vision. Moving stealthily toward the fireplace, he too, inadvertently trips on the other end of the COLONEL almost, but not quite, dropping the logs.)

HAROLD: Oh shit!

(He teeters his way to the fireplace and dumps the logs in the grate then, tuckered out, flops into the easy chair.)

HANNAH: *(Re-entering)* What's all the bloody noise, Harold?

HAROLD: It's the logs in't?

HANNAH: You should use a little less quiet.

HAROLD: A little less quiet!? What kind'a grammar is that?

HANNAH: Don't be narky. You get my meaning.

HAROLD: 'Less quiet' me backward bovine, would mean more noise—
in common English parlance, that is.

HANNAH: It's enough to make you drop yer ovaries, all that bleedin'
noise. And y'know the Colonel is very jumpy these days.

HAROLD: I got me chores, haven't I?

HANNAH: You got a bleedin' cheek, that's what you got. Stompin'
around this place like you was Lord of the Manor.

HAROLD: Crampin' your style, is it?

HANNAH: Don't get cheeky with me, Harold. I've got seniority here.

HAROLD: You're so bloody long in the tooth, my gal, you'd have seniority in the Old Folks Home.

HANNAH: *(Slyly, delightedly)* You got flogged by the Colonel again last
week, din't you?

HAROLD: None of yer business, gasbag.

HANNAH: I heard him thwackin' your tushi.

HAROLD: My peccadillos concern only the master and me'self.

HANNAH: A few more peccadillos like that, my fine friend, and you'll
be sittin' from a standin' position.

HAROLD: Before you start on about me, you ought to be on the lookout
for yer own misdemeanors.

HANNAH: And what's that supposed to mean!?

HAROLD: Leavin' shoes all over the bloody room! That's a lovely habit.

HANNAH: Shoes? In the drawing-room?

HAROLD: The Colonel would just love to see that, especially on a week-end when the place is full 'a houseguests. That would really endear you to 'im.

HANNAH: What are you on about, shagface?

HAROLD: If you'll cop a gander to me right, you'll see exactly what I'm on about.

(HANNAH *looks behind the easy chair where* COLONEL CALVARLEY's *feet and shoes are just jutting out from behind the easy chair. She walks behind the chair to inspect, discovers the corpse, bends down to check its pulse, then draws back in horror.* HAROLD *is oblivious.)*

And the Colonel is always gassin' on about neatness in the home, and how a tidy house is the symbol of a tidy mind. If you ask me, the only reason he keeps you round the place is cause he knows that no one else would hire someone as sloppy and superannuated as yourself. Seniority, my gal, what good is seniority when you can't tell the difference between a pile 'a washin' and a pile 'a shit? Which, not to put too fine a point on it, is exactly your problem. *(Turns and sees for the first time her horror-stricken face)* What *are* you gapin' at? Surely the sight of your own negligence is not all that bloody mesmerizin'?

(HANNAH *motions to the sight behind the chair.)*

What'chu playin' at, whale blubber? Don't you think that all this arsin' about is going to . . .

(Sees corpse. Stops in his tracks. Bends down, now invisible, to check body. Straightens up, now visible again, equally horror-stricken. He turns to Hannah who, finally unable to sustain her horror, topples over in a faint as HAROLD, *boggle-eyed, turns to the front and shoves his finger-nails into his mouth.)*

Blackout

A few hours later.

*There is a thump at the door. After a moment, a very distracted HAR-
OLD comes wheeling out and opens the front door to a rotund nonde-
script-looking stranger.*

MAN: Potts.

HAROLD: No, not today! *(Slams door in man's face and rushes off.)*

(There is another thump at the door. Nothing. Then another. HANNAH
comes dashing out of the kitchen, also distracted. She opens the door.)

MAN: Potts.

HANNAH: We don't need any! *(Slams door and rushes out)*

(The thumping now becomes more insistent, loud and thunderous. HAN-
NAH *and* HAROLD *dash out together and simultaneously open the door.)*

FARCUS: *(Stepping in front of Potts and flashing credentials)* Farcus of
the Yard, this is Potts my special assistant and I wouldn't slam that
door again if I were you.

HAROLD: I'm so sorry, Inspector. I thought . . .

FARCUS: Come in, Potts.

*(*POTTS, *rather wary, pokes his head around the door and gingerly enters.)*

You are . . . ?

HAROLD: Harold. Minks. I work—worked—for the Colonel.

FARCUS: In what capacity?

HAROLD: Sort of houseboy, personal valet. I suppose you could call me
a go-fer.

FARCUS: No matter how physically unendowed you may be, young man, I would never sink that low. On the other hand, neither would I dispute your own findings in that matter. And you?

HANNAH: I'm Hannah. The cook, the housekeeper. I was the first to find the body, y'know.

INSPECTOR: There are no prizes for that, my good woman. Potts, have you examined the cadaver?

POTTS: *(Surfacing from behind chair)* Face is contorted and blue. Clear signs of strychnine poisoning. Body is cold. Just a little clammy. Eyes staring. Mouth agape.

INSPECTOR: Dead is he?

POTTS: *(Melancholic)* 'Fraid so, Inspector.

INSPECTOR: Come, come Potts. It's none of your doing. *(Beat)* I expect. Who else is in the house?

HANNAH: We're all full up. The colonel had a houseful of weekend guests. Business friends and associates.

INSPECTOR: And where are they?

HAROLD: Still asleep.

INSPECTOR: *(Looks at watch)* Make a note of that, Potts. Suspects asleep at 11:30 A.M. What is the usual wake-up call, Minks?

HAROLD: Breakfast is usually at 11:00 sir.

INSPECTOR: How decadent.

HAROLD: But everyone went to bed very late last night, so I expect they're all having a lie-in.

INSPECTOR: Lot of carousing last night, was there?

HAROLD: It was the Colonel and Lady Calvarley's anniversary. There was quite a bit of tippling. Expect everyone will have a bit of a hangover today.

INSPECTOR: Everyone except the Colonel. Potts, are you quite sure of your diagnosis?

POTTS: I think so, Inspector. He's beginning to pong a bit.

INSPECTOR: Then rigor mortis can't be far behind. Eh, Minks?

HAROLD: *(Surprised to be consulted)* I really couldn't say, Inspector.

INSPECTOR: Of course not. You're not a coroner, a G.P. or a necrophiliac, are you Minks?

HAROLD: I'm certainly not a coroner or a G.P.

INSPECTOR: Well two out of three's not bad. And you, Hannah. I expect you don't have much truck with dead things, eh?

HANNAH: No sir. Not at all.

INSPECTOR: Not at all?

HANNAH: Well I kill chickens of course, when we're havin' chicken.

INSPECTOR: And turkeys?

HANNAH: Sometime. When we're havin' turkey.

INSPECTOR: And bulls?

HANNAH: No, I can't say as I've ever killed a bull.

INSPECTOR: Good. People should draw the line somewhere. Potts, have you got all that? Chickens, turkeys, no bulls.

POTTS: *(Efficiently)* Got it all down, Inspector.

HANNAH: Now wait a minute. I hope you don't think . . .

INSPECTOR: Rest easy, my good woman. Routine inquiries, nothing more.

HANNAH: I don't see what's so routine about my killin' chickens 'n turkeys 'n bulls.

INSPECTOR: *(Suddenly)* So you admit to killing bulls?!

HANNAH: I do not! I have never killed a bull in my life!

INSPECTOR: *(Relieved)* Good girl. Just checking. *(Checks watch)* As it is closer to lunchtime than it is to breakfast, I think we'd better have a look at all these houseguests, eh Minks?

HAROLD: We didn't know whether to wake them or not. We didn't quite know what to do about . . . about the Colonel.

INSPECTOR: Leave all that to us. We're old hands at this sort of thing. Potts, can you dispose of the body?

POTTS: There's a bit of a problem there, chief. The ambulance men've been on a go-slow for the past two weeks and it might be a while before any stretchers arrive.

INSPECTOR: That's a bit of a pickle.

HANNAH: We can't just leave the Colonel there.

INSPECTOR: Certainly not. *(Beat)* Have you got a freezer ma'am?

HANNAH: You mean, put him in cold storage?

INSPECTOR: I don't expect you'd want him propped up on the verandah.

HANNAH: Haven't you got arrangements for this kind'a thing?

POTTS: We're not morticians, y'know.

HANNAH: Isn't there a drill of some kind? You can't just leave stiffs, beggin' your pardon Colonel, lyin' around the house.

INSPECTOR: Which is why I am inquiring about your freezer, ma'am.

HANNAH: There's lots of foodstuffs and drink in that freezer.

INSPECTOR: I don't expect the Colonel will be tempted. Minks, give Potts a hand like a good fellow.

(MINKS *looks agitatedly at the* INSPECTOR *and then with* POTTS, *carries the corpse into the kitchen.*)

HANNAH: I think this is most irregular, Inspector.

INSPECTOR: Don't blame us, my good woman. It's the British trade unions that are at fault. Last year a strike at the mortuary caused a pile-up that effectively prevented funerals throughout London and the Home Counties. They were stashin' stiffs into every available cubicle. I found two cadavers in the boot of my own Morris Minor. Some poor distracted lady from Cheltenham shoved her grandfather into a safe deposit box and he'd be there still if they hadn't started charging 'er a double digit rate of interest. This, unfortunately, is the society in which we now find ourselves. In Winnie's day, it would have been unthinkable.

HANNAH: What's that?

INSPECTOR: A double-digit rate of interest! Now, be so good as to wake the sleepers, ma'am.

HANNAH: I do hope the Colonel will be all right. It don't seem right to put a well-bred Englishman in the freezer like that.

INSPECTOR: Au contraire, madame. It is probably the aptest place in the house for a stiff upper lip. Now go and rally the rest of the guests.

(HANNAH *leaves.*)

POTTS: *(Confidentially)* What do you make of it, Inspector?

INSPECTOR: *(Likewise)* Clearly the Colonel was poisoned by someone who is still on the premises. Whoever the culprit may be, it is more likely than not, one of those persons who are, at this very moment, rousing themselves in the upstairs bedrooms. You're sure about the cause of death?

POTTS: *(With bottle)* The poison must've been in this bottle of California Sauterne.

INSPECTOR: Or indeed, the Sauterne itself might be the cause of death. From all I hear, this foreign stuff can be pretty lethal.

POTTS: I don't like these kinds'a cases, Inspector. It makes me queasy dealin' with the upper middle classes.

INSPECTOR: Fundamental working class angst, Potts. It's because your father is a Welsh collier and you spent most of your childhood down the mine. Anything that happens on or above surface level makes you uneasy. It's a normal reaction.

POTTS: I know I'm a victim of me upbringing, Inspector. For twelve years I couldn't have dinner unless I first lit a lamp in my hat. Even now, I can't bear bread puddin' less it's got coal dust sprinkled over the top.

INSPECTOR: It took us nine months to get you to stop touchin' your forelock and salute properly. The toffs have got a lot to answer for in your case, Potts. You can just thank your lucky stars you were taken onto the Force.

POTTS: That's your doin', Inspector, and I'll never forget it.

INSPECTOR: Come, come, you're a pride to the regiment, Potts. And you've improved so vastly these past few months, your old dad wouldn't recognize you. Until last Whitsun, you'd never go out on a case without first wiping soot all over your face, do you remember?

POTTS: It dies hard, Inspector, all the old ways.

INSPECTOR: Every time it thundered, you'd rush down to the cellar and cry: Trouble in pit! Get out the shovels!

POTTS: You cured me of all that, Inspector. I'm eternally grateful.

INSPECTOR: Nonsense, Potts. In fact, fifteen or twenty years underground is probably the best qualification a man can have for workin' in Scotland Yard. God knows, police work can be the pits sometimes. Ah, here come the first of our suspects.

(ALAN HOBBISS *and his wife,* BERENICE, *enter. She is a man dressed and made up as a woman and despite her masculine appearance, plays female throughout.*)

ALAN: Inspector?

INSPECTOR: Farcus of the Yard, here. My assistant, Potts. And you are?

ALAN: Hobbiss, Alan Hobbiss; this is my wife, Berenice. I'm Colonel Calvarley's business partner. I can't believe what I've just heard.

BERENICE: Is it really true, Inspector? The Colonel poisoned—right here in the house!?

INSPECTOR: *(After a take)* The Colonel appears to be deceased, madam and, as far as we can ascertain, strychnine was the cause of death.

ALAN: But he was perfectly well last night. Singing and carousing. It's just incredible.

INSPECTOR: The crime appears to have been committed in the early hours of this morning when, presumably, you were a'bed, Mr. Hobbiss?

ALAN: Why yes. We went to bed about three, wasn't it Berenice?

BERENICE: Yes, I remember listening to Willie the Night Owl until about then.

INSPECTOR: *(Beat, checks with* POTTS) Bird-watchers, are we then?

BERENICE: Willie the Night Owl is a late-night radio programme. It goes off the air at three.

INSPECTOR: I see. And you heard nothing strange in the middle of the night?

BERENICE: Why no. A few snores perhaps. But then, Alan always snores.

ALAN: *(Uptight)* Not really, Berenice. I know you think that when you wake up suddenly, but the fact is, it's *you* who snores—as you indeed were snoring last night.

BERENICE: *(Wounded)* I—snoring?

ALAN: I'm afraid so, darling.

BERENICE: Are you quite sure of that?

ALAN: It kept me up most of the night, dear.

INSPECTOR: I see. So you were not exactly a'bed.

ALAN: Would you be with a Black 'n Decker in your earhole?

INSPECTOR: My nocturnal habits are not relevant to this inquiry, Mr. Hobbiss. Yours, on the other hand . . .

ALAN: Surely you don't suspect that I . . . or my wife . . . ??

INSPECTOR: *(With pad in hand)* You are Colonel Calvarley's partner, are you not? And the beneficiary of his business in the event of his death?

ALAN: That's true, I suppose.

INSPECTOR: Supposition, my dear Mr. Hobbiss, implies some uncertainty or doubt, but there is neither uncertainty nor doubt in the fact that you are now the full possessor of the Calvarley Business. And what precisely is that business, Mr. Hobbiss?

ALAN: Calvarley Cavalry Clothes. It's the nation's largest equestrian outfitters.

INSPECTOR: Horses and saddles 'n things.

ALAN: Yes.

POTTS: *(Darkly)* Leather and thongs and such like?

ALAN: Yes. *(Checks them out)* This is preposterous, Inspector. Are you trying to say that you suspect us of committing this atrocious crime?

INSPECTOR: In a case of this kind, Mr. Hobbiss, I would suspect me own grandmother of being a guilty party. And indeed, in a similar set of circumstances, my grandfather *did,* and the old lady made a clean breast of the whole affair and would have swung for it if the prison shrink hadn't proved she was only tryin' t'get back at the old man by dyin' with her insurance premiums unpaid.

ALAN: What has that got to do with the Colonel's death?

INSPECTOR: I am only tryin' to demonstrate Mr. Hobbiss, that in a criminal investigation, *everyone* is a suspect! With the possible exception of the murder victim. The crime was committed at a time when you or your wife—or you *and* your wife—were up and about.

BERENICE: I was certainly not up and about, Inspector. Although come to think of it Alan, didn't you complain about not being able to sleep and say you were going downstairs for a hot drink?

ALAN: No, Berenice. You are constantly imagining that I am up brewing hot drinks when I'm doing nothing of the kind. Like the time you dreamt our water-bed was sinking in the Mediterranean and woke up in such a state.

BERENICE: But the next morning the water had gone!

ALAN: You'd been bailing it out all night.

BERENICE: Did I?

ALAN: Don't you remember the mattress was dripping wet?

BERENICE: Was that me?

ALAN: The maid thought it was incontinence and fitted those rubber sheets.

BERENICE: I must say, it's all rather hazy.

ALAN: It always is. I'm afraid Inspector, my wife suffers somewhat from delusions. I've learned to put up with it. Indeed, living with delusions is all part and parcel of married life, don't you agree?

INSPECTOR: I couldn't say, Mr. Hobbiss, since, to the best of my knowledge, there is no Mrs. Farcus.

BERENICE: *(Flirtatiously)* Really Inspector, that seems so incredible. *(Throws a seductive glance to* POTTS *who quakes discernibly.)*

ALAN: *(Turning)* Oh dear, it's Lillian—Lady Calvarley. I do hope we can soften the blow, Inspector.

LADY C: I'm so glad you were able to make it. One has become so accustomed to tradesmen letting one down. You'd better start with the hall and work your way up to the bedrooms. I see you've met my guests. Good morning, all.

INSPECTOR: I'm afraid I have some rather distressing news, Lady Calvarley.

LADY C: Now don't tell me you can't start straight away! I've been planning these changes for months and cannot abide another week with that puce wallpaper in the foyer. Do be a darling and strip it away immediately. I've found some lovely Oriental tiles we can put in its place. Third Dynasty stuff, or so I'm told. It's all Greek to me— although I am assured it is, in fact, Oriental.

INSPECTOR: *(Piqued)* I am not here to wallpaper the foyer, madam.

LADY C: Do keep a civil tongue in your head, sir. You'll be paid exactly what we agreed—plus your travel expenses. If you finish before tea-time, I'll even consider giving you a testimonial.

INSPECTOR: I need no testimonials from you, Lady Calvarley, for my work!

LADY C: *(To* ALAN *and* BERENICE) Aren't they all boringly predictable, these sordid working classes. Arrogance and inefficiency, arm in arm like Hansel and Gretel. The Egyptians had the right idea—keep them in chains and footlocks and pretend the pyramids are a low-income housing development.

POTTS: *(Who has been fuming)* Shall I cosh her round the head, Inspector?

INSPECTOR: Restraint, Potts. Don't let the old working-class angst get the better of you.

LADY C: But you've brought your 'mate' along. Why in Heavens' name can't you start as planned?

INSPECTOR: Because, my dear lady, I am not a worker!

LADY C: God bless us, we know *that* but you'll muddle through as best you can.

POTTS: *(Boiling)* We are not decorators, ma'am!

INSPECTOR: Easy, Potts, easy.

LADY C: It doesn't matter to me what you call yourselves. As long as you get on with it.

INSPECTOR: *(Measuring his words)* Lady Calvarley, may I, calmly and reasonably, attempt to explain the situation. I am Farcus of the Yard.

LADY C: It's just around back.

INSPECTOR: What is?

LADY C: The yard. If you'd like to bring in the ladders'n things.

INSPECTOR: The yard to which I am referring, Lady Calvarley, is Scotland.

LADY C: Well I'm not paying travel costs all the way from Scotland! What kind of fool do you take me for?

INSPECTOR: Scotland Yard, ma'am, which I'm sure you know, is the center for police inquiries in the City of London and I am here on official business from that Yard—*Scotland* Yard not 'the' yard—namely, the murder of your good husband Colonel Calvarley who was poisoned in the early hours of this morning and is, at this very moment, reposing in the deep freeze compartment of your kitchen.

LADY C: *(Looks to* INSPECTOR *blankly, then quietly to* ALAN *and* BERENICE) Alan, call the police, the man may be dangerous.

INSPECTOR: I *am* the police!

LADY C: *(Whispering)* I'll humor the fellow till the wagon comes.

POTTS: *(In a huff)* You are behaving monstrously to a leading member of Her Majesty's Police Force and although I recognize the immense gap in our social stations, I am obliged to risk offending your ladyship by pointing out that you are carrying on *like a bloody pratt!*

LADY C: *(After a beat)* There's two of them escaped together.

ALAN: I'm afraid they're speaking the truth, Lillian.

LADY C: *(Looks incredulously to* ALAN, *then turning warily to* BERENICE) Berenice, would *you* make the call?

BERENICE: I don't know how to tell you this, but the Colonel has been murdered. He drank a poisoned bottle of Sauterne in the early hours of this morning.

LADY C: Nonsense, the Colonel never drinks before breakfast.

INSPECTOR: I am sorry to incommode you, ma'am, but the truth must out. Your husband was found a few hours ago by your servants who, in turn, telephoned the police.

LADY C: *(After a pause) Where* is he?

INSPECTOR: *(A bit uptight)* We've had to put him in the deep freeze for the moment as it may be some time before the appropriate removal services arrive.

LADY C: In the deep freeze!? *(Shoots a look to* HANNAH)

HANNAH: I moved all the beef to one side, ma'am. There was plenty of room beside the strawberry ice cream.

LADY C: My husband? Between the beef and the strawberry ice cream!?

INSPECTOR: I apologize for the unorthodox arrangement, Lady Calvarley, but it seemed the most appropriate thing in the circumstances. Would you care to identify the body?

(LADY CALVARLEY *imperiously surveys the assembly then sweeps out to make her inspection.)*

BERENICE: She's going to take this very badly, I fear.

ALAN: Who can blame her, poor devil. Last night he was boisterous and gay and today he's just a frozen fish finger.

(CHARLES APPLEY *arrives from upstairs.)*

CHARLES: I say, is it true?

ALAN: You've heard.

CHARLES: Harold's told me the most extraordinary tale.

INSPECTOR: Farcus of the Yard, my assistant Potts, and you are?

CHARLES: Charles Appley.

INSPECTOR: Of?

CHARLES: Appley, Appley, Appley and Plum.

INSPECTOR: Which I take it is either a chronic stutter or a law firm in the City.

CHARLES: I'm the legal adviser to Lady Calvarley and the Colonel. But is it really possible that . . .

INSPECTOR: It becomes wearisome to repeat what for us have become mundane events, Mr. Appley, but in trying to further the investigation of this unfortunate crime, let me reiterate—yet again—that Colonel Calvarley is dead—the victim of strychnine poisoning, and let me further add that it is quite likely the person responsible for this tasteless caper is in our midst and has been at the manor since the start of this fateful weekend.

CHARLES: Are you saying the murderer of the Colonel is in this house?

INSPECTOR: A slightly more economical summation of the facts than me own, but essentially identical in import.

CHARLES: Alan, what do you say to all this?

ALAN: I am grieved, shocked, flabbergasted, distressed and Inspector, rather hungry. Do you mind if we have some breakfast?

INSPECTOR: Go right ahead. In fact, Mr. Potts and I may join you for a cuppa, if you will permit.

POTTS: *(Uptight)* Do you think we should, Inspector. At the same table?

INSPECTOR: *(Aside to* POTTS) Come, come, Potts. Fight that angst. These people are exactly like ourselves—except for the fact that their annual income is four or five thousand times greater and they own more property than the Vatican and the Queen of England combined.

BERENICE: Do come, Inspector. We can set up a small table in the pantry for you and your friend. Charles?

CHARLES: I don't think I can swallow a thing at the moment.

(They exit, leaving POTTS *and* FARCUS *together.)*

POTTS: *(Confidentially)* That Mrs. Hobbiss, Inspector. Do you think there's something peculiar about her?

INSPECTOR: Peculiar, Potts, in what way?

POTTS: Somethin' a bit queer there. I can't put me finger on it.

INSPECTOR: Nonsense, Potts. A typical British upper middle class specimen. Girton, Swiss Boarding School, house in the country, flat in town, well spoken, well connected, turgid, vapid, frigid.

POTTS: There's something about 'er look, Inspector.

INSPECTOR: Come along, Potts. We've got more important things to do than gawk at the toffs. Let's get in there before they devour all the muffins.

(INSPECTOR FARCUS, POTTS, ALAN *and* BERENICE *retire to the kitchen. When they have gone,* LADY CALVARLEY *re-enters.* CHARLES *glances toward where the others have exited, then hotly embraces* LADY CALVARLEY.)

LADY: *(Stunned)* He's quite blue, Charles. Quite, quite blue.

CHARLES: And dead?

LADY C: *(Cool)* Don't be silly, dear boy. Of course he's dead. He wouldn't be blue if he weren't dead.

CHARLES: Lillian. *(Checks to see that the others are out of earshot)* I have to ask you this, and I hope you will be absolutely straightforward in your reply. *(Looks her straight in the eye)* Did you do it?

LADY C: Don't be stupid, Charles. The bloody temperature's turned him blue.

CHARLES: I'm not talking about that. Did you kill him? I know we both talked about being rid of him so that we could go away together, but I never thought in my wildest dreams that . . .

LADY C: Do you think I'd ruin a perfectly good bottle of Sauterne by lacing it with strychnine? Of course I didn't kill him. He was a harmless old stick anyway. Never dreamt we were carrying on under his nose and if he lived to be a thousand, would never have suspected. I quite liked the entire arrangement. Infidelity has a certain tang when carried out before the eyes of the cuckold. It will never be quite as deliciously naughty again, I fear.

CHARLES: But who could have . . . ?

LADY C: There's no shortage of suspects. Alan has loathed him for years, ever since he wangled the company away from him and made it his own. And Berenice is a rejected lover of long standing. She made a stupid play for the Colonel while they were on an archaeological dig near Vesuvius. No sooner had she bared her breasts than the volcano erupted. Her timing was always rotten. The Colonel took it as a sign from heaven and resisted all future advances. And even Harold is on the list. The Colonel flogged him on the slightest pretext. If the boy weren't so perverse, he would have hobbled away long ago. And of course, we haven't even begun to probe your motives.

CHARLES: *My* motives? You don't think for a moment . . .

LADY C: I don't wish to alarm you, Charles, but if the nature of our relationship should be revealed, you would be the police's very first suspect.

CHARLES: I, but what have I done?

LADY C: You're 'knocking off' the Colonel's 'old lady' aren't you. And the British public always suspects an adulterer is capable of even darker crimes—like picking his nose or spitting in public places.

CHARLES: But *you* seduced *me!*

LADY C: It was pure altruism, Charles. It was clear you hadn't had a good poke in a very long while, and as I had nothing better to do . . .

CHARLES: *(Aghast)* You mean, you were only doing it out of the kindness of your heart?

LADY C: *(Shocked)* You don't think I took any pleasure from it? What *do* you take me for?

CHARLES: But *will* the police find out?

LADY C: Have you told anyone?

CHARLES: Only my analyst.

LADY C: Is he a Freudian?

CHARLES: Yes.

LADY C: Good. He'll keep his mouth shut; they always do. Oh, this is so like the Colonel, to do the unexpected thing at the most inopportune moment.

CHARLES: I must say, Lillian, you don't sound very broken up.

LADY C: He was a thoroughly vapid old codger who cared more about his horse than his wife. He never made love. Always busy buffing the bloody stallions. There was more foreplay in the stables than ever took place in our bedroom.

CHARLES: Lillian, you are absolutely callous.

LADY C: He wanted a housekeeper in the mornings, a hostess during the day and a hot water bottle at night. I served all three purposes admirably and, as it was a full-time job, I exacted a full-time salary. And it was cheap at the price.

CHARLES: Lillian, I am seeing you in an entirely new light. It's frightening.

LADY C: Not as frightening as it will be when they try to pin this murder on you. You clearly have a motive.

CHARLES: *(Proclaiming a principle)* I haven't had a motive in my entire life! You know I went to Oxford.

LADY C: I know it, dear boy, but no one else will understand. Don't be distressed. Come to Mummy and she'll give you a nice big kiss and cuddle.

CHARLES: It is obscene thinking of sex when your husband's body isn't even cold.

LADY C: On the contrary, if he gets any colder, they'll have to thaw him out to get him into his coffin.

CHARLES: *(Shocked)* Lillian!

LADY C: As it is they'll have to use an icepick to get him out of the fridge.

CHARLES: Lillian, you are a thoroughly insensitive and unfeeling person without a shred of warmth.

LADY C: Nonsense, everyone in the Conservative Party seems that way at first. Now, we'll have to be cunning, Charles or they'll try to pin this thing on you.

CHARLES: Oh God, and I've never even had a parking ticket!

LADY C: I doubt that will pass as mitigating circumstances in a murder trial.

CHARLES: I am *not* a murderer.

LADY C: Of course you're not, dear boy. But the police don't care a damn about that. If the shoe doesn't fit, they lacerate the toes of the suspect until it does.

CHARLES: But I'm innocent!

LADY C: Don't keep saying that, Charles. It just makes you sound like a pregnant virgin. You need an alibi.

CHARLES: An alibi?

LADY C: Where were you at seven in the morning?

CHARLES: In your bed.

LADY C: I'd keep that under your hat if I were you.

CHARLES: I knew all this would come to a bad end. My analyst told me I was looking for a swift and severe punishment.

LADY C: When did he say that?

CHARLES: When I refused to pay his bill.

LADY C: They can't hang you for non-payment of bills, poisoning, on the other hand . . .

CHARLES: I haven't poisoned anyone!!!! Why do you keep saying that?

LADY C: I'm trying to put myself in their place.

CHARLES: I wish you would put yourself in my place.

LADY C: Your place may be a death cell, Charles, unless we keep our wits about us.

CHARLES: *(Squeamish)* There, you've said it again!

LADY C: If that oafish flatfoot questions you, refer all inquiries to me.

CHARLES: Won't that look suspicious?

LADY C: Not when I explain about Oxford. With a little luck, we should be able to throw him off the scent.

CHARLES: What scent? I am innocent, I tell you. I did not murder your husband!

LADY C: Just stick to that story, Charles, no matter what! Remember, I'm behind you whatever you've done and no matter what becomes of you.

CHARLES: Go to hell.

BERENICE: *(Appearing from kitchen)* Do come and have some breakfast, Lillian. Mourning on an empty stomach is positively barbaric.

LADY C: Come along, Charles. A few kippers and marmalade will do us both a world of good.

CHARLES: It sounds like the condemned man's last meal.

(LADY CALVARLEY *ushers* CHARLES *into the kitchen.* BERENICE *is about to return to the kitchen as well when* HAROLD *appears from the opposite side of the stage and 'psst's' her.)*

HAROLD: Psst!

BERENICE: *(To the others)* I'll be right along.

(BERENICE *and* HAROLD *dash into each other's arms and have a hot, sultry embrace.)*

BERENICE: Oh Harold, why didn't you come this morning?

HAROLD: Are you daft? The Colonel's been murdered.

BERENICE: I was in the barn for almost an hour. The smell was overpowering.

HAROLD: Well it would be, woon' it?

BERENICE: I was up all night, squirming with expectation. How could you be so callous?

HAROLD: You really are sump'in. Don't you realize what's happened?

BERENICE: I've dreamt all night along about your lovely white pancakes.

HAROLD: *(Looking toward kitchen)* Hang on, I'll get you a microphone, you can broadcast it to the whole bleedin' house.

BERENICE: They're all at breakfast. We've got at least half an hour. *(Moves to his belt-buckle.)*

HAROLD: Now listen, Berenice, the Colonel has gone to the Great Bridle Path in the Sky and there's a bloke from Scotland Yard tryin' t' find out who nudged him on his way. This is no time for slap 'n tickle.

BERENICE: You're so imperious, Harold.

HAROLD: Lay off, will ya.

BERENICE: *(Whispering, hotly)* Come into the linen closet. I've put a brand new woollie on the ironing board.

HAROLD: Will you kindly fuck off, Berenice.

BERENICE: *(Turning on him)* It's the Colonel, isn't it? You're heartbroken. You just can't live without it, can you?

HAROLD: Get 'a hold of yourself, woman.

BERENICE: I know what's been going on all these months. Do you think I'm blind? All those black and blue marks all over your back.

HAROLD: Don't say things you'll be sorry for.

BERENICE: Upstairs with him hour after hour, lashing yourself insensible.

HAROLD: The Colonel was a very strict taskmaster. You know that.

BERENICE: And you loved every minute of it.

HAROLD: He was wont to inflict some corporal punishment when he was particularly put out.

BERENICE: Which was three or four times a day judging by the state of your buttocks.

HAROLD: My buttocks are none of your concern.

BERENICE: *(Amorous)* But I love your buttocks. The flesh, the freckles. Oh, Harold, I dream about them. Two warm French rolls emblazoned with poppy seeds. *(Goes for belt buckle)*

HAROLD: Berenice, you are beginning to vex me.

BERENICE: *(Turning nasty again)* Oh yes, that's what you say now. But before, when we were in the linen closet, you sang a different tune.

HAROLD: We were both of us a little tipsy in the linen closet.

BERENICE: And in the coal shute, were we tipsy then?

HAROLD: The coal shute was entirely your doing.

BERENICE: And the attic cupboard, when you were bristling with desire?

HAROLD: There was no bloody air in that cupboard. I was just asphyxiating.

BERENICE: And the belfry, the silo, under the harvester, the side of the paddock, the back of the trough—did none of that mean anything to you?

HAROLD: Not very much—with hindsight.

BERENICE: *(Aroused)* Oh, say it again.

HAROLD: What?

BERENICE: *Hind*-sight.

HAROLD: You're a bloody pervert, Berenice. Do you know that?

BERENICE: *(Attacking)* You adored the Colonel's thong, why don't you admit it?

HAROLD: You are working yourself up into a right old state.

BERENICE: You worshipped the master's bull-whip.

HAROLD: The Colonel's thong, the master's bull-whip, my buttocks— are none of your bleedin' business. I tell you this, Berenice. You have been gettin' worse 'n worse these past few weeks and I've been meanin' to have a good old natter with you. It's unfortunate that other priorities, like the Colonel's untimely passing, have made it awkward to discuss this at present. But I am telling you, Berenice, and I hope you are taking it in: things cannot go on the way they have in this house. Everything comes to an end sooner or later and sometimes sooner than later.

BERENICE: *(Checks watch)* We have about ten minutes. What about the chimney stack?

HAROLD: *(Checks watch)* This is the last time, Berenice. The very last —*(He takes her arm and they dash up the side stairs)*

ALAN: *(Entering from kitchen area with* POTTS *and* INSPECTOR*)* I can't think where Berenice has got to.

INSPECTOR: I expect she's taken the Colonel's death rather badly. Women are so much less resilient in matters like this.

ALAN: I hope she's all right.

(HANNAH *appears from another door.* ALAN *catches her eye. Before she can move away, he intercepts her.*)

Could you do me a little favor, Hannah?

HANNAH: *(Fearful)* What's that, Mr. Hobbiss.

ALAN: My wife needs a certain article of clothes—you know, the black thing with the satin stuff. It may be in the car or upstairs. Could you fetch it?

HANNAH: If that's all right, Inspector.

INSPECTOR: Business as usual, Hannah. We don't want the Colonel's death to cause any gossip with the neighbors that might impede our inquiries.

(HANNAH *looks strangely at* ALAN *and exits.*)

INSPECTOR: *(With pad)* So, you say there were strained relations between Harold Minks and his master.

ALAN: The Colonel was very put out by the boy. He was constantly being reprimanded.

POTTS: It's very clear to me, Inspector. If I may?

INSPECTOR: Go ahead Potts. Exercise your initiative.

POTTS: The boy is a typical, downtrodden working class youth. Seethin' with envy over his master's social superiority. Constantly bein' ticked off for minor offenses and petty peccadillos. *(Starts dramatizing)* Little by little, his working class hatred is growing like a big black mushroom in his belly. Ekin' out a livelihood only by his master's leave. Livin' in *his* house; walkin' on *his* grounds; eatin' from *his* plate. Always at the mercy of the bloody boo'jois capitalist pig who's rubbin' 'is nose in the dirt, his soul in the mud. One day, he can bear it no longer. He mixes the poison into his master's favorite Sauterne —the wine he keeps especially for hisself and that's never offered to the workers who have to make do with stale ale and warm beer. The bloody, insensitive, hard-hearted Lord of the Manor gulps it down after a night of wild carousal and the houseboy triumphs at last. *He's free of the mines forever!!!*

(HOBBISS *and* INSPECTOR FARCUS *regard the end of* POTTS' *maniacal performance.* ALAN *turns questioningly to the* INSPECTOR *who feels the need to justify his colleague's embarrassing fanaticism.*)

INSPECTOR: Sound theory, Potts. A few gaps here and there; a bit thin on hard evidence but, on the whole, a pretty creditable performance, wouldn't you say, Mr. Hobbiss?

ALAN: *(Warily)* Well . . . uh . . . yes . . . I suppose so. Of course, Harold, despite his rough manner is, in fact, the son of very well-to-do country folk and graduated from Eton and Sandhurst.

POTTS: *(Slowly adjusting to the bombshell)* That lout!?

ALAN: Some pretension he picked up in primary school. He's always emulated the working class, so much so that he gave up his entire inheritance, his social station and even his middle class speech habits, adopting instead this rather crude and theatrical working class diction. He could have had a manor of his own—the family owns half of Cheshire, not to mention the iron and coal mines, but he preferred to work as a lowly houseboy for the Colonel.

POTTS: *(Slowly, seething)* Bloody working class impostor!

INSPECTOR: Easy, Potts, easy.

POTTS: Pretendin' to fish 'n chips when he's noshin' bloody caviar from a silver spoon; puttin' on airs and graces. *(Recovering)* I think I need a bit of fresh air, Inspector. If I may?

INSPECTOR: Certainly, Potts. Take ten.

POTTS: *(Grumbling under his breath)* Bleedin' boo'jois bastard. *(Tearful)* What is the bloody world comin' to!?

ALAN: Is he all right, Inspector?

INSPECTOR: Potts? Don't mind him. Mild case of working class angst. Touch of pneumoconiosis as a child. Never quite at home without the pit pony, the miner's lamp and the smell of stool on his Wellies. Still, he's my right arm.

ALAN: In any case, there was bad blood between Harold and the Colonel. Everyone knew that.

INSPECTOR: Obviously then, a prime suspect, wouldn't you say?

ALAN: If the shoe fits, Inspector . . .

INSPECTOR: Precisely, and if it doesn't, lacerate the toes of the suspect until it does, eh?

ALAN: What?

INSPECTOR: A bit of an in-joke at the Yard, Mr. Hobbiss. Give it no mind. *(Checking the pad)* I see from my notes that originally you were a major investor in Calvarley Cavalry Clothes, but that at a stockholders' meeting a few months back, the Colonel acquired seventy-five percent of the business as well as chairmanship of the board.

ALAN: Well, yes, there were some changes a few months back.

INSPECTOR: And further, that Calvarley Cavalry Clothes was originally Hobbiss' Harnesses 'n Hostlery. Is that not so?

ALAN: Well, yes, I did start the company but . . .

INSPECTOR: It also appears from my notes that there was a bitter feud between you and the Colonel which left him completely in charge of a thriving concern and you out in the cold.

ALAN: *(Confronting it)* We had a difference of opinion, Inspector.

INSPECTOR: What about?

ALAN: *(Beat)* He wanted to replace all the British mounts with Western-style American saddles and I absolutely refused to accept the alien horns. It was uncalled-for, non-British, anti-traditional—and the horses didn't want it.

INSPECTOR: *(Beat)* You consulted the horses, did you?

ALAN: I've been in horses all my life, Inspector. I know when a horse is discontent. As soon as the new Yankee saddles came in, they didn't touch their hay and refused to wear their feedbags. They stopped whinnying and there was nothing in the buckets when the grooms came to muck out in the morning.

INSPECTOR: *(Beat)* You mean they stopped . . . *(mimes 'shitting')*

ALAN: Exactly, Inspector. It was their way of demonstrating.

INSPECTOR: *(Beat)* Curious form of protest, wouldn't you say?

ALAN: Unless you understand horses.

INSPECTOR: Common practice, is it?

ALAN: When a horse is unhappy, the very first sign is constipation.

INSPECTOR: Do tell?

ALAN: Any horseman will tell you that.

INSPECTOR: And diarrhoea indicates contentment, does it?

ALAN: Good healthy muck is always a sign of equestrian pleasure. You check the stalls of some of the greatest race track winners in history, Inspector, and you'll find there were good, healthy, brown symbols of contentment all over the place. Man 'o War was so prolific you could barely enter the stable of a morning. They had to turf it out with a bulldozer.

INSPECTOR: This is all very interesting, Mr. Hobbiss, but . . .

ALAN: You show me a full heap and I'll show you a happy steed.

INSPECTOR: But I put it to you that . . .

ALAN: You show me an empty pail and I'll show you a constipated horse.

INSPECTOR: *(Pushing his way through)* I put it to you that there might have been a bit of bad blood between you and the Colonel as well— and since under the present agreements, you now stand to inherit the entire business . . .

ALAN: This was my business to start with.

INSPECTOR: Of course it was, Mr. Hobbiss . . .

ALAN: And when I ran it, the stench of horse manure was so strong it would make your head spin.

INSPECTOR: Granted, Mr. Hobbiss, but . . .

ALAN: There would never have been Calvarley Cavalry Clothes without Hobbiss Harnesses 'n Hostlery.

INSPECTOR: And the change was not much to your liking, was it?

ALAN: *(Suddenly sobered up; the penny drops)* If you're looking for a motive for murder, Inspector, I would suggest you interrogate Charles Appley who has been consorting with Lady Calvarley behind the Colonel's back for years.

INSPECTOR: Are you insinuating that . . .

ALAN: If the shoe fits, Inspector . . .

(POTTS *comes dashing in.*)

POTTS: Inspector, there's an animal of some sort stuck in the chimney-stack. I shinnied up the roof and distinctly heard it breathing.

INSPECTOR: An animal—in the roof?

POTTS: It's a pretty big one too, by the sound of it. It's shakin' all the brickwork loose.

(There is a loud, thunderous noise off stage. LADY CALVARLEY *and* CHARLES *enter in a state.)*

INSPECTOR: I shall have to ask all of you to accompany me up to the attic. No one, I'm afraid, can be left on his own.

CHARLES: The attic is full of dirty old objects, Inspector.

INSPECTOR: No more than the parlor, Mr. Appley, if you ask my opinion. All right. Everyone. Quick march. Potts, you bring up the rear.

(INSPECTOR *leads them all through the door that leads to the attic,* POTTS *bringing up the rear. When all have exited,* HAROLD *and* BERENICE, *covered in soot, their clothes blackened, emerge from the side door.)*

HAROLD: Look what you've done, you randy cow. Practically demolished the whole house!

BERENICE: How could I know the bricks would give way?

HAROLD: The Eiffel Tower'd give way under all that 'arsin' about.

BERENICE: You know you bring out the tiger in me.

HAROLD: Sounded more like a bloody elephant stampede. Quick. We've gotta get washed and out'a these clothes before the copper's back. Hurry up, hurry up!

(They exit as INSPECTOR, LADY CALVARLEY *and* CHARLES *reemerge from the side.)*

INSPECTOR: Just a minor roof-collapse. Nothing to fret about.

LADY C: Are we safe, Inspector?

INSPECTOR: A touch of cement and everything will be as good as new.

CHARLES: What could have made that chimney give way like that?

INSPECTOR: War-time construction, I expect. Most of the houses were put up with suet and semolina in those days. Are you all right, Potts?

POTTS: *(Utterly shaken)* It felt just like a bloody pit cave-in. I thought they'd be diggin' us out for days.

INSPECTOR: Attics rank fairly low as potential sites for pit cave -ins.

POTTS: But what was that breathin', Inspector? I heard it clear as day. Like two pigs ruttin' away in the mire.

INSPECTOR: You've had a few nasty jolts today, Potts. The mind playing tricks on you, I suspect.

POTTS: It sounded almost human—grunts and groans and all.

INSPECTOR: 'Arf a mo'. We seem to be lacking your wife, Mr. Hobbiss, and that grotty little houseboy. Where can they be I wonder? Potts, I think you'd better . . .

BERENICE: *(In fresh clothes, enters from bedroom stairs)* What's all that racket? It sounded like an explosion.

HAROLD: *(Entering from the kitchen side, now spotless)* Blimey Inspector, did you hear that kafuffle?

INSPECTOR: *(To* BERENICE*)* A mild structural mishap, nothing more. *(Then to* HAROLD*)* And where have you been, Twinkle?

HAROLD: To the chapel. I always like to get in a few Hail Marys before the day starts.

INSPECTOR: A rich spiritual life, eh?

HAROLD: The Colonel was a firm believer in early mornin' mass. Some days we had only the eucharist instead of breakfast.

POTTS: Shall I work him over in the garage, Inspector?

INSPECTOR: There'll be plenty of time for routine interrogations, Potts. And you, Mrs. Hobbiss?

BERENICE: I was upstairs, Inspector. Then I heard the crash.

INSPECTOR: Took you quite a while to descend.

BERENICE: I was busy getting in and out of things.

HAROLD: *(Aside)* There's the bleeding understatement of the century.

INSPECTOR: I should be most obliged if you all went to your rooms and remained there until further notice. Except for you, Mr. Appley, and you, Mr. Minks. I should like you two gentlemen to stay behind and help us with our inquiries, if you have no objection.

(POTTS *whispers to* INSPECTOR FARCUS, *as if to say: You take* APPLEY *and leave* HAROLD *to me.* LADY CALVARLEY *and* CHARLES *are uneasy at the prospect of an interrogation of* CHARLES *and show it.)*

INSPECTOR: *(To* APPLEY) If you'd be so good as to accompany me on a little stroll around the grounds while Mr. Potts has a little chat with Mr. Minks here.

CHARLES: That might be misconstrued, Inspector. I'd better not.

INSPECTOR: Misconstrued?

CHARLES: Two grown men strolling around the grounds together. You know how the villagers like to gossip.

INSPECTOR: I think we can fend off any allegations of misconduct, Mr. Appley. We will, after all, be fully clothed.

CHARLES: I don't know . . . what do you think, Lady Calvarley?

LADY C: If the Inspector has no objection, I'd be quite willing to act as chaperone. That would effectively disarm any possible criticism.

INSPECTOR: I've no need for your chaperone services, Lady Calvarley, and would in fact prefer my chat with Mr. Appley to be entirely private and confidential.

LADY C: Well, I certainly don't wish to interfere with any intimate plans you might have.

INSPECTOR: *(Getting steamed)* I have no intimate plans other than a brief conversation with Mr. Appley—and I resent the allegation that an Inspector from Scotland Yard might be guilty of an impropriety with a suspect who happens to be a member of the same sex.

LADY C: *(Reasonably)* You *are* a bachelor, after all, Inspector. One can't be too careful.

INSPECTOR: *(Boiling)* Would you do me the kindness to retire to your room until further notice, Lady Calvarley.

(Reluctantly and with maximum waves of suspicion as to the INSPEC- TOR's *intentions, she leaves.)*

INSPECTOR: And now Mr. Appley, with at least twelve inches of day- light between us, would you be good enough to accompany me out- side. (INSPECTOR *gives high sign to* POTTS) If there are any shrieks or sounds of scuffle, Mr. Potts, feel free to notify the Rape Squad at once.

(INSPECTOR FARCUS *exits with* CHARLES APPLEY.

There is an awkward pause while POTTS *and* HAROLD *eye each other and jockey for position. After a long while,* POTTS *begins.)*

POTTS: Like a fag?

HAROLD: Thanks. *(Looks at pack)* Got any wi'vout filters?

POTTS: No, sorry. *(Beat)* Prefer 'em that way, do you?

HAROLD: Yeah, like to feel the smoke's goin' straight to me lungs, y'know.

POTTS: Umm. *(Beat)* Like a little wine: A Dom Perignon p'raps?

HAROLD: No thanks. I only drink beer.

POTTS: Like yer pint of an evening, do you?

HAROLD: Yeah, it settles me insides y'know. *And* a game 'a darts.

POTTS: Like darts too, d'yuh?

HAROLD: Yeah, I fancy a game 'a skill now 'n again.

POTTS: Yer father play darts, did 'e?

HAROLD: *(Slowly and warily)* No, I don't fink so.

POTTS: And was *he* a big beer drinker?

HAROLD: No, not as you might say a beer drinker. Liked 'is tankard now 'n again.

POTTS: *(After a beat)* Wha'd you do as a nipper, 'Arold?

HAROLD: 'Ow'd yuh mean?

POTTS: School 'n that. Studied lots of Greek and Latin 'n such like, I expect.

HAROLD: *(Slowly and warily)* No . . .

POTTS: *(Surprised)* No?

HAROLD: Not really. Did a little carpentry, lathe-operator, wood-workin'.

POTTS: Lots of summers in the south of France, I expect. At the tables in Monte Carlo. Skiin' in the Alps. Lausanne? San Moritz?

HAROLD: Packed crates in Stepney for a while. Some coon-exporter got the bright idea of makin' coconut-shells into brassieres and sellin' 'em cheap to the native girls. The bristles gave 'em all tit-rash so it never caught on. Sold headstones door-to-door for six months till I got a hernia and had to pack it in.

POTTS: Frantic social life, no doubt. Lots of swingin' little heiresses in Chelsea, I s'pose?

HAROLD: No, not really.

POTTS: No? No little Mayfair dollies in Morgans and Porsches?

HAROLD: Went wiv a scrubber for a while. She used to earn fivers goin' down on sailors out Wapping way. She died 'a clap when she was eighteen. Scared dee 'ell out 'a me. If I even got so much as a pimple, I'd shoot me bum full 'a penicillin.

POTTS: *(Ignoring all of this)* Mummy and Daddy're quite well off, I understand. Little bit 'a property here 'n there?

HAROLD: *(Slowly and warily)* No . . . not really.

POTTS: *(Surprised)* Is 'at so?

HAROLD: Yeah.

POTTS: Not comfortably off then?

HAROLD: Dad kips in a coal-bin beside the British Rail shed at Saint Pancras Station. He's all right till they tip in the rubbish—then it's a bit tight. The last I heard 'a Mum, she was a bag-lady in Walthamstow. Some of the locals had a whip-round for 'er on account 'a the bottom fell out'a her carrier and it was givin' all the other old crones a bad name.

POTTS: *(Ceasing all subterfuge)* Who do you think yer foolin', Sonny-Jim?

HAROLD: I ain't tryin' t'fool no one.

POTTS: Droppin' your aitches like you was a navvy!

HAROLD: What I do with my aitches is none of yer business.

POTTS: *(Suddenly earnest)* You can level with me, boy. I'm your friend.
   I don't care if you are one of the Four Hundred and went to the best
   Public Schools in the land.

HAROLD: What are you on about?

POTTS: It don't make no odds with me if you got your own private
   enclosure at Ascot and your own opera box at Covent Garden. I
   don't look down at that!

HAROLD: I ain't never been to Ascot and Covent Garden's just a vege-
   table market 'far as I heard.

POTTS: *(Taking him around, emotionally)* It's all right, Sonny! We can't
   all be worms in the dust. Some of us have got to have clean finger-
   nails and lunch with the vicar.

HAROLD: I don't know no vicars and I chewed me fingernails away
   years ago. *(Growing hysterical)* You tryin' to spook me out or
   sump'in?

POTTS: *(Almost tearful)* Don't fight it 'Arold. Confess to your gilt-
   edged securities, your numbered bank accounts in Switzerland, your
   blazers and your cricket bats. No one's goin'a hold any of that
   against you. *You're just as good as the next man!* Can't you see, I'm
   openin' me 'eart t'you?

HAROLD: *(Warily)* Are you some kind of a pervert or sump'in?

POTTS: *(Sensing the conversion is near)* Just take that first step 'Arold.
   That's all it needs!

HAROLD: *(Picking up vase)* Stay away from me or I'll brain yuh!

POTTS: Take your courage in both hands and say it straight out: I'm a
   poncy, posh, piss-elegant middle class shit, and *proud of it*!

(HAROLD *throws the vase at* POTTS *just as he is starting to bear down on him. At that moment,* INSPECTOR FARCUS *and* APPLEY *appear at the front door. The* INSPECTOR *nonchalantly catches the vase.*)

INSPECTOR: Calm down, Minks. Easy, Potts.

POTTS: *(Mopping brow)* I almost 'ad 'im, Inspector. Almost.

HAROLD: I've a good mind to have you up for Grievous Bodily Harm.

INSPECTOR: I'd consider that charge if I were you, Minks—especially as how it might stack up against Resisting Arrest, Refusal to Comply With An Officer's Orders and Wilful Destruction of Private Property. *(Nonchalantly shatters the vase in his hand)* And now, Mr. Appley, apropos of our nice little chat outside, I think we should have a little natter with Lady Calvarley. Minks, you'd better come along as well.

HAROLD: Why is everyone pickin' on me?

INSPECTOR: Tut, tut, Minks, we mustn't give way to paranoid fantasies. Only unreformable criminal types do that.

HAROLD: What d'yuh want from me?

INSPECTOR: Just a little corroboration of facts recently acquired from Mr. Appley regarding the Colonel's lady. We won't keep you long. Hannah!

(HANNAH, *clutching a small parcel, appears immediately from behind the kitchen door where she has obviously been listening.*)

On tap twenty-four hours a day, are we?

HANNAH: Did you call, Inspector?

INSPECTOR: Where's the good lady of the house?

HANNAH: Out back, doin' some gardening. She says it calms her down.

INSPECTOR: Very therapeutic. I've known several mass-murderers who found great relaxation planting their victims in allotments throughout the Home Counties. Nothin' ever sprouted though. Come along, Mr. Appley, Mr. Minks. Potts, bring up the rear.

(FARCUS, CHARLES *and* HAROLD *troop out the front door followed by* POTTS, *leaving* ALAN *alone with* HANNAH. *As soon as everyone has left, a strange glint comes into his eye.* HANNAH *appears to recognize it and recoils.*)

ALAN: *(Transformed)* Have you got it?

HANNAH: *(With parcel)* This is the last one I'm getting for you, Mr. Hobbiss. The very last one.

ALAN: Is it the one I asked for?

HANNAH: Lady Calvarley is getting very suspicious. She keeps askin' me about the dance gowns and I keep tellin' 'er they're at the cleaners. They've been at the bleedin' cleaners now for eighteen months.

ALAN: *(With dress)* This is it. The satin, the lace, the zips. Oh, Hannah, I can't wait, I must try it. *(He begins to undress.)*

HANNAH: *(Frantically turning towards the door)* I don't think this is the best place for a fittin', Mr. Hobbiss. The Inspector might . . .

ALAN: He'll be out there for hours asking his fool questions.

HANNAH: Mr. Hobbiss, why didn't you see that doctor I got for you?

ALAN: Don't be silly, Hannah. There's nothing the matter with me.

HANNAH: He could've given you some sort of prescription for all this. He told me all about it—aversion therapy or sump'in. They put you in frocks and give you a sort of an electric shock and if you try dressin' up after that, you barf all over yourself.

ALAN: Give me a hand with the zip.

HANNAH: This goes right against my upbringing, Mr. Hobbiss. I'm Church of England, and there's four or five commandments against this kind'a thing.

ALAN: *(Now in the dress)* What do you think?

HANNAH: *(Braving it out)* It does sort of suit you.

ALAN: Sort of? It's magnificent. I knew it the moment I spotted it. What line! What a cut! And the shoes set it off perfectly. *(Looks to her)* Now you! Get the jodhpurs, the shooting jacket, the riding boots. It's your most magnificent outfit.

HANNAH: They're just outside, Mr. Hobbiss, in the garden.

ALAN: *(Threatening)* I can't wait any longer, Hannah.

HANNAH: Try to calm down, sir. The Colonel's only just passed over. It don't seem right to . . .

ALAN: Calvarley was an ass. Serves him right whoever polished him off. *(Beat)* Was it you, Hannah? You can tell me. You needn't be afraid. It would only make you more deliciously desirable in my eyes.

HANNAH: Poison the Colonel? The man who pays me wages each month?

ALAN: Now that the whole business is mine, I will take you into my service. Would you like that, Hannah?

HANNAH: I'm thinkin' of visitin' some relatives in Bora Bora actually. Might be gone for some little time.

ALAN: *(Rummaging in closet)* Here, put on this anorak, these corduroys. The rugged outdoor look—one of your finest ensembles.

HANNAH: *(Peering out window)* Mr. Hobbiss, I've been meaning to have a long talk with you. I don't mind extra little duties, but I think you've been takin' liberties these past few months as . . .

ALAN: Do it, Hannah. Do it!! *(He is bending the riding crop ominously in his hands)* I can't hold out much longer.

HANNAH: 'Housekeepin' and light domestic chores', that's the understanding I had with the Colonel.

(ALAN cracks the riding whip. HANNAH dons the anorak and stuffs her skirt into the oversize corduroys.)

I think it's exploitin' the labor force, Mr. Hobbiss, to add modelin' and messin' about to all me normal duties. It don't somehow seem right to . . .

ALAN: And the boots, Hannah. The boots!

HANNAH: It ain't decent wearin' the master's things and him nestlin' amongst the ice cubes like that.

ALAN: The boots! *(Cracks whip)*

(HANNAH is now in anorak, corduroys and boots. ALAN moves slowly and sensually towards her.)

ALAN: It's breathtaking, Hannah. A bit casual and devil-may-care but that only adds a certain rustic *Je ne sais quoi. (He sits on her lap.)* Begin, Hannah, and don't leave anything out.

HANNAH: I ain't even put out the dustbins yet, and the breakfast things are all stacked up in the . . .

ALAN: BEGIN!

HANNAH: *(After a beat, in a gruff voice)* 'Where have you been all night? What's the idea of comin' in at three in the morning? What do you think you're playing at, my lovely?'

ALAN: *(In a woman's voice)* 'I'm sorry. I just wasn't watching the time. I don't know what got into me. You're angry—I can hear it.'

HANNAH: *(In her own voice)* You're bleedin' heavy, Mr. Hobbiss.

ALAN: *(Giving cue)* 'You're angry—I can hear it!'

HANNAH: 'You're bloody right I'm angry. This is the last time you make a fool out of me—sleeping around with other men—two-timing me on every side!'

ALAN: *(Craven, pleading)* 'Not the whip! Not the whip!'

HANNAH: *(Begging off)* Mr. Hobbiss . . .

ALAN: *(Prompting)* The whip! The whip! *(Acting)* 'Not the whip! Not the whip!'

HANNAH: 'You asked for it, dearie, and now I'm going to tan your hide so's you won't be able to sit down for a month of Sundays.'

ALAN: *(Kneeling before her)* 'No, no—don't. I'm only a fragile little thing. Have mercy, mercy!' *(Prompting)* Get on with it! Get on with it! *(Acting)* 'Please, dear God, spare me, spare me.'

(As HANNAH *raises the riding crop, the door opens and the* INSPECTOR *appears in the doorway facing away. As he speaks,* HANNAH *and* HOBBISS *are rapidly changing back to their original clothes.)*

INSPECTOR: *(Faced away)* Thank you, Lady Calvarley, and you, Mr. Appley. *(Issuing instructions)* Potts, check the garage, the barn, the silo, the birdhouse, the gazebo. If there's a clue anywhere on these grounds, I want it in my dossier. Leave no stone unturned!

(The INSPECTOR *is about to turn into the room but turns away again.)*

No, not the bloody rock garden. Don't be so literal, Potts. And there's nothing under that crazy paving. Leave it alone. Good man, Potts. No need to go overboard.

(INSPECTOR FARCUS *is about to turn again, but turns back to* POTTS.)

And report here as soon as you're through. We're going to wrap up this case in a matter of hours. I'm coming in for the kill, Potts.

(He finally turns and as he does so, HANNAH *and* MR. HOBBISS *are standing before him normally attired. Their 'other' clothes are in a heap on the floor.)*

What's all this then?

HANNAH: I was turfin' out the hall closet, Inspector. Oxfam comes every Thursday morning and we always try to leave 'em a little bundle.

INSPECTOR: Every item in this house is evidence in what may turn out to be the biggest murder trial of the century. It all stays where it is. And besides, this isn't Thursday, it's Sunday.

HANNAH: Sometimes they're a bit early.

INSPECTOR: Conscientious little buggers, aren't they? Have always suspected those Oxfam volunteers of operating one of the biggest re-sale rackets in the country. Ever since I found a blue gabardine suit I gave them selling in Selfridge's window at twice the price. *(Beat)* Are you all right, Mr. Hobbiss?

ALAN: It's all got a little too much for me, Inspector. I think I'll have a little lie down. Hannah, perhaps you could bring me a little cocoa.

HANNAH: I've still got me chores, Mr. Hobbiss. Better be getting on with them.

INSPECTOR: I'm afraid, Mr. Hobbiss, I shall require your attendance in the drawing room—along with everyone else. Hannah, be good enough to summon everyone into the drawing room.

(HANNAH *exits.*)

ALAN: *(Irked)* This is getting very tiresome, Inspector. You can't just come in here and throw your weight around. Everyone is still in a state of shock over the Colonel's death. No one is quite back to normal yet.

INSPECTOR: The more I learn about this household, Mr. Hobbiss, the more I dread to think what the norm is. It's clear that one murder has been committed and, from what I can gather, about half a dozen moral misdemeanors.

ALAN: May I remind you, Inspector, we are living in a free society which tolerates different codes of social conduct?

INSPECTOR: Don't you believe it, Mr. Hobbiss. There are two Good Books in this country. The first contains the word of our Lord and the second, roughly the same information, translated into the provisions of the Criminal Code. I consider it a holy calling to administer justice in this land for I know that behind the boot, the truncheon and the Black Maria stand the vicar, the priest and the Archbishop of Canterbury. It gives me an enormous sense of confidence.

ALAN: I take it then you do not recognize the separation of Church and State.

INSPECTOR: They may be separated, Mr. Hobbiss, but I can assure you they are still living together. For someone of my persuasion, the Queen of England is only the Commissioner of Police in royal regalia.

ALAN: What a fanciful idea—a woman in man's clothes.

INSPECTOR: Please be seated.

(THE GUESTS *have now entered the room. They distribute themselves throughout the room.)*

INSPECTOR: *(Calling)* Potts! We shall require you indoors for the moment.

(POTTS *re-enters carrying two stones. The* INSPECTOR *regards them as does everyone else.* POTTS *places them on a nearby side table and once again looks officious.*

When all are seated, INSPECTOR FARCUS, *sensing his 'big moment' sternly views the assemblage before him. He then consults his notes, eyes the assembled guests, takes up a prominent position like a lecturer about to deliver an oration, and begins.)*

INSPECTOR: I do not wish to cause any more distress than that already caused by the unfortunate events of this fateful weekend—nor do I wish to alarm any of the persons in this room—except the murderer of course, who I hope is shitting bricks at this very moment!!!

(Everyone rustles uncomfortably. The INSPECTOR, *pleased by his effect, continues.)*

In any routine investigation of homicide, a policeman considers himself fortunate if he manages to dig up even one likely suspect—which is to say, an individual who, for nefarious motives of his or her own, has good reason to wish the decease of the deceased and stands to benefit, in some way or other, from that act of deceasement.

Well now, in our present circumstances, we have a positive feast of riches for, as far as I can ascertain, there is almost nobody in this room who did not have a fairly compelling reason to wish the deceased to cease and desist, as indeed the deceased *did* cease and desist by becoming the deceased.

Take all of this down, Potts. Some smart-alec M.P.'ll probably want a verbatim copy for the record.

(Roams around the room, gravitating towards MR. *and* MRS. HOBBISS.)

I put it to you, Mrs. Hobbiss, that, motivated by carnal desires which are quite repugnant in a woman of your age and appearance, you mounted—at some time in the not too distant past—a small campaign to snag the affections of the late Colonel which was soundly rebuffed, I might add, causing a certain rancor, bitterness and even hatred for that very man who refused to succumb to your erotogenic advances.

(All have turned accusingly to BERENICE. *She quails quietly and inwardly shrivels up.)*

And you, Mr. Hobbiss, as we have already demonstrated, stand to gain the most from the Colonel's death as you are now the beneficiary of a thriving business in leather and saddlery—from which the Colonel had originally barred you—an action which was bound to exacerbate the feelings of rivalry which already smoldered between you. And, if that were not motive enough, there is the fact that there was suspected hanky-panky between your wife and the Colonel, which may well have fed that secret desire for revenge which burns in the coccyx of all cuckolds.

(The group has now shifted its look of accusation to MR. HOBBISS *who wilts under its stare.)*

As for you, Mr. Appley, it appears to be common knowledge that an illicit union existed (and probably still exists) between yourself and Lady Calvarley, leading one to suggest that the removal of the good Colonel might have facilitated your desire to bang the Colonel's lady without let or hindrance.

(The group now wheels around on APPLEY.*)*

And likewise suggests that you, Lady Calvarley,

(The group now wheels upon her.)

despite your elaborate show of grief, may well have aided and abetted the deceasement of the deceased for craven, licentious and filthy-minded reasons of your own.

And, as if this is not sufficient grounds for a dozen murder trials, there remains the fact that you, Mr. Minks . . .

(All wheel toward him.)

were subject to excessive and unnatural punishment by the late Colonel over an extended period of time, and that it is quite likely these castigations developed in you a murderous desire to rid yourself of that tyrant directly responsible for your bruised limbs and sore bum.

Which brings me to my last and most subtle suspect, the lady who first discovered the body and would appear to reap no apparent advantage whatsoever from the Colonel's death. A brilliant ruse designed to divert attention away from herself—which would be quite clever if we didn't already know from many decades of detective fiction that it is the Innocent, the people with no apparent motive or treacherous design, who invariably turn out to be the blackest villains of all!

(Everyone wheels around to HANNAH.*)*

The evidence in the case of *this* suspect, being virtually non-existent, is perhaps the most damning of all!

*(*HANNAH *shrinks before the glare of others.)*

All of which seems to beg the question—who then is the murderer of Colonel Calvarley; the very question, no doubt, that is circulating wildly in the minds of every person in this room at this very moment.

We shall not keep you in suspense very much longer. For our inquiries have now come to a successful conclusion and I am at liberty to announce the name of the guilty party.

(Everyone stirs in their seats. They look sheepishly at one another and then back to the INSPECTOR.

Now in a central position, towering over all in his authority.)

The murderer of Colonel Calvarley is none other than . . .

(There is a knock from the kitchen door. All turn toward the door. POTTS *looks fearfully to the* INSPECTOR, *then rises and, pistol in hand, approaches the door. The dull thudding continues.* POTTS *gets right up to the door and suddenly swings it open. Behind it is revealed:* THE COLONEL, *very blue in the face, frost on his hair and icicles hanging from his nose.)*

COLONEL: *(Hoarsely)* Whose bloody idea was it to stick me in that fridge???

Sensation. Shock. Tumult.

Curtain

Act 2

A short while later.

THE COLONEL is now seated in the easy chair, wrapped in blankets and surrounded by hot-water bottles. The others are grouped around him.

INSPECTOR: You say you remember imbibing the drink and then . . .

COLONEL: I felt a constriction in my throat, a terrible pounding in my chest and then everything went black. The next thing I knew I was lying on this godawful shelf and couldn't feel a thing. This is it, I told myself, I've expired and am now in the morgue waiting to be shipped to the next world. No direct routes to heaven or hell, only a tedious passage through all the stops in between: the morgue, the funeral, the burial, the decay and eventually, I suppose, the divine dispensation. Just like the bloody Almighty to procrastinate right up to the last minute.

INSPECTOR: And while you were entertaining these metaphysical speculations, what were you feeling?

COLONEL: Bloody cold, I can tell you that!

INSPECTOR: I've already apologized for the unorthodox arrangements, but was there anything else?

COLONEL: I still felt pretty queasy of course—and hungry. I hadn't had a bite of breakfast remember. Well, in the dim light of that refrigerator . . .

POTTS: (*A revelation*) Ah, so the light stayed on when we closed the door, did it?

INSPECTOR: Don't interrupt the Colonel, Potts. Go on.

COLONEL: I could dimly see some food. There was yogurt, ice cream and a lot of frozen strawberries. That was all I could actually reach, so I wolfed it all down, one after the other, and to my astonishment, I started feeling rather better.

POTTS: *(Snapping his fingers)* Of course, Inspector! It just so happens that yogurt, ice cream and strawberries are the antidote for strychnine poisoning. What a stroke of luck!!

COLONEL: Well, it certainly brought back my strength. And that's when I found that by manipulating the sharp end of the icicles, I could just barely move the catch on the inside of the door. After snapping five or six icicles in the attempt, I finally managed to twist the lock, lift myself in one vertical piece out of the freezer and into the drawing room. *(Sneezes)*

INSPECTOR: An amazing escape, Colonel, which, if I may say, out-Houdinies Houdini. You're very fortunate the ambulance services did not arrive. Getting out of the mortuary is no snap. The paperwork alone would have kept you incarcerated for six weeks at least.

COLONEL: It was all rather distressing of course, but it does give certain spiritual insights I shall keep with me to the end of my days. I don't expect I'll ever again be able to look a frozen chicken in the face without quailing, and every time I defrost a lamb chop, I'll be prepared for the intervention of God.

INSPECTOR: Divine intervention notwithstanding, a diabolical villain is still in our midst and we must redouble our efforts to find him—or her—aided now by direct testimony from the deceased himself, as it were. Therefore, I must ask all of you to repair to your rooms while I question the victim and try to unearth the perpetrator of this dastardly and, if you'll pardon the expression Colonel, cold-blooded crime.

LADY C: You don't mean to simply continue your investigation, do you? With my husband only barely alive from this shattering experience.

INSPECTOR: The Colonel appears to be something of a survivor and in rather chipper form. Am I correct in this, Colonel?

COLONEL: *(Sneezes)* Well, these hot water bottles have certainly got the old blood percolating again and, Inspector, I agree with you. The villian must be uncovered and, groggy as I am, I shall co-operate to the utmost.

INSPECTOR: Spoken like a True Brit.—Was it in the last Great War against the Boche you won your spurs, Colonel?

COLONEL: No, I was in charge of routing the wogs out of Rangoon, actually.

INSPECTOR: A campaign, if I may say so, just as laudable as hunting the Hun. Therefore, to reiterate: I should like everyone to repair to their rooms and await further word. And no one had better attempt to flit from these premises as that will be taken as a sure sign of incrimination. All right, ladies and gentlemen?

(Everyone slowly and nervously leaves the room.)

INSPECTOR: Potts, go upstairs and check that everyone is where they ought to be. I do not wish the ensuing interrogation to be overheard by anyone.

POTTS: Right, chief.

INSPECTOR: Then get right back, Potts.

POTTS: Right, chief.

(HE *exits upstairs.)*

INSPECTOR: *(Puts the brandy-flask and glass on side table beside* COLO-NEL) I think a bit of brandy would now be appropriately medicinal, Colonel. I am going to check the outside of the house to make sure that our interview is entirely private. Back in a jiff.

(INSPECTOR *darts out the front door.*

THE COLONEL *sneezes again, then draws the blankets around him for greater warmth. As he does so, one of his hot water bottles falls to the floor. He leans over to pick it up. While he is bent over, we see a hand dart out from the curtains which are directly behind the side table. Deftly, it raises the brandy flask, pours in some invisible contents, shakes it, then replaces it on the table. This done, the hand disappears.* THE COLONEL, *now having retrieved the hot water bottle, wedges it behind his back. Turning to the brandy, he pours himself a stiff drink and knocks it back. He then settles back in the chair, luxuriating in the warmth of the drink, closing his eyes and relaxing. After a moment, his eyes pop open and a terrifying expression distorts his face. He raises himself up in the chair toppling two or three hot water bottles onto the floor, gasps, gurgles, coughs, sputters and then, with a series of deadly shivers, expires in the chair.*

After a moment, POTTS *comes down the stairs.)*

POTTS: All tucked away nicely, Inspector.

(Sees the INSPECTOR *is not there. Turns to* THE COLONEL *now resting in the easy chair. Notices his eyes are closed and that several hot water bottles have fallen to the ground. He begins to pick them up and tuck them around* THE COLONEL's *body.)*

POTTS: Got to keep warm, Colonel—even if we are havin' a little kip. What an ordeal, eh? I don't know too many men can say they've been back from the dead. Although there's some that say they buried me grandpa prematurely. The will had been read. The insurance payments made. It was all a fait-accompli y'might say, and at the graveside, they hear this peckin' in the coffin. The gravedigger says to my grandma: 'I think we've made a terrible mistake,' and he starts pullin' the nails out of the box. 'Leave off,' me grandma says, 'I've paid to bury his body not exhume it!' The digger was real put out. 'He might be alive in there,' he says. 'Too bad if he is,' she says. 'Should'a thought of that before the will, shouldn't he? Now get on with it!' She was a real stickler for routine, me grandma. Well this here gravedigger was a real church-goer, y'know; sang in the choir'n all. 'I ain't damnin' my soul t'hell for no twelve quid a day,' he says and with that, he begins pryin' open the coffin lid. 'Leave 'im be,' me grandma is screamin'. 'He's had his bloody innin's and he's out now!' Well the digger got half the lid off when all of a sudden, a little chipmunk jumps out'a the box and cavorts over to the gravestones. 'I told you 'e's a bloody stiff,' me grandma says, 'now get hold'a some maskin' tape and repair the damage you done to that lid!' It took all the piety right out'a the occasion and the Vicar got so rattled he started in on the christenin'-service. Everybody was supposed to throw one shovelful of dirt into the grave and pass on, but when it came to me grandma's turn, she just stood there pitchin' one shovelful after the other like a bloody navvy. The family was right cool to grandma after that.

(The dead COLONEL, *of course, does not react to the story. The* INSPECTOR *returns.)*

INSPECTOR: Right. The coast is clear on all sides and we can now get to the bottom of this . . .

*(*INSPECTOR *stops short as he sees the* COLONEL's *face. Listens to his pulse, heartbeat, puts magnifying glass to his mouth.* THE COLONEL *is clearly inert.* THE INSPECTOR *turns accusingly to* POTTS)

INSPECTOR: What you playin' at, Potts?

POTTS: Inspector?

INSPECTOR: Our miraculously resuscitated survivor is now as stiff as a donkey's rod.*(Continues to peer suspiciously at* POTTS:)

POTTS: It weren't me, Inspector. *(Beat)* You don't think that . . .

INSPECTOR: Everyone is a suspect, Potts, and when a man is standing over the body of a dead man who was alive only two minutes ago, he is *more* than a suspect, he is practically an accomplice!

POTTS: I thought he was havin' a kip. I just been standin' here reminiscin'. Tellin' him about me granny.

INSPECTOR: Boring a man to death is still grounds for prosecution if the subject actually expires.

POTTS: Honest to God, Inspector. It weren't me.

(Notices the brandy flask beside THE COLONEL. *Inspects it, smells it.)*

It's the brandy. It's laced with poison.

*(*INSPECTOR *grabs the flask and sniffs it.)*

And you gave him that bottle, didn't you, Inspector?

INSPECTOR: *(Registering* POTTS' *accusing look)* I hope you are not insinuating that to avoid redoing my original paperwork, I have returned the Colonel to his former state.

*(*POTTS *looks curiously at the brandy flask.)*

Men have been hung for smaller innuendoes than that.

POTTS: *(Snapping himself out of it)* I'm sorry, Inspector. I must'a lost me head.

INSPECTOR: Obviously someone, presumably neither you nor I, has switched a harmless bottle of brandy for a poisoned bottle within the two or three minuters which elapsed between our exit and return. *(Checks the curtain behind the side table)* Ah ha, you see! A sliding panel in the wall directly beside the table on which the brandy stood.

POTTS: Blimey Inspector! I didn't think there was such things as sliding panels outside of Agatha Christie novels.

INSPECTOR: As a direct result of their unprecedented popularity, they have now been widely installed throughout the country and that twisted old lady has got a lot to answer for. *(Beat)* Well, Potts, this puts us into a rather delicate situation.

POTTS: How so, Inspector?

INSPECTOR: This morning the Colonel was poisoned, was he not? *(*POTTS *nods)* This afternoon, he was miraculously resuscitated. *(*POTTS *nods)* Now he has unfortunately been poisoned again, and since the entire supply of yogurt, ice-cream and strawberries is exhausted, there is no chance of any last minute rallies. *(*POTTS *nods)*

When we came onto the case, he was dead. As soon as we began our investigations, he revived. Just as we were concluding our work, he was murdered again. Don't you see?

POTTS: No sir.

INSPECTOR: To the casual observer, it might appear that his second murder, occurring as it did under the noses of two senior police officers, is the result of gross negligence on our part.

POTTS: On *our* part?

INSPECTOR: Well yours anyway, since *you* were actually with the deceased.

POTTS: But *you* gave him the brandy.

INSPECTOR: *You* were the last one to see him alive.

POTTS: I thought he was asleep.

INSPECTOR: It'll never stand up in court, Potts.

POTTS: Who's goin'a court?

INSPECTOR: Both of us, if we don't come up with something.

POTTS: But I can't be a criminal, Inspector. I'm a member of Her Majesty's Police Force.

INSPECTOR: It's a novel twist of logic, Potts. In any case, let's put an end to these mutual recriminations. If you swear you didn't knock him off, I'll believe you.

POTTS: By me father's lamp and sainted shovel, I did not!

INSPECTOR: Good man, Potts, I didn't think for a moment you'd gone over to the other side.

POTTS: What about you? *(Beat) I* swore.

INSPECTOR: *(Embarrassed, but knowing it must be done)* By the spirit of the blue lamp, the Queen's corgies and anything else you like. *(He crosses himself)*

POTTS: *(Pumps his hand warmly)* I knew you wouldn't break up the old team, Inspector.

INSPECTOR: Our mutual trust, Potts, in no way alters the fact that in the eyes of the Yard—and perhaps even the Press, our permitting the decease of the deceased so soon after his resurrection may look like a dereliction of duty.

POTTS: We've got to find the blighter that's done this. Twice!

INSPECTOR: We have one advantage.

POTTS: What's that?

INSPECTOR: No one but we know the Colonel is dead. We may even speculate that the murderer himself, though he administered a second dose, is not absolutely certain it has taken.

(THE INSPECTOR *places guilty brandy flask into inside breast pocket.*)

POTTS: How's that help matters?

INSPECTOR: In a little-known tale by Sax Rohmer entitled, 'The Second Coming'—have you read it perchance?

POTTS: We was never allowed sexually explicit material in Wales, Inspector.

INSPECTOR: In any case, in Rohmer's little story the detective, being in custody of the murder victim and, like ourselves, wishing to capitalize on it, arranges for the cadaver himself to interrogate the suspects through an ingenious device not very far removed from ventriloquism. Look.

(INSPECTOR *inspects the easy chair.*)

This is a rather ample easy chair with a deep groin of a seat. If someone were to place themselves underneath the Colonel, hidden by a mountain of pillows and blankets, and manipulate his head and arms accordingly, he might well pass for the Colonel himself.

POTTS: You mean sit with that stiff on top of you?

INSPECTOR: No, Potts. Sit with that stiff on top of *you.*

POTTS: Me? *(The penny drops)* I'm too squeamish to have a corpse on me lap. I'd just keel right over.

INSPECTOR: Not if the alternative were an official reprimand and possible demotion.

POTTS: Demotion? But I've only just been promoted.

INSPECTOR: Life in the Yard's a veritable yo-yo, Potts. Up today, down tomorrow—all at the whim of civil service mandarins whose jobs are so secure, they'll still be getting their pension cheques ten years after they're dead and buried.

POTTS: Do you mean sit with that body on top 'a me and try to conduct a normal conversation?

INSPECTOR: I'll field all interference.

POTTS: Me ole dad wouldn't like it if he heard about it.

INSPECTOR: I promise you, I'll make no mention of it in my monthly reports to him.

POTTS: I don't know, Inspector. I've never before assumed a position of close intimacy with a deceased.

INSPECTOR: In the line of duty Potts, the police are often asked to perform strange and unnatural acts. When I was tracking down a gang of gay abortionists who took refuge in a health club, I was myself obliged to shower with ten or twelve of the loathsome sodomites, and I must say, though dreading the encounter, it was nothing like as disgusting as I'd been led to believe.

POTTS: He's gonna start to pong again any minute.

INSPECTOR: A little cotton-wool up the nostrils and that problem is easily sidestepped. The point is, Potts, whoever it is who has spiked the Colonel's brandy is certain to show his hand in a private dialogue with the man he has twice murdered. And I have a fairly good hunch who that might be.

POTTS: Couldn't we just book 'im Inspector and avoid all the rest of the folderol?

INSPECTOR: You don't seem to grasp, Potts. Our credibility has already been strained to breaking point. If we add False Arrest on top of Negligence and Making A General Balls-Up, we'll both of us be pounding the beat.

POTTS: But a while back, I thought you'd worked out who the murderer was.

INSPECTOR: A conventional ploy in criminal investigations which, if properly executed, makes the pressure so unbearable it brings the guilty party springing to his feet.

POTTS: That didn't quite happen, did it?

INSPECTOR: The culprit reasoned there was no mileage in confessing to a crime which the Colonel's unexpected revival rendered null and void. Without the habeas corpus, he rightly concluded, he was home and dry. Well, what do you say, Potts?

POTTS: *(Regarding the dead* COLONEL*)* I don't like it, Inspector. I can't pretend as I do.

INSPECTOR: Your revulsion does you credit, Potts. If you fancied the idea of entering into a grisly embrace with the cadaver, I'd have no alternative but to suspect the worst of you. Now let's rig this thing up.

(INSPECTOR *removes pillows and hot water bottles from chair as* POTTS *lifts up the dead* COLONEL. THE INSPECTOR *then motions* POTTS *to hand the corpse over to him, which* POTTS *does.*)

INSPECTOR: Now, sit down as deep as you can.

(POTTS *sits in the cavernous easy chair.*)

Get your head down a bit further.

(POTTS *does so.*)

Right, comin' in.

(INSPECTOR *places* THE COLONEL *on top of* POTTS, *effectively obliterating* POTTS *so that only* THE COLONEL *is visible. He then restores pillows and hot water bottles and places the blankets over* THE COLONEL's *legs masking* POTTS' *as well.*)

POTTS: He ain't no lightweight.

(INSPECTOR, *like a studious window designer, steps back to admire the arrangement.*)

INSPECTOR: Try a bit of mime, Potts. To see if you've got the hang of it.

(POTTS, *now unseen, gestures with* THE COLONEL's *arms and manages to nod* THE COLONEL's *head up and down.*)

INSPECTOR: Good show, Potts. Puts Edgar Bergen and Charlie McCarthy right in the shade. If you put your mind to this, it could develop into a headline act at the London Palladium.

POTTS: I've no aspirations in that direction, Inspector.

INSPECTOR: *(The astute director)* Now don't forget the voice, Potts. The Colonel was rather posh.

POTTS: *(Assuming upper middle class voice)* 'Is it more this kind of thing, do you think?'

INSPECTOR: *(The perfectionist)* A bit in the lower register.

POTTS: *(Very bass)* 'A bit down here, d'you think?'

INSPECTOR: He's not a bloody darkey, Potts. Bring it up a bit.

POTTS: This ain't my speciality, Inspector.

INSPECTOR: Get the hang of it as best you can. I'll bring in the first client. Try to lead the conversation into the right areas. We are trying to unmask a murderer, remember.

(THE INSPECTOR *exits.* POTTS *tries to get the hang of the dead* COLONEL.)

POTTS: *(From underneath)* What a friggin' caper. *(Makes some mime, nods* THE COLONEL's *head, etc.)* Blimey, he's gettin' stiff. If rigor mortis sets in, they'll have to part us with a bloody buzzsaw.

(THE INSPECTOR *ushers in* HAROLD.)

INSPECTOR: Just sit down over there, Harold *(Motioning to seat away from* COLONEL) The Colonel'd like a little word with you.

HAROLD: Over there?

INSPECTOR: That's right. We don't want you too close to the Colonel as he's particularly susceptible to germs in his present condition.

(HAROLD *sits uneasily.)*

INSPECTOR: It's Mr. Minks, Colonel. He's right here, like you asked.

POTTS: *(With posh voice)* 'Oh yes, Minks. I meant to ask you . . . when precisely was it you brought that Sauterne into the drawing room?'

HAROLD: *(Beat, taking in odd voice)* But Colonel, you always kept the California Sauterne in your own rooms, don't you remember? We was never allowed to touch that.

POTTS: 'Quite right, Minks. Quite right. Inspector, could you leave us to have a private word, if that's all right?'

INSPECTOR: As you like Colonel. I'll be just outside, if you need me. *(He exits.)*

HAROLD: *(Moving closer)* Are you all right, Colonel?

POTTS: 'Don't come too close boy. I'm still not geared up for human contact.'

HAROLD: I can imagine, Colonel. It must'a been a terrible ordeal.

POTTS: Words can't describe it, my boy. It's like your whole life streaming before you in a snowstorm. You took it badly, did you boy?'

HAROLD: I was beside me'self, Colonel. And then those moronic flat-feet tryin' to implicate me. You should'a seen it. If they wasn't so stupid, it'd be laughable.

POTTS: 'A bit slow, are they?'

HAROLD: There's somethin' right sly about that ugly one; the one they call Potts. He looks like he's escaped from a correctional institution.

POTTS: 'Seemed a nice enough chap to me, still I'm not completely with it yet.'

HAROLD: *(Looks about, then, confidentially)* I have to tell you this Colonel—even though I know it will put you out a bit.

POTTS: 'What's that, Harold my boy?'

HAROLD: When I heard you'd buggered off for good, I sort of lost me cool. I went out to the privet hedges and trimmed them all crooked, all cock-eyed like. Different lengths. I don't know what got into me. You was always so particular about them, I felt like a right villain cuttin' 'em up every which way. But I kind'a went off me head. *(Waits for* COLONEL's *reply)*

POTTS: 'Uh hm.'

HAROLD: It was very naughty, Colonel, and I know I deserve a stiff reprimand.

POTTS: 'Well they'll grow again no doubt, my boy. You can trim them properly later on.'

HAROLD: But it'll be years before they grow out, Colonel. And meantime, they look bloody awful. A right embarassment to the whole Manor. *(Beat)* I know I was in the wrong, Colonel. And I deserve every lash that's comin'.

POTTS: 'It's not all that terrible, Harold.'

HAROLD: But it *is,* Colonel. It makes you look silly in the eyes of the neighbors. A cock-eyed privet-hedge! They'll be saying all kinds of dark and treacherous things about you, Colonel. And it's all my fault. And I accept full blame for this wanton act of sacrilege. *(Beat)* Would you like me to go upstairs and drop me pants?

POTTS: 'I don't think that will be necessary, Harold.'

HAROLD: Of course it will, Colonel, and I ain't askin' for no favors. I know when I done wrong and I'm ready to take me punishment. *(Beat)* Should I slick the oil over the cat-o'-nine-tails?

POTTS: 'I'm still a bit tuckered out, Harold, from all the icing, y'know.'

HAROLD: *(Whispering)* This might be just what you need to get you back on form, Colonel.

POTTS: 'Perhaps . . . but . . .'

HAROLD: *(Whispering)* A few good strokes of the lash and you'll be your crackin' old self again, eh Colonel?

POTTS: 'The fact is Harold, I'm . . .'

HAROLD: *(Intensely)* I've rethreaded your black thong. The one that got all ragged and wispy. It's got a nice silver stud now right at the tip of each lash.

POTTS: 'I think I need a few minutes' nap, Harold. To gather my strength.'

(THE COLONEL's *dead head nods off as* BERENICE *enters.*)

HAROLD: What you doin' down here?

BERENICE: The Inspector said the Colonel wanted a word with me. *(Sees* THE COLONEL*)* Good God, what's happened to him?

HAROLD: He's having a little kip, isn't he? He's not completely with it, y'know. Wouldn't be surprised if there's parts of 'is brain not even thawed out yet.

BERENICE: *(Looks about furtively)* I hope all this hasn't changed things for us, Harold.

HAROLD: What are you on about?

BERENICE: I hope the Colonel's unexpected return doesn't mean we'll be strangers again, Harold. *(She makes for his crotch)*

HAROLD: *(Sharp)* Keep your bleedin' paws off'a me, Berenice!

BERENICE: *(Shocked)* Harold. You've never spoken to me in that tone of voice!

HAROLD: We are through, Berenice. You better get that through your thick libido.

BERENICE: Through?! You mean . . .

HAROLD: I mean no more linen closets, no more coal shutes, no more attics—through! I'm zippin' up me pants for good and throwin' away the key.

BERENICE: *(Trying tenderness)* But Harold, what's brought all this on?

HAROLD: We ain't compatible, Berenice, and, if you want the truth, we never was.

BERENICE: Not compatible.

HAROLD: There's not only a great gulf in our social stations, our intellects and our income, but the fact is, you just don't turn me on any more.

BERENICE: *(Hurt)* But Harold, the crotchless drawers? The nippleless bras? The luminous G-strings?

HAROLD: Don't mean a thing, Berenice. It don't raise a flicker in me no more.

BERENICE: The transparent corsets, the goose-down bloomers, the barbed-wire nighties . . .

HAROLD: It's no use goin' on. It don't do a thing to me.

BERENICE: *(Suddenly turning)* You're all his, aren't you? You're wedded to the whip and the manacle, admit it!

HAROLD: My preferences are no concern of yours. And I resent you treatin' me like I was your goods and chattels. I've bundled up all your gifts and you'll find them outside your door in the mornin'.

BERENICE: My gifts!? You're returning all my gifts?

HAROLD: All of 'em, Berenice! The autographed copy of 'Justine', the smelly aphrodisiacs, the rubber inflatables, the designer-condoms, everything!

BERENICE: But Harold . . .

HAROLD: Since the Colonel's death and hasty resurrection, I've found a new direction in my life. A new destiny is beckoning and there's no place in it for you.

BERENICE: *(In tears)* But Harold . . . Harold . . .

HAROLD: It's no use, Berenice. I've written 'finis' to this sordid chapter of me life.

BERENICE: *(Trying again)* Couldn't it just say 'To Be Continued'?

HAROLD: *(Harshly)* More like 'Out of Print', Berenice! 'Return to Sender!' *(He turns on his heel and exits)*

BERENICE: *(Bitterly to herself)* Another failure! This means back to the personal columns of The New York Review.

(HANNAH enters hurriedly as if chased by ALAN who follows hard upon. When they both see BERENICE, they stop short and assume a nonchalant air.)

ALAN: Comforting the Colonel, Berenice?

BERENICE: He's asleep. Might be best to leave him to it.

(As BERENICE and HAROLD exit, HANNAH and ALAN return to the hostility which brought them into the room.)

ALAN: Why are you being so damned stubborn, Hannah?

HANNAH: Shush, you'll wake him. *(Regards THE COLONEL)* He looks almost like a baby lying there so peaceful.

ALAN: Don't try distracting me, Hannah.

HANNAH: *(Whispering to avoid waking THE COLONEL)* I'm not goin'a do it, Mr. Hobbiss. The Colonel's just back from the brink of death and this is no time to be riflin' Lady Calvarley's lingerie closet.

ALAN: *(Whispering)* What has the one thing got to do with the other?

HANNAH: *(Whispering)* There's too much goin' on here, Mr. Hobbiss. Police, poison, detections, erections, resurrections. It's makin' me head spin.

ALAN: It's only a little black corset, she'd never miss it.

HANNAH: If the Colonel has a relapse and dies, she may well want it
for the funeral.

ALAN: It would go so beautifully with the black stockings and
garterbelt you gave me.

HANNAH: That was only a loan, Mr. Hobbiss. You promised to return
that as soon as you was done with it.

ALAN: *(Irate)* Well, I'm not 'done with it', am I? And you're getting
very uppity and insubordinate for a menial.

HANNAH: I'm not *your* menial, Mr. Hobbiss. I work for the Colonel,
bless 'is soul, and I don't think he'd approve of me dressin' up in his
riding britches just so's you can have a cheap thrill.

ALAN: You're getting very out of hand, Hannah.

HANNAH: I'm fed up to the teeth with all this lark. The Colonel poppin' off and poppin' back, coppers crawlin' all over the house,
sneakin' frilly underwear from the closet to the hall. It's all too much
for a workin' girl.

ALAN: *(Raising his voice)* If you don't get this for me . . .

HANNAH: *(On her high horse)* I may only be a servant here, but I won't
be part of no slinky-kinky hanky-panky. *(Marches out.)*

ALAN: *(Rhetorically)* Oh, for a rod of fire to . . . *(Mimes shafting*
HANNAH, *then rushes out, chagrined.)*

(POTTS, *finally, climbs out from under the dead* COLONEL *as* THE IN-
SPECTOR, *dazed, wanders in from his hiding place.)*

INSPECTOR: *(Shattered)* You needn't say a word, Potts. I've heard the
whole sickening exchange.

POTTS: I couldn't believe me ears, Inspector. What's it all mean?

INSPECTOR: It means, Potts, we have stumbled into the lowest den of iniquity in the Home Counties. A positive paradise of perversion.

POTTS: Makes me sick to me stomach, Inspector.

INSPECTOR: Nothing more nor less than I expected from their class. And it throws a whole new light on the murder of the Colonel.

POTTS: What do you mean, Inspector?

INSPECTOR: I mean I wouldn't be surprised if he was done in simply to satisfy the unnatural craving of some resident necrophiliac.

POTTS: *(Aghast)* Good God Inspector, you mean a sex crime?

INSPECTOR: In this society, Potts, there's nothing *but* sex crimes. They bugger each other, they bugger the workers, they bugger the state. It's like the last days of the Roman Empire with Nero fiddlin' and everyone else diddlin'.

POTTS: But we still don't know who's knocked off the Colonel?

INSPECTOR: *(Utterly disillusioned)* Does it even matter any more, Potts? Whoever it is, it's just a murderer in the midst of transvestites, flaggelants, sodomites and lechers. Nothin' to choose between 'em.

(He sits staring desolately into the middle distance. POTTS *is unnerved by his uncharacteristic decline.)*

POTTS: Shouldn't we do somethin' about the Colonel?

INSPECTOR: What's happened to the world, Potts? In Winnie's day, everyone mucked in for the war effort, went to church on Sunday, to the pub in the evening, back to their own beds at 11:00 when the gov'nor called 'time'. Life was decent, people were straight, the spirits were never watered down, God was in His Heaven. Where did it all go wrong? *(He stares blankly ahead)*

POTTS: *(After an uncertain beat)* Do you think we ought'a move the body, Inspector?

INSPECTOR: We all listened to the Queen's speech at Christmas, danced the hokey-cokey on New Year's Eve, did our neighbors as they did us and brushed the tear from our eye as we sang "There'll Always Be An England". *(Goes blank again)*

POTTS: *(After another uncertain beat)* Should we call the Vice Squad, p'raps?

INSPECTOR: *(Resolutely)* The Beatles!

POTTS: *(Beat)* Eh?

INSPECTOR: They're the ones started cocking their snook, takin' the mickey, refusin' to have their hair cut. They started the rot. The hippies, the weirdos, the long-haired gits with bandanas on their heads and beads around their necks.

POTTS: *(Beat)* There might be a patrol car in the neighborhood.

INSPECTOR: *(Seething to himself)* Christine Keeler. Mick Jagger. Jeremy Thorpe. Joe Stalin. Richard Nixon.

POTTS: *(Checking watch)* It *is* getting on a bit, I suppose.

INSPECTOR: The Pakis, the pansies, the Irish, the Yids, the I.R.A., P.L.O., C.I.A., I.U.D.

POTTS: Do you think, Inspector, we ought'a . . .

INSPECTOR: *(Gone)* Ban the Bomb, oh yes, and why? Because Black is Beautiful, that's why! And so it follows we must Save the Whales, Protect the Seals, Free the Battery Hens, give Equal Rights to Women and Let the Sikhs Wear Turbans Instead of Crash Helmets. Make Love Not War, right? We shall not only 'come', We Shall Overcome. I shall 'lay me down'; you shall 'lay you down'; we'll all get bloody laid! And where? On the Bridge Over Troubled Waters, where else? Queen and Country? Love Honor and Obey? Not on your nelly! All it is is turn off, switch on, drop out, bend over and fuck off!

(POTTS, *now genuinely concerned, taps* THE INSPECTOR *on the shoulder to bring him round.*)

POTTS: Everything all right, Inspector—

INSPECTOR: *(Recovered)* Almost fell in that time, Potts. Good chap. *(Grasps hand fondly)*

POTTS: I knew you'd catch yourself in time, Inspector. Should we store the Colonel back in the deep freeze?

INSPECTOR: Better not take any chances. Let's lay him out in the garage and lock the door.

(POTTS *and* INSPECTOR *lift the body of* THE COLONEL. *They walk only a step or two when they encounter* CHARLES *and* LADY CALVARLEY, BERENICE *and* ALAN *entering.*)

LADY C: We've had quite enough of this incarceration. We're now taking this matter into our own hands and . . . *(Discovering* THE COLONEL's *body)* What do you think you're doing?

(Sheepishly, POTTS *and* THE INSPECTOR *put down* THE COLONEL's *body. Everyone is regarding them with fierce suspicion.)*

INSPECTOR: I've some bad news, I'm afraid. I fear the good Colonel has had something of a relapse. *(Beat)* This just isn't your day, Lady Calvarley.

(All stand aghast regarding the body of THE COLONEL, *then slowly turn to* LADY CALVARLEY.)*

LADY C: A relapse?

POTTS: We only left him alone for a couple of minutes and then, I don't know exactly how it happened but . . .

INSPECTOR: What my colleague is endeavoring to convey is that, strange as it may sound—and it's certainly a first in my experience—

the Colonel appears to have expired once again—victim, I fear, of yet another lethal drink.

(LADY CALVARLEY withers THE INSPECTOR and POTTS with her look. Everyone else regards them with open, unconcealed looks of accusation.)

INSPECTOR: It is, as I'm sure we all agree, an extraordinary sort of coincidence given the adage that lightning never strikes twice in the same place. Although there is the counter theory that History Always Repeats Itself.

(This in no way convinces the assembly.)

CHARLES: How could this have happened, Inspector? Everyone was upstairs.

INSPECTOR: Except the villain who, using this sliding panel, administered the fatal refill.

CHARLES: But you were with him all the time.

INSPECTOR: Save for a matter of seconds when I went to check outside the house.

CHARLES: You left him alone?

INSPECTOR: Barely long enough to say 'Jack Robinson'.

ALAN: But long enough for the Colonel to imbibe another draught of poison.

(They all look darkly and with grave suspicion at THE INSPECTOR and POTTS who shifts uneasily.)

INSPECTOR: May I remind you all that I am a member of Her Majesty's Police summoned here in the line of duty to investigate a homicide?

ALAN: How do we know that?

INSPECTOR: Eh?

ALAN: How do we know you are who you say you are?

INSPECTOR: I think you will admit I have all the salient characteristics of a Scotland Yard inspector; grubby raincoat, oversize shoes, shiny waistcoat and an officious, blunt, mildly obnoxious manner.

BERENICE: Anyone can simulate that.

INSPECTOR: I beg to differ, Mrs. Hobbiss. I doubt that anyone can reproduce that unique blend of courtesy and obtuseness which is characteristic of the Yard.

CHARLES: How is it you got here so quickly? Within minutes of the first crime?

ALAN: And on a weekend at that?

INSPECTOR: I grant you that kind of punctuality in government employees *is* suspicious, but the fact is, Potts and I were motoring through the countryside on our day off when the call came on the short-wave and being the officers nearest to the scene of the crime . . .

CHARLES: You were on your day off, *together*?

INSPECTOR: The close proximity of our daily employment encourages a camaraderie which has spilled over into our private life. I don't see why that should cause any raised eyebrows or unsavory speculation. We are still living, thank God, in a society where the stag party, the turkish bath and the daisy-chain are traditional British pastimes.

ALAN: *(To* CHARLES) I must say I've never heard of any Farcus of the Yard.

CHARLES: I knew a Farcus in Dunstable once.*(To* ALAN) You remember old Charley Farcus of Pigeon-Drop Lane.

ALAN: That was Farrakus, and besides he was Greek.

CHARLES: You're right, come to think of it. *(Turns to* INSPECTOR*)* You're not Greek, are you?

INSPECTOR: I am not Greek, and I do not come from Dunstable.

CHARLES: Well, you wouldn't do if you weren't Greek.

INSPECTOR: I am, as I have previously stated, an employee of Her Majesty's government from Scotland Yard and shall be happy to show you my credentials.

ALAN: But aren't such credentials in your experience, Inspector, as forgeable as passports or any other form of documentation?

INSPECTOR: Well, yes, it is certainly true that any official papers can be . . .

ALAN: And Scotland Yard being, on the whole, a civilian branch of the police force with no conspicuous markings, almost anyone can claim an official connection and no one would be the wiser.

CHARLES: If you were a constable, of course . . .

ALAN: Right, wearing a blue uniform and silver buttons that would be more reassuring. The British bobbie is, nine times out of ten, unmistakable.

INSPECTOR: I am not a British bobbie, and I have no uniform!

ALAN: Well, there you are. That's the problem, isn't it?

INSPECTOR: What problem?

ALAN: You have no way of conclusively identifying yourself.

POTTS: *(Stepping forward)* I have known the Inspector for over seven years and can positively vouch for his authenticity.

ALAN: But who can vouch for yours?

INSPECTOR: I have known Special Assistant Potts for a like period of time and am prepared to swear an affidavit to that effect.

ALAN: *(To* INSPECTOR*)* But since your credibility is in question, how can you possibly verify someone else's and vice versa?

INSPECTOR: My identity, Mr. Hobbiss, like anyone else's has got to be taken on trust.

ALAN: You mean like an article of faith—as one believes in the existence of God?

INSPECTOR: *(After a moment's consideration)* Yes, if you like.

CHARLES: Let me get this straight, Inspector. Does that mean that if I am an atheist, you need not exist in my eyes?

ALAN: Or contrariwise, if I am a lapsed Catholic say, I could believe that you once did exist but no longer do. I must say, a Papal canon to the effect that you do would go a long way towards removing my doubts. Do you happen to have one?

INSPECTOR: Have what?

ALAN: A Papal canon to that effect.

POTTS: *(Trying to be helpful)* Is it something we might be able to get from the Home Office, Inspector?

INSPECTOR: *(Fuming)* I have no intention of standing around here trying to prove that I exist!

CHARLES: Why should you be any different from anyone else?

INSPECTOR: Eh?

ALAN: Charles does have a point. You barge in here presuming to be some kind of government official, brandish documents which you concede are probably forgeries, haven't a scrap of Papal evidence to support your claims and then expect everyone to jump to and do your bidding. Who do you think you are, God Almighty?

POTTS: *(Confused)* They may have a point, Inspector.

INSPECTOR: The hell they have! I say I'm Inspector Farcus of the Yard. Grubby raincoat, oversize shoes, shiny waistcoat, officious manner! It's up to you to disprove it! Can you!?

(ALAN *and* CHARLES *look at each other.)*

Point made! Up to and until such time as some official communique, sacred or secular, appears to alter these suppositions, I intend to proceed in the identity of the aforementioned Inspector Farcus. *(Turns to* POTTS) How about you?

POTTS: Can I be your Special Assistant?

INSPECTOR: I see no earthly reason why not. We still live in a society, thank God, where Free Choice can allow a man to be whoever he thinks he is. That's what our boys died for on the beaches of Normandy! And while we are indulging in this pointless dialectic, the good Colonel's body is awaiting removal and storage.

LADY C: Are you certain he's dead?

INSPECTOR: I fear this time the diagnosis is quite incontestable. I know this comes as a great shock, Lady Calvarley. The only thing worse than sudden bereavement is unexpected recovery, and you've had your fill of both today.

LADY C: *(Fuming)* This is simply too much. Too much!!

INSPECTOR: Try to calm yourself. The Lord giveth and the Lord . . .

LADY C: It was hard enough having to muster some sympathy for the old bastard the first time 'round, I'll be damned if I go through all that again! Charles, pack up our things, we're leaving for Majorca immediately.

POTTS: *(To inspector)* The shock has affected her mind, Inspector. I've seen this happen a lot at pit disasters. They just go off their rocker.

INSPECTOR: It might be a good idea, Lady Calvarley, if you had a good stiff drink and a little lie-down.

LADY C: Did you hear me, Charles?

CHARLES: But what about the house, the funeral arrangements?

LADY C: Hannah will see to the house as she always does, and I'm sure the insurance company will arrange a convenient resting place somewhere behind the stables.

CHARLES: But Lillian . . .

LADY C: If we start now, we should be at Heathrow in an hour and in Nuova Palma by dinner time. Luckily I had the foresight to put a down payment on that charming little hotel we stayed at last year. We'll rename it the Calvarley Arms and make it a refuge of British cuisine in the midst of all that chilli and garlic.

CHARLES: Our own little place, at last.

LADY C: Hurry, Charles, and don't forget to pack the Kaopectate.

(INSPECTOR *and* POTTS *look aghast at each other.)*

INSPECTOR: You don't really mean that you are running off to Majorca with a man not your legal spouse at the very moment of your husband's demise?!

LADY C: As far as I'm concerned, my husband's demise took place twenty years ago.

POTTS: *(Trying to sort it out)* Are you, as it were, romantically linked to Mr. Appley?

LADY C: Certainly not. We simply sleep together.

(INSPECTOR *and* POTTS *turn sharply to* APPLEY.)

CHARLES: The Colonel didn't mind. He was into horses, you know.

POTTS: Sleepin' with 'em?

CHARLES: I never pried into the Colonel's personal affairs.

POTTS: *(Sinking into a chair)* I don't think I can take too much of this, Inspector. Me middle class morality is crumblin' on all sides.

(HAROLD, *now dressed in a blue blazer and trim slacks, skips into the room carrying a cricket bat and a small hold-all. He now speaks in a posh, upper middle class accent.)*

HAROLD: I'm afraid I shall have to give notice immediately, Lady Calvarley. As a result of a rather dramatic personal revelation, I've decided to leave for Cheshire and take over the manor house my parents were good enough to bequeath me some years ago.

LADY C: Good for you, Harold!

HAROLD: It's rather silly to cling to thirty bob a week and a life of drudgery because of some misguided attachment to proletarian purity, don't you think?

LADY C: Couldn't agree more.

HAROLD: I may not be happy with 6000 acres, a life of leisure and an unlimited bank account, but by golly, I'm going to give it a bash. Thanks for all you've done and . . . *(Discovers the body of the Colonel)* I say, is the Colonel . . . ?

LADY C: He's done it again, I'm afraid. It may simply be a chronic addiction to poison in which case even the rehabilitation programmes would be of no use.

HAROLD: *(Mourning)* The last lash. *(Recovers)* Well that only confirms me in my new decision. All the vestiges of my former life are metaphorically, in some cases actually, dying off. The verdant fields of Cheshire beckon.

POTTS: *(Mesmerized)* Are you going to take over your own manor house then?

HAROLD: Precisely the fate planned by my parents which I have foolishly tried to escape but, like Oedipus, I bow to the power of the gods and, casting off my blindness, now recognize the bourgeois bliss for which I was always intended.

POTTS: It's big then, is it, this place in Cheshire?

HAROLD: From the front porch, there is an unbroken view of plush greenery interspersed with some of the fattest cattle in the land. To the west, some of the richest coal and iron pits in the whole of England.

POTTS: You'd need lots'a help in a place like that.

HAROLD: No doubt, but since my fortune is second only to the Saudi sheiks, I see no problem in recruiting some staff.

POTTS: I wonder if you might consider my verbal application pending the proper submission of a written form.

HAROLD: You?

POTTS: The fact is, Har—, uh Master Harold, ever since I first encountered you in these uncharacteristic surroundings, I felt an immediate tug of attraction. Something in your brusque and callous manner told me this man is suffering the agonies of hell and I felt impelled to try to drag you from that pit. Now, since you've rescued yourself, as it were, I feel an even stronger impulse to stay by your side and render you the services I am sure you will require in your new life. You can count on me for anything: aide-de-camp, valet, gardener, handyman and—if you should deign to consider it, foreman of your coal and iron works where, I must say, my oldest and deepest sympathies still lie.

INSPECTOR: *(Who has been transfixed)* Potts, are you quite right in the head?

POTTS: I am, Inspector. I knew there was something wrong with me at the Yard but only now have I discovered what. I'm not made to lord it over me betters. I was born to serve, Inspector. I'm a congenital working class flunky and proud of it!

HAROLD: *(Pumps him by the hand)* Good show! There's nothing warms my heart more than a proletarian who knows his place! You're hired!

POTTS: *(Touching his forelock)* Thank yuh, guv'nor.

HAROLD: We'll discuss terms at a later stage. Like all workers, I know you'd rather put in a full day's work than bother your head about the higher mathematics of proper compensation.

POTTS: It would be an honor to be underpaid by the likes of you, Master Harold.

INSPECTOR: Potts, I can't believe my ears. Are you going to throw away the seven best years of our lives? The staff picnics, the day trips, the booze-ups after the all night identity parades?

POTTS: *(Dramatically)* I've been livin' a lie, Inspector.

INSPECTOR: And what about me? I found you, I trained you, I sat up nights nursing your working class angst. I turned you into the man you are.

POTTS: I've taken the wrong turning, Inspector, and I must straighten me'self out while there's still time.

INSPECTOR: *(Cracking)* Why Potts, you were the light of my life in the duty-room. I looked forward to your rosters as I did nobody else's.

POTTS: We've all got our crosses to bear, Inspector. I can't wait to get into me clogs and overalls and be the man that nature intended.

(THE INSPECTOR *is speechless. Aghast, he looks from one to the other.*
BERENICE *finally breaks the silence.*)

BERENICE: *(To* LADY C) It's really been a lovely weekend, Lillian, but
we really must be going. I'd convey my condolences, but I know
you're delighted to be rid of the old bounder, so all I can say is: Asta
la Vista and drop us a card when you get to Majorca.

(ALAN *and* BERENICE *turn to go.*)

INSPECTOR: Just a moment! I don't mean to interfere with anyone's
travel plans, but you are conveniently overlooking the fact that a
murder has been committed in this house and the criminal is still at
large.

ALAN: Don't carry on, Inspector. It was only the old Colonel and no
one will really miss him.

LADY C: Indeed, I am considering establishing a scholarship in the
name of the Unknown Assailant to insure there will always be people
around to rid the world of such unsavory characters.

INSPECTOR: *(Coming in for the kill)* Since we are on the subject of
unsavory characters, Lady Calvarley, I feel impelled to express my
repugnance and disgust at the unsavoriness of this entire household.

LADY C: I haven't a clue what you're on about.

INSPECTOR: Have you not, my dear Lady? Then allow me to enlighten
you. Am I incorrect, Mr. Hobbiss in contending that you and the
housekeeper pass the time of day performing slimy little charades
with one another which are centered around a variety of intimate
female attire, the wearing of which is an aberration which inspires
disgust in the minds of most respectable people?

ALAN: I do have an interest in fashion, if that's what you mean. I am,
after all, in clothes.

INSPECTOR: More often than not, in someone else's and almost invariably of the opposite sex. And you Mr. Minks, despite your new-found

social station, you must admit you pursued a perverse form of pleasure with the late Colonel which involved a variety of leather articles, the nature of which cause winces of disgust in those upright citizens who are unfortunate enough to encounter them in the windows of the more sordid sexual boutiques which have now mushroomed throughout the length and breadth of Britain.

HAROLD: The Colonel was in equestrian supplies, and leather was certainly a tool of his trade.

INSPECTOR: And from what I can gather, you and the Colonel traded tools at every opportunity. But when you switched your attentions to Mrs. Hobbiss, an even more beastly form of licentious behavior came to the fore.

BERENICE: Harold and I are only good friends.

INSPECTOR: I should hate to be a fly on the wall during those friendly encounters in which you experimented with every erotic trick in the book—the book being The Collected Works of the Marquis de Sade!

HAROLD: What consenting adults do in private is none of your business.

INSPECTOR: Au contraire, Master Harold. Once the public gets wind of it, any consenting adult that does not first obtain my consent and that of people like me, are in for a very rough ride in this land, I can tell you. Clean fingernails, flushed drains, and conventional sexual practices are the principles of public decency in Great Britain. That is how we measure civilization and, by that measuring-rod, almost everyone in this house is grubby to the point of barfing.

ALAN: You really think you *are* God Almighty!

INSPECTOR: If I was and took a look at you lot, I'd think I'd made a right balls-up of the world.

ALAN: I've no intention of being preached to by a philistine whose perversion is dressing up in grubby raincoats and pretending to be a member of Her Majesty's Police Force.

INSPECTOR: Pretending?

LADY C: Let's go, Charles. The motorway's bound to be chock-a-block.

INSPECTOR: I forbid you to leave this house. Potts!

POTTS: Sorry, Inspector, I've turned in me billy-club, metaphorically speaking.

INSPECTOR: *(Dramatically putting his hand into his inside breast pocket as if to draw a revolver)* No one in this room is to make a move! *(Removes hand which brandishes brandy flask instead of pistol)* Where's the bloody pistol, Potts?

POTTS: The armory's always locked on the weekend, Inspector.

CHARLES: Go easy Inspector. We've already established that you have no authority in this matter.

INSPECTOR: No authority?

CHARLES: You've not been able to prove your identity to anyone's satisfaction, including your own.

ALAN: And furthermore, if you don't mind my saying so, you appear to me to be suffering from delusions of grandeur.

INSPECTOR: Delusions . . . ?

ALAN: You have been making wild comparisons between the Deity and yourself, you must admit.

INSPECTOR: *(Fuming)* Christ almighty!

ALAN: *(Under, to* CHARLES) There he goes again.

CHARLES: You're among friends here, old chap. If you want to tell us who you really are, I don't think anyone here will be vindictive.

INSPECTOR: I am Inspector Farcus of the Yard.

LADY C: *(As to a child)* Of course you are. Would you see that all the lights are off when you leave. Just pull the front door to. I'll leave it on the latch.

*(Everyone starts to leave. They begin chatting casually—*BERENICE *and* LADY CALVARLEY, HAROLD *and* POTTS, ALAN *and* CHARLES. THE INSPECTOR *cannot grasp the turn of events. As* POTTS *prepares to go off with* HAROLD, *he darts forward.)*

INSPECTOR: Potts, I ask you for the last time. Consider this rash and irreversible action. You are leaving the world of decent people for a life of orgy and licentiousness, carnal desire and indiscriminate sexuality.

POTTS: A change is as good as a rest.

(He puts his arm in HAROLD's *as they start to go.)*

INSPECTOR: What shall I tell your father?

POTTS: I'll send him a dirty postcard.

(They go. THE INSPECTOR, *his world-view in fragments, sits heavily in the easy chair. He is dazed and defeated. Only* HANNAH *remains.)*

HANNAH: Don't take it so badly. You could always *apply* to be an Inspector. You're still a young man.

INSPECTOR: *(Exhaustedly, undefensively)* But I *am* an Inspector.

HANNAH: Course you are, love. *(Starts clearing up.)*

INSPECTOR: And what about you?

HANNAH: Me? Oh, I'm no Inspector. Girl Guides is the closest I ever got to a uniformed position.

INSPECTOR: I mean, why haven't you left? With the others?

HANNAH: Well the fact is, Inspector—is it all right to call you Inspector?

(THE INSPECTOR *gestures wearily as if to say: I'm not going into all that again.)*

When the Colonel's will is read, I think you'll find I am the major beneficiary. He never much liked the wife, nor she, him. Kind of mutual contempt, you might say. If you're goin'a have something like that, it's always best if it *is* mutual. That way nobody feels left out.

INSPECTOR: *(The penny dropping slowly)* The will? But how do you know what's in the will?

HANNAH: The Colonel showed it to me many times. He even consulted me in the wording of some of the clauses. He loved in-put, did the Colonel.

INSPECTOR: *(Dawning on him)* Why then, you've got the strongest motive of all for having the Colonel killed. *(Beat)* Hannah? *(Pause)* Did you . . . ?

HANNAH: *(Cheshire-cat smile)* That'd be tellin' now, woon' it?

INSPECTOR: *(Recoiling)* Do you mean to say . . . ?

HANNAH: I'm not saying a thing, Inspector. Me dad always told me, Hannah, don't you go admittin' anything at all. Even if you're caught red-handed—just say you was cleanin' the salmon or peelin' the beets. And how about you, Inspector? What are your plans?

INSPECTOR: Me?

HANNAH: You don't have to dash away, I hope. It'll be quite lonely with Harold off for good and her Ladyship gone to Majorca. I could fix a nice place for you in one of the guest rooms. Or, if you fancied it, there's always the Colonel's master bedroom. The mattress is practically new as the Colonel and Lady Calvarley was never very high on canoodlin'.

INSPECTOR: Are you suggesting I stay here—in the Colonel's manor—and the Colonel lying right there?

HANNAH: I was just thinking, once the Colonel's will is read, the whole of this manor house will be mine, and there's quite a lot of cash comin' as well. And the fact is, I've never been very good on me own. I could never be like Lady Calvarley y'know—just restin' on me laurels. I've always enjoyed *doin'* for people—a bit'a washin', a spot 'a cookin', dustin' and sweepin' 'n that. And I sort of thought, if you've nothin' better to do, you could stay on here for a while—as me guest if you like—and see how we go. You never know what can happen when Fate brings two people together. *(Pause)*

(THE INSPECTOR *speechlessly and painfully considers what is being proposed. Meanwhile,* HANNAH *dusts and puts the house in order.)*

It'd be more comfortable than police work. Wouldn't be on your feet so much of the time. And there'd be nobody lordin' it over you. I've been too long in me place under the guv'nor to want to do that. And I can quite see Potts' point of view. There are some people who just enjoy servin' others. Sort of social workers to the upper classes. Gawd knows, they need someone to look after 'em.

Well, I'll bring you a nice cuppa tea while you think it over, eh? I know you've had a hard day.

(THE INSPECTOR *sits somewhat stunned, regarding* THE COLONEL *who is propped up beside him—as if having a silent communion with the corpse. He looks towards where* HANNAH *has exited, then again at* THE COLONEL.

He then starts examining the furnishings of the drawing room, silently comparing them with his own grubby condition. After silently mulling for a few more minutes, he moves to the telephone and dials a number.)

INSPECTOR: Hello Wilkinson, Farcus here. I'm at the Colonel's manor. Yes. Bit of a false alarm. Colonel's popped off all right, but it seems to be a case of food poisoning or p'raps misadventure—not quite sure as yet. Foul play? No, not as far as I can see. . . . Yes, I'll file my report in the normal way. No hurry though. May be a little while before I get back. Take all the messages, will ya like a good chap? Right. *(Hangs up)*

(THE INSPECTOR *studies the house again. He now rises and inspects the room as if he were a prospective purchaser. Finds* THE COLONEL's *tweed jacket hanging on the back of the closet door. Tries it on. Finds crumpled tweed hat. Puts that on his head. A swagger-stick which he picks up as well. Finding a hunting rifle, he straps that over his shoulder, then stands back to gauge the effect of his new 'country' persona. While he is admiring himself,* HANNAH *re-opens the kitchen door and regards him admiringly for a moment.* THE INSPECTOR, *sensing her return, turns towards her.)*

HANNAH: *(Smiling)* It *does* do something for you, Inspector, and that's the truth.

(THE INSPECTOR *flattered by* HANNAH's *compliment, straightens up and swaggers a bit, feeling every inch the country squire. At just that moment,* THE COLONEL's *body slumps from the chair onto the floor. Both* HANNAH *and* THE INSPECTOR *do an immediate 'take' of alarm. In a few seconds they realize it is just the corpse twitching as is its wont.* THE INSPECTOR, *reassured, smiles faintly at* HANNAH. HANNAH *beams back a great big affectionate smile.* THE INSPECTOR's *smile similarly broadens, and as* HANNAH *and* THE INSPECTOR *are smiling broadly at one another,*

The curtain falls

Epilogue

(Spoken by Inspector Farcus)

Should you complain, as patrons sometimes do,
Exaggeration's all the players gave 'ya
And nothing we've enacted strikes you true

Or in the realm of plausible behavior,
We must concede the criticism's sound
And we wouldn't think to challenge or refute it.
But a work of art's not measured by the pound;
You can't just punch it in and then compute it.
So if you want to see your next-door neighbor—
His Dramas, Dreams, his Tragedies and Hopes,
And all that muck that telly-plays belabor,
You should'a stayed at home and watched the Soaps.
A play is not a mirror on the wall
Reflecting back our bosoms and our phalluses.
If indeed, a looking-glass at all,
It's much more fanciful—like Alice's.
If a Thriller's what you want, Godammit,
With twists and shocks and such like elec'tricity
There's rubbish heaps galore by Dashiell Hammet
And all that crap by, what's-her-name, Miss Chris-i-tie.
We hope you find the moral in our tale.
The subtle one. The one that we've planted
That simply put says: Pleasure should Prevail
and Immorality be ta'en for granted.
For if we let them close up every chink
Wherein may breed peculiar liaisons,
Disdaining this man's folly and that man's kink
And frowning on our sexual persuasions,
A time may come, and sooner than you think,
When Those that Frame the Law may soon disparage
The tendency of boys and girls to link
Within the bounds of *hetro'* sexual marriage.
So turn upon the Farcusses of life
The full and flowing juices of Contempt.
Let people go wherever Pleasure's rife
And from Hypocrites like me, you'll be exempt.

Now words are done and time has come to break up
And like the likes of Bernhardt or of Duse,
I stow me clothes and pack away me makeup
And dance with nimble tread into the boozer.
And there I'll raise my pint-pot to the skies

And say in words not fancy or prolix:
'Here's to all us geezers that are wise
To them that *claim* to be the Clever Dicks!'

(THE CAST *raise their glasses and drink to* THE INSPECTOR'S *toast.*)